BUTCHERVILLE

CHRIS KELSEY

Black Rose Writing | Texas

This is a work of fiction. Names, characters, businesses, places, events, and
incidents are either the products of the author's imagination or used in a
fictitious manner. Any resemblance to actual persons, living or dead, or
actual events is purely coincidental.

ISBN: 978-1-68433-425-4
PUBLISHED BY BLACK ROSE WRITING
www.blackrosewriting.com

Printed in the United States of America
Suggested Retail Price (SRP) $18.95

Butcherville is printed in Chaparral Pro

*As a planet-friendly publisher, Black Rose Writing does its best to eliminate
unnecessary waste to reduce paper usage and energy costs, while never compromising
the reading experience. As a result, the final word count vs. page count may not meet
common expectations.

In memory of my dad, Barry Kelsey, who heard it first.

BUTCHERVILLE

PROLOGUE

If I had to cite one quality that defines where I live (that would be Burr, Oklahoma, population 1,276—down from 1,280 after we sent two father & son pairs of miscreants to the state penitentiary in McAlester last year), it would be the natural inclination of my fellow citizens to do the direct opposite of anything a person in authority says, regardless of whether or not it's in their best interests. President Lyndon Baines Johnson himself could drop a hint to one of our farmers that it would be a good idea to water his crops. More likely than not, the farmer'd flip LBJ the bird and piss all over his own soybeans or sorghum or whatever it is he grows just to be contrary. He might even invite over the neighbors and let them join in.

Anyone who pretends to understand anything about us Oklahomans knows we can be mulish and self-reliant, sometimes ridiculously so. Nobody—and I mean *nobody*—tells an Okie what to do.

I reckon to an outsider, our nature might seem a little hypocritical, since, after all, if our ancestors hadn't been willing to accept a government handout (or two or three), the state we know as Oklahoma might instead be called Sequoyah, and a majority of its citizens would comprise descendants of men named Geronimo and Standing Bear and Black Kettle.

That wouldn't do at all.

Nah, this wonderful land of black gold and waving wheat and championship football teams was gifted to us on the cheap by the boys in Washington D.C. on behalf of the much-tread-upon and lied-to American Indian, and it cannot be convincingly argued otherwise.

Indeed, our representatives' generosity didn't end with the gift of pilfered real estate.

Back in the Dirty '30s, a good number of farmers swallowed their pride and accepted a share of Franklin Roosevelt's New Deal money, or what was left of it after the sitting governor got his cut. I don't mean to suggest they weren't right to take the cash. It hardly rained a drop for almost a decade and the wind didn't stop blowing just because the ground was parched and turned to dust. Most of what few crops managed to poke through got eaten by grasshoppers and jackrabbits. Nah, those fellas accepted help because they had no choice. They had mouths to feed.

But now it's 1966, and the big money brought here by oil and gas interests has rendered memories short and Oklahomans cocky. That noted bootstrap-puller and shantytown-inspirer Herbert Hoover coined a name for the attitude that infects our state. He called it "rugged individualism," which means if we're going to do something, we're going to do it our way or not at all. I'm not stretching things much when I say a lot of folks these days would rather quench their thirst with Drano than admit the boys in Washington or Oklahoma City know what's best for them. Our lizard-brained politicians know that, which is why they've made appealing to a general distrust of government into an art form. Any candidate who can convince voters that he only wants to get elected so he can tear things down from the inside can write his own ticket. Some people love the sound of that bull crap so much that—whether out of stubbornness, meanness, or a lack of common sense—they're happy to look the other way while the fella saying it picks their pockets. I believe the most common descriptive phrase is: "Cut off your nose to spite your face."

Would-be nose-less bastards like that inhabit every corner of this state. It's a part of who we are, for better or for worse. Here in Tilghman County, however, a few miles north of Burr in a town called Butcherville, we've got ourselves an especially peculiar concentration of that sadly unendangered species.

Butcherville's founding fathers believed that man is endowed by his creator with an inalienable right to do whatever he damn well pleases and to hell with anyone who tries to tell him otherwise. Feel like adding a second floor to your outhouse? Be my guest, although I'd advise you to take an umbrella or at least wear a hat when you go do your business. Got an urge to paint your ding-dong orange and drive a tractor naked past a schoolyard of first-graders? Enjoy the ride, buddy. No true-blue Butchervillian would dream of spoiling your fun. Just don't forget the Coppertone.

All in all, it's probably good that most lack ambition and are inclined to settle for milder forms of rebellion, such as parking broken-down cars and tractors in their yards for years at a time. Watching discarded and disabled machinery fall prey to the elements is a favorite local spectator sport.

To be fair, there is a subset of Butcherville residents who enjoy such challenging pursuits as hunting squirrels with machine guns and fishing for bass with hand grenades. Drinking copious amounts of Schlitz while operating farm equipment is about the safest thing they do.

From the laziest to the craziest, however, the most important thing is: no one tells them they can't.

It's no surprise that Butcherville doesn't have a police department, since by-and-large nothing short of murder or horse-thievery will get you put away. On the other hand, some laws of God and Oklahoma still apply there, same as they do other places. Do something like tie a person up, tape a burlap sack over his head, and run him over with a pickup, you'll answer to someone.

In Butcherville, more often than not, that someone is me.

My name is Emmett Hardy. I carry a badge.

And a flask of Old Grand-Dad bourbon in my glove compartment, for reasons that will become apparent, if they haven't already.

CHAPTER ONE

When my dispatcher and trusted aide Karen Dean isn't scolding me about something else—like my drinking, for instance—she's finding fault with my tendency to exaggerate. Her word for it is "hyperbole," which I take to mean telling fish stories. Guilty as charged.

That said, I'm not exactly claiming to have hooked Moby Dick with a bamboo rod when I say what's obvious to anyone who grew up around here: pretty near every Oklahoman with a pulse gets a hot and tingly sensation in the crotch of their Lee Riders when the first Friday in September rolls around.

In towns like Burr, the local high school football team's first game of the season is a secular holiday on a par with New Year's Eve and Independence Day. Get one of our local good ol' boys to chug enough beer, he might even risk eternal damnation and admit what most of us know, but are embarrassed to say out loud.

Baby Jesus's birthday ain't got nothing on the season opener.

Football season snuck up on me this year. A long, hot summer during which hardly anything happened lulled me into a false sense of security. For three months, it felt like everyone in town had decided to become law-abiding by unspoken but unanimous consent. I was beginning to think that henceforth my job would consist solely of helping little old ladies cross the street and catching speeders out by the city limits. About the only thing of note to happen occurred the day after Memorial Day, when a couple of numb-nuts teenage boys set off a bottle rocket on ground surrounded by dry switchgrass, sparking a blaze that took several hours of hard work by Burr's Bravest to extinguish.

We were lucky. Most places, a grass fire wouldn't rate too high on a list of summer calamities. In July, *The Daily Oklahoman* ran a story about some crazy bastard in Chicago who killed eight student nurses. Closer to home, a group of negroes marched from Oklahoma City to Lawton to protest the fact some redneck amusement park owner wouldn't let colored folks use his swimming pool. Some peckerwood in Mississippi shot the first negro admitted to Ole Miss for being so uppity as to encourage others of his race to vote. People all over the country—even a few here in Burr—are starting to fidget over this war in Viet Nam, which is looking increasingly like its own kind of criminal enterprise, if you ask me (few around here do, knowing my pinko propensities).

Fortunately, I don't need to concern myself with those places. As the chief of police in Burr—the third-largest (and fourth-smallest) town in the least-populous county in the state—I only have to worry about my little corner of Oklahoma, which in the Summer of 1966 was as lazy as a box of toads.

•　　•　　•　　•　　•

It started out like every other opening day I can remember, going back to when I played tailback for Burr High in the '40s. Everywhere you went, people debated the team's prospects: from Miller's Drug (where people fill their prescriptions and drink root beer floats while trying to ignore the fact the place smells like a bowling alley men's room) to Bill Haygood's barber shop (where I don't get my hair cut, but where I do go to hear a bunch of old men exegete on subjects they don't know a damn thing about), to the Jesus Is Lord Hair Salon (where I *do* get my hair cut, and listen to the beauticians complain about Bill Haygood, who bought the place a few months back and therefore has a monopoly on all the haircutting in town). The red white and blue of the Burr Patriots adorned every light pole and store window on Main Street. Optimism and happiness reigned.

People couldn't stop talking about the new wonder boy destined to lead the team to the promised land. There's a new one every fall. This year's model was Marlon Truitt, Jr., a transfer sophomore from Temple City, the county seat and a town ten times larger than Burr. From what I've been told, Marlon might not be an Einstein in the classroom, but on the football field he's Bronko Nagurski and Red Grange and Jim Brown, all rolled into one.

As a freshman in Temple City, Marlon backed up an All-State halfback on a team that won its third Class 2A state championship in a row. Folks expect him to blossom as a Patriot, especially since Burr only picks on schools our own size. We play eight-man football rather than traditional eleven-man. There'll be fewer bodies standing between our young hero and the end zone, which—if all goes to according to plan—folks hope he'll be visiting three or four times a game.

I told my people to be at the station by 4:30, thinking I'd start the meeting at 4:45, allowing for stragglers. There's always at least one. On football Fridays, it's all-hands-on-deck, me included, although my duties are largely of a supervisory nature—meaning I sit in the press box and pretend to watch the game while my people on the ground direct traffic and guard against whatever minor malefaction results from gathering most of the town's population into a small space and whipping them into an emotional frenzy.

My personal game-day preparation had consisted of going home at lunchtime, flopping down in my worn-out La-Z-Boy, and sleeping off my intake of alcohol from the night before. Considering all the extra lifting I had to do in the run up to the game, my conscience was clear. I was able to stroll into work reasonably refreshed at more or less the specified time.

The officers under my command—Deputy Chief Bernard Cousins, part-time patrolmen Kenny Harjo and Jeff Starns—were in attendance, as was the aforementioned Miss Dean, who said, "Look what the cat drug in," like she always does.

"You need to come up with another expression," I said. "If I had a nickel for every time you said—"

"If I had a nickel for every time you said, 'if I had a nickel,' I could retire and move to Hawaii."

"Go ahead. I assume you'll be taking me with you."

"Promise me you'll never wear one of them itty-bitty bathing suits, and maybe I will."

Everyone got a kick out of that.

"I don't know what makes you think such a thing is even a possibility," I said, "but that's a promise I'm willing to keep."

Jeff nudged Karen and winked. "C'mon, wouldn't you like to see him in some of them *Beach Blanket Bingo* shorts?"

"Chief don't look anything like Frankie Avalon," said Kenny.

I tipped the fedora I wear instead of a cowboy hat.

"I appreciate you saying that, son."

Karen rolled her eyes. "I was thinking about something more itty-bitty than that, but never mind," she said. "Can we get down to business, please? I got a football game to go to."

"Alright, we go through this every year," I said. "Who's doing what, and where're y'all doing it?"

Kenny spoke up first. "I'll be parked out on Franklin Street with Jerry Chrisco, coordinating parking," he said. Jerry's a town councilman, but his primary job is being Director of Maintenance for Burr High School, which is just a fancy name for head janitor. Jerry doesn't appreciate it when you point that out.

"I'll be working the home sideline, of course," said Jeff, dressed in khaki slacks and a Burr Patriots t-shirt. Jeff doubles as an assistant football coach, so he'd be splitting his chores in half. He's my least dedicated officer and, in terms of intelligence, has, at most, only a couple of brain cells to rub together. Let's just say, whatever law enforcement he provided would be a bonus.

"I'll be roaming," said Bernard, my only full-time officer, who, in contrast to Jeff, takes being a cop as seriously as a preacher takes the Sunday offering. "I'm going to park the Fury down by the south end zone this year. It's close to the road by the bus shed, so it should make it easier to get in and out in an emergency. I'm having 'em park the ambulance there, too."

In past years we parked our cruiser and the combination ambulance/hearse from Pate's Funeral Home behind the grandstand—I guess for no other reason than that's what we've always done. Bernard's idea made so much sense, I felt silly for not thinking of it myself. I told him so. He puffed up, but not in a conceited way. He just likes to be told he's doing a good job.

Karen's the only one of us who never works game nights. She's graduated almost twenty years ago, but God help her, she still loves Burr High School football.

"Did you get someone to man dispatch?" I asked her.

She blew me a raspberry. "If by 'man,' you mean 'Did I get someone to handle the dispatching so I can go to the game?' then yes, I got Cindy Bartlett to come in." Cindy's a telephone operator for Southwestern Bell who moonlights with us when Karen needs a break. Besides being a great dispatcher and my semi-secret girlfriend, Karen's also an outspoken agitator for the rights of the fairer sex.

"If you need me, you know where to find me," she added.

"You'll be in the press box, Chief?" asked Kenny.

"Yeh, I guess," I said, not trying very hard to hide my lack of enthusiasm. I'm not a football fan, despite having played it with some distinction in my misspent youth. My disaffection has partly to do with a personal dislike for dealing with large crowds of people. At games, I stare at the field and pretend to be so engrossed that I can't be bothered to talk. In fact, my eyes glaze over and I daydream about skinny dipping in the Arctic or standing in line at the post office or a million other things I'd rather be doing instead of watching high school football. It's not easy to do, but over the years I've had lots of practice.

"Who're we playing?" asked Bernard, which was a silly question, since everybody's been talking about it for weeks and anyway we've got a Burr Patriots schedule taped to our front window.

"Carmen," said Karen, meaning the town, not the opera. Although if anyone in Burr has actually heard of an opera by that name, it would likely be her. She might even know who wrote it.

"Carmen any good?" I asked for some reason. I didn't care one way or the other.

"We'll handle them," Jeff said. "That new boy we got is unstoppable." I assumed he was referring to Marlon Truitt, Jr. I was tempted to suggest the jury's out on young Marlon, but I held my tongue.

"Didn't Carmen win the state championship last year?" asked Kenny.

"Nah, Carmen ain't won nothing," grumped Jeff. "That was Cherokee won State."

"Cherokee didn't win State," said Karen. "Balko did."

"That's right. Balko," said Kenny. "But Carmen beat us, right?" Kenny gets a kick out of bursting bubbles. I'm a bad influence on him in that respect.

"Not this year," Jeff muttered.

I didn't care if we were playing Bullwinkle and Rocky the Flying Squirrel.

"What's the weather going to be like, Kenny?" He's our resident meteorologist and tornado-chaser.

"Channel four says we're in for heavy rain tomorrow," he said, "but tonight should be high and dry."

Like it has been for months. We could use some rain.

"Everybody got fresh batteries in your walkie-talkies?" I asked.

They nodded. We affirmed the correct frequency.

"Alright, y'all can go, then. I'll hang around until Cindy gets here."

"You sure you don't want me to stay?" asked Karen.

"Not necessary. Go grab yourself a good seat," I said. There aren't really any bad seats in a stadium as small as ours, and she sits with the Pep Club, which always gets prime viewing real estate.

They filed out: Bernard businesslike as always, Jeff and Kenny laughing and poking each other like little kids. Football seems to put everyone except me in a good mood.

Through the front window, I watched Jeff and Kenny climb into Kenny's pickup. Bernard commandeered his much-beloved 1961 Plymouth Fury Police Cruiser, with Karen riding shotgun. The Fury was our only squad car until about a year ago, when the town government approved the purchase of a used 1964 Ford Galaxie Police Interceptor. The Galaxie is not nearly as slick as the Fury, but it runs fine, which is all I care about. My officers don't like it because it looks like the car on The Andy Griffith Show. They get called "Barney Fife" enough as it is, especially Bernard, because of his name. In any case, I wanted a car of my own, so custody of the Galaxie fell to me. I don't mind what it looks like, as long as it runs, and no one dares call me anything but Chief Hardy. I take it, and let the boys fight over the Fury. Bernard usually wins.

I grabbed a magazine and plopped down in Karen's chair. I slid her dispatcher's microphone and typewriter to one side, leaned back and put my boots up, in a calculated gamble she wouldn't forget something, come back and catch me with my feet on her desk.

The magazine was called *Down Beat*. Karen bought me a subscription for my birthday. It covers jazz music, which I like a great deal. I'm fairly sure I'm the only reader they have in Tilghman County. Jazz is a taste few of my fellow western Oklahomans have acquired.

I'd just cracked it open when the phone rang. It was Ona Ray Collins. Ona Ray lives with her husband Merle and their son Earl in a small house on a plot of land out on Butcherville Road, near the natural gas processing plant. I knew the family slightly but hadn't seen them in a while. Ona Ray called because her boy was late coming home from school and she was starting to worry. Butcherville's too cheap to build their own schools. They bus their kids to Burr. Earl's an eighth-grader, 12 about to turn 13, so he goes to our junior high. Like most kids not old enough to drive, Earl takes the bus back and forth to school. Ona Ray said he typically gets home a few minutes past four. Today he was over an hour late. I didn't think it was a very big deal, but you know how mothers are.

She asked if I'd seen him. I said no, I didn't think so, although I couldn't exactly remember what he looked like. I asked if he'd been planning to go to the game.

"He is," she replied, "but he was supposed to come home and eat dinner first. We were going to go as a family."

"Could he have gone home with a friend?"

"Well, I thought about that. I called up every single one of his friends. They all planned to meet-up at the game, but they split up after school, and no one's seen Earl since." She paused. I heard the snap of a cigarette lighter and the sound of her inhaling and exhaling a lungful of smoke. "Well, almost no one," she continued. "Will Boston rides the bus with Earl. He said Earl got off the bus at the Butcherville Store, like he's been doing all week." The first week of school was just coming to an end. "Earl says the bus driver likes it when he does that, because it cuts ten minutes off his route, since Earl's the only student out this way. Most days, Earl goes in the store and buys himself a pop, then walks home ..." Her voice faded and I thought I could hear her choke back a sob.

"But today he didn't," I said. "Walk home, that is."

"No, Chief, at least he ain't stepped through the door yet."

Cindy Bartlett stepped through my own front door, flushed but not flustered, accompanied by a cloud of dust whipped up by one of those hot thirty-mile-an-hour winds that appear out of nowhere. She saw I was on the phone and mouthed a silent apology for being late.

I winked at Cindy and asked Ona Ray if she'd called the store.

"Nobody answers the phone," she said, sounding annoyed. "I don't know what to do. Merle is at work and I don't have a car. I'd walk down to the store, but it's almost a mile away and I don't want to leave in case Earl calls or comes home."

I asked if Earl could've met his daddy at work. She said no, Merle works in a small-engine repair shop in Seiling, twenty miles away. I asked her for the names of Earl's friends, since at some point we might need to question them ourselves. She rattled them off, and I wrote down the names and phone numbers on Karen's yellow legal pad. "I'll tell you what, Ona Ray," I said, "I'll drive out to the store myself, talk to whoever's running the place, and look around. I expect Earl's with some other friends you don't know about or just didn't think to call. Maybe he's got a girlfriend you don't know about."

The idea seemed to cheer her up a little. "I don't know about a girlfriend, but he might rather go to the game with his friends. He's getting to be that age where he's embarrassed to be seen with us."

"There you go, I'll bet that's all it is." I told her I'd stop by in a little while, and we said our goodbyes.

"Sorry I'm late, Chief," Cindy said. As always, she was dressed for success: a light-blue jacket over a white blouse, a matching skirt, tan high heels, with her light brown hair wound into a bun. Cindy's age is a mystery. Most people around here have lived in Burr all their lives, so I can usually remember when they were born or when they graduated from high school, or—if they're older than me—how old they are in relation to my parents. Cindy moved here a few years ago to work for the phone company, however, so her looks are about all

I have to go on. She could be anywhere from twenty-five to forty. She reminds me a little bit of Miss Jane Hathaway from *The Beverly Hillbillies*, except Cindy's prettier and more level-headed.

"My relief was late," she said. "I couldn't leave until she got there."

"That's ok, I'm not in any hurry. At least I wasn't until I got that phone call."

I explained about Earl and said I was going out to look for him. I asked her to first radio Bernard and tell him I might be late to the game, then call the boys on the list of Earl's friends and ask them directly if they'd seen Earl, or if they had any idea where he'd be. In particular, I told her to ask if Earl had a girlfriend, and, if so, who she was and where she lived.

I thanked Cindy and headed to Butcherville, thinking of the trip as a welcome excuse to miss the opening kickoff.

I didn't mind, so long as it was just an excuse and nothing more serious. I didn't expect it would be.

CHAPTER TWO

Butcherville didn't exist when I was a boy, at least not officially. Back then, the thirty-square-mile part of Tilghman County north of Burr called Butcherville wasn't much more than a scattering of farms and houses, home to more stray dogs and cats than people. It didn't incorporate and become an official town until the late '40s.

Butcherville got its name long before it was a dot on the map, although how it got the name is a matter of some dispute. Some say it was named for a local pig farmer who butchered his own hogs, but no one seems to have known or met or even heard such a person mentioned in conversation until a few years ago. I say he's a figment of some bacon-lover's imagination.

Others say the name comes from a massacre of ex-slaves who tried to settle the area in the years between land runs and statehood. That theory is plausible, inasmuch as white folks in these parts have on occasion demonstrated an inclination to do grievous bodily harm to their negro brothers and sisters. There's no evidence it ever happened, though. Most agree that it's just a story bigots tell to scare off any colored folks who might want to live there.

That's not the only origin tale with a racial element. One spring day in 1931, a colored railroad porter left the train in Burr, intending to jump off, buy a newspaper, then jump right back on. For some reason, the train left without him, and the next day someone found the poor man alongside a dirt road south of town, his dead body bearing signs of torture and split almost in half by what the authorities conjectured was a fireman's axe. Some of those authorities claimed he was killed by Bonnie and Clyde.

He wasn't.

I was little at the time, so I don't remember the incident, but according to my father, everyone in town knew the killer was Rufus Kenworthy, a local Klansman. Kenworthy's cross-burning buddies invented the Bonnie and Clyde yarn to relieve the district attorney of having to go through the motions of prosecuting their friend. The DA went along with the charade, despite the fact there wasn't a thimble's full of evidence to support the theory.

The Barrows did undoubtedly wreak havoc elsewhere in the state, but it can definitely be said they never set foot nor rubber in Tilghman County.

Their bullet-ventilated death car does make annual appearances at the county fair, however.

A history professor from Southwestern State College in Weatherford gave me the real lowdown on how Butcherville got its name, and it's about as exciting as the midday farm report. The name comes from a man named Jim Butcher, who back in the '20s opened a general store on the corner of US 14 and what we now call Butcherville Road, three miles north of Burr. The store became a community center of sorts, and eventually people started calling the surrounding area Butcherville. No pig farmer, no slave massacre, no Bonnie and Clyde. Just some old boy selling butter and eggs to his neighbors. I could tell you plenty of bizarre and entertaining stories about Butcherville. The true story of how it got its name isn't one of them.

The Butcherville Store has taken a few body blows over the years, but for the most part it's withstood the ravages of time. It still looks much as it did in the old days—a square, flat, one-story structure with black asphalt siding, a sheet-metal roof, and a front porch with a green awning that slumps precariously on one side. A 7-Up thermometer gets pride of place beside the front door. Pepsi-Cola, Coca-Cola, and Royal Crown Cola signs are afforded equal time on the east and west sides of the building. The porch is framed by a couple of Skelly gas pumps, one Ethyl and one Regular. Butcher sold the place during the Great Depression, and it's changed hands several times since—more frequently in recent years, as it lost business after the Piggly Wiggly opened in Burr a few years back. At some point I lost track of who ran the place. I stop in for gas sometimes, but hadn't in a while.

I parked the Galaxie off to one side so as not to block the pumps for paying customers. I climbed a set of rickety steps. Stretched out all comfortable in a patch of shade to the right of the front door was the uncrowned King of Butcherville, an ancient, one-eyed tabby cat named Cyclops. Opinions differ as to whether Cyclops is original equipment or the descendent of another cat—or cats—from days of yore, identical right down to the torn ear and monocular vision. One thing for sure, Cyclops has outlasted several of the store's human owners. It goes without saying that whoever buys the store also assumes responsibility for feeding him.

I said hello. He gazed at me with his one squinted eye, stuck a rear leg up in the air at a ninety-degree angle and licked his privates.

I refrained from asking if he'd seen Earl Collins.

The sound of music came from inside. The lyrics said something about "summer in the city." I doubt any city gets hotter than Butcherville on a late summer afternoon.

I walked in the door. A small bell over the door rang, but I could barely hear it over the music. At first glance, nothing seemed much changed since my last visit, whenever that was. An ancient pot-bellied stove sat in the middle of the room. The floor planks bowed underneath. A gas furnace had long-ago rendered the stove obsolete, yet there it sat, too expensive or impractical to remove, I expect.

Most of the goods sat on shelves behind counters running along the four walls. Glass display cases held a variety of candy and chewing gum. Bottles of pop chilled on ice inside an open-topped cooler. The only other weapon against the stifling heat was a ceiling fan that would've had to run backwards if it turned any slower. Lysol fought a losing battle against the odors of tar paper and gasoline.

Other than myself, the only person present was a young girl standing behind the register, leaning forward with her elbows on the counter, reading a book. She put it down when she saw me.

I could tell she was saying, "Good afternoon," by reading her lips, but I couldn't hear. The music was too loud.

I responded in kind. Her lip-reading must not have been as good as mine. She scrunched her eyes and cupped a hand to her ear. I said it again but it didn't help. She walked out from behind the register and over to the jukebox, reached behind it, and pulled the plug.

Now, the only noise was the whine of tires on asphalt from a passing car.

She marched back to her spot behind the cash register. "Sorry about that," she said. "I couldn't understand what you were saying." Her footsteps were heavy. She wore heavy black lace-up combat-type boots, with gum rubber soles and bright yellow stitching.

"I was just saying 'hello' back at you."

"Oh, ok," she said. "Hello again. Or I think I said, 'good afternoon,' but it doesn't matter."

"Alright then, now that we got that settled."

I tried a grin on for size. She smiled back faintly.

"They got you holding down the fort?" I asked.

"I suppose you could say that."

She produced a folded newspaper, tore off a scrap and stuck it in her book. She set it on the countertop beside her.

"Can I help you with something?" she asked.

When I first walked in the door, I thought she looked about 12. Up close, however, she looked four or five years older. She wore a black-and-white-striped, short-sleeved crew neck shirt and dark blue Levi's. She was on the tallish side, with long, dark-brown hair parted in the middle and tied into a ponytail. These days, not many high school girls wear their hair like that.

The book was *In Cold Blood*, by Truman Capote. It's a true story about a couple of drifters who, back in 1959, murdered an entire family in Holcomb, Kansas, a town even smaller than Burr, and only a couple of hours away as the crow flies. Area newspapers—including the *Burr Gazette*—made a big deal about it when it happened. Before those killings, people in towns like Burr felt safe inside their homes. Afterwards, they started locking their doors at night. The book was published only a few months back. I'd been meaning to read it and asked Kate Hennessey over at the public library to order me a copy. She called me that morning to tell me it'd come in the mail. I wondered if this young lady had beaten me to it.

I was fairly sure it wasn't something I'd want any teenaged daughter of mine to read. Not that it matters, since I don't have a daughter, teenaged or otherwise.

"We haven't met," I said. "My name's Emmett Hardy. I'm the police chief over in Burr."

"Bonnie Hubbard," she said, and offered her hand. She had a firm grip. Young as she was, she seemed as out of place in Butcherville as a Porsche in a demolition derby.

"Aren't you a little young to be running a big business like this?" I asked.

"It's not very big and I am old enough, but I don't." Miss Hubbard did not appreciate being patronized. "My mom is the manager," she said. "I just work here."

I vaguely remembered hearing that Clyde Raymer's recently-divorced daughter had taken over running the place a few months back, although I expect it might be more accurate to say Clyde had bought it and put her in charge. Clyde owns WestOK Petroleum, a natural gas processing plant in Butcherville. If what I heard was true, that means he was Bonnie's grandfather. I'd have known if I'd ever gone out to say hello after they moved in, but I never did, which was an inexcusable lapse on my part.

I asked to speak to her mother, but Bonnie said she'd gone home. I asked when she'd left.

"About four," Bonnie said. "That's when the school bus drops me off. I work until closing and let her go home."

I asked Bonnie if anyone else got off the bus when she did.

"A boy named Earl Collins."

"Anyone else?"

"No. Just me and Earl."

"Did he come in with you?"

"No. He usually comes in and buys a pop and talks to me, but he didn't today. I think he might have a little crush on me."

"Of course he does," I said. "You're a gorgeous older woman."

"Older, maybe," she said, abashed. "I don't know about the gorgeous part."

"Did he come in later?"

"No, I haven't seen him since we got off the bus. I guess he walked straight home."

"Any idea why he didn't come in today?"

She frowned. "I didn't really think about it. Tell you the truth, I was kind of glad. I like him well enough, but when there are people here, I can't read." I could relate to that, being a lover of books myself. "Why're you looking for Earl?" she asked.

"His mama called and said he didn't come home when he was supposed to, so I told her I'd look around for him."

She nodded. "Well, I haven't seen him since we got off the bus."

"You got a restroom around back, don't you?" I asked.

"Yes sir."

"Could Earl have used it after he got off the bus?"

She pushed a few stray hairs behind her ears. "Maybe," she said. "I think I might've heard the restroom door slam right after I got here. When the music's not playing I can always hear people go in and out, but today the music was so loud, I can't really say for sure."

The jukebox reminded me of the robot from that TV show, *Lost in Space*—an extra-wide version, with the words "Seeburg Select-O-Matic" written across its face.

I asked why they played it so loud. She sighed and rolled her eyes. "It's my grandfather's idea. He wants to turn this into a place kids will come after school and hang out and buy stuff. He thinks the jukebox will help."

Clyde Raymer never met a penny he wouldn't bend over and pick up.

"It hasn't helped so far, but my mama still makes me play it, in case grandpa walks in."

She leaned forward and lowered her gaze. I couldn't hear any cars drive by, but I did hear birds chirping. "Yeh, that might've been Earl going to the restroom," she said quietly, as if to herself.

I asked if anyone else was here when she arrived.

"Besides my mother," she said, "there were some men in trucks parked out front."

"Anyone you knew?"

She hesitated for a fraction of a second. "I know one of them," she said. "His name's Darryl Martin."

The name rang a bell, but I couldn't place it.

"What about the others?"

"I didn't get much of a look, but no, I don't think I knew them."

I asked for a description of the trucks. She reeled off the information with the kind of authority you don't question, even if it's coming from a teenage girl. Hell, *especially* if it's coming from a teenage girl.

"One was a red '54 Kaiser Willys. Darryl's was a **Chevy C-10 four-by-four pickup** with a fancy blue-and-white custom paint job and Cragar S/S wheels." She smiled shyly. "I really like that truck," she said. "Darryl's let me ride in it a few times."

"And the Willys belonged to the man you didn't recognize."

"Men, actually," she said. "There were two."

"Could you describe them?"

"No, I mainly just saw the back of their heads." She plucked a soda straw out of glass dispenser and started playing with it.

"How 'bout the color of their hair?"

"I'm sorry, I wasn't paying any attention at all. If I had to guess, I'd say their hair was dark."

Not much to go on there. "Darryl Martin was in his truck?" I asked.

She smashed the straw flat and started rolling it around her index finger. "Yes, he was."

"Alone?"

She let the straw fall to the counter, where it sat coiled like a small paper snake.

"Yes," she said, and added: "He's got a big cast on one of his legs. He broke it a little while ago."

I asked if she'd mind if I went out back and checked the restroom. She told me to go right ahead. Cyclops still sat in the same spot on the porch, but the shade had shifted and he now sat in the sun. I reckon he was too old and lazy to move. I walked around to the side of the building. A dirt path was worn in the grass, leading around back.

The restroom was a small wooden hut painted white, without the black siding that covered the main building. It wasn't much bigger than an outhouse. It looked like it had been slapped on as an afterthought to the original construction. To open the door, you had to pull a metal handle. A long spring bolted to the frame held it closed. I stepped in and let it slap shut.

At first glance the room was spotless except for some fine dust that had blown in from the outside. Faded brown linoleum covered the floor. The walls were painted a color so ugly, I doubt it has a name, but if you pinned me down, I'd say it was pinkish-green. There was a sink, a toilet, and a towel on a roller hung on the wall. In one corner was a tall metal trash can with a flat top and a swinging lid. I saw something sticking out from underneath. I bent over and picked it up, banging my head on the sink in the process.

It was a piece of splintered wood attached to the eye part of a hook-and-eye latch. I turned to look at the doorframe. There was a gash where the eye had been torn off. Someone had bashed the door in. The hook still hung by a few splinters.

I pulled the trash can away from the wall. I heard something fall to the floor. A school textbook had apparently slid down and gotten wedged between the can and the wall. I picked it up. It was protected by one of those heavy paper covers meant to save wear and tear. This one was grayish-blue, with dark blue and red printing. It had advertisements for local businesses, and a picture of the Burr High School mascot: a scowling fella dressed in a Revolutionary War uniform, about to hike a football between his legs to an invisible quarterback. Burr stole it from a professional team, but I guess what the Boston Patriots don't know can't hurt them.

I opened the book. It gave off that gluey new-book smell, and for a second, I flashed-back to my own school days. It was a seventh-grade science text called *Our Planet Earth*. Under "Issued To" on the inside front cover was signed "Earl Collins." Under that was a single word, written in hastily scrawled capital letters:

HELP

CHAPTER THREE

A long time ago, when I was young and stupid and just starting to get the hang of this job, I found myself drinking in a bar alongside a veteran Oklahoma State Highway Patrol investigator. I'll change his name to protect the guilty and call him Dale.

I'll never forget something Dale said.

"The beginning of a case is like making the break in a game of pool," he said with the kind of over-the-top sincerity and self-consciously precise enunciation the too-rapid consumption of illegal alcohol can produce. "The way them balls bang around against each other and arrange themselves after that first whack go a long way toward determining how things shake out in the end."

We were both three sheets to the wind, but at the time I thought what he said made a lot of sense.

It made even more sense several years later, when I was informed of Dale's death.

He was shot to death by his wife, who got off scot-free for reasons having a lot to do with the observation he had shared with me.

A barebones account goes something like this: Dale had been out drinking. He came home late. Apparently, he couldn't find his housekey. Rather than knock and wake the little lady, he climbed in through an open bedroom window. It turned out to be the last bad idea Dale ever had.

According to the tale the wife told officers on the scene, Dale had said he'd be working the overnight shift so she shouldn't expect him home until daylight. When she woke in the middle of the night and saw the shadow of a large man stumbling around in her darkened bedroom, she did the logical thing and vaporized his head with the 12-gauge shotgun she slept with on the nights Dale worked late. Only after she turned on the lights and recognized the bolo her husband had worn to work that morning did she realize her mistake.

That was her take, anyway.

Later, investigators came to find Dale wasn't working late but had instead been on a date with a dancer from the Red Dog Saloon—one of Oklahoma City's finest naked lady bars—with whom he'd been keeping illicit company for several months. There were whispers that his wife had known, and the shooting was her revenge. She insisted otherwise. Convincingly, as it turned out. Or convincingly enough.

Let's just say, the cops and prosecutor were receptive to her plea. They knew Dale. Most hated his guts. He kissed bosses' asses and abused everyone else. Dale was the kind of guy who'd kick you in the balls then blame some guy in a wheelchair. No one had a good thing to say about him. Hell, that one time I met Dale, the SOB skipped out on his tab.

The thing is, had the investigators on the case put forth a little more effort, they might've determined that the wife acted with criminal intent. They were disinclined to do so, however, because the victim was a notorious piece of shit. Her initial explanation set things up, and the cops ran the table. She was never charged with a crime. A tragic accident, everyone said, trying hard not to smile.

I bring up this story to make a point, albeit in an admittedly roundabout way that may or may not be relevant to the telling of this story:

I've always been a lousy pool player.

•　　•　　•　　•　　•

As I pondered the scene in the restroom, I thought the smart thing to do would be to call Cindy and have her notify the Tilghman County Sheriff's Department. Pass the buck to them, then get back to town and pretend to watch the game. I'd be perfectly justified, since we were in Butcherville, where I technically had as much authority as a school crossing guard.

I'm the police chief of Burr, not Butcherville. Butcherville isn't a part of Burr, even if it might like to be when it suits its purposes. At best, Butcherville's my patch by custom, not by law.

Officially, I have no power there—a fact hammered home by a vote taken several years ago in which the notoriously disputatious citizenry turned down our kind offer of annexation. If they wanted a police force, they could hire one, but they'd rather let their residents hunt coyotes with bazookas and light Marlboros with sticks of dynamite. Butcherville's town fathers decided a long time ago to leave matters of law enforcement to other entities, specifically and especially the county sheriff.

That's the way they feel, and normally I'd say goody for them, except Tilghman County is the least populous in the state, meaning it has the smallest sheriff's department. A handful of deputies are expected to patrol over twelve-hundred square miles. They can't afford to pay special attention to one stubborn little hole-in-the-wall under their jurisdiction that declines to provide for law and order.

Usually, a deputy can take his time attending to a call in Butcherville. Occasionally, however, someone with a badge and gun is needed—to break up a fight, referee a shouting match before it gets physical, or talk an irate homeowner out of shooting his neighbor's dog for getting in his trash—sooner than the half-hour it might take a deputy to get there.

Somewhere along the line, Butchervillians got in in the habit of calling the Burr police, which usually means me. I guess maybe they figure that since their children go to our schools they're entitled to my services. Occasionally, I tell them they're wrong about that, but mostly I show up when they call, trusting they don't know or care that I'm not legally empowered to do much of anything.

•   •   •   •   •

My first reaction upon opening that textbook and seeing what I saw was the kind of adrenaline rush you get when you're a little kid walking home from a Boris Karloff movie in the dark and someone in a Frankenstein mask comes up behind you and taps you on the shoulder and you turn around and almost pee your pants. That actually happened to me once.

This time, the shock was transitory. Besides being a little cockier than my abilities warrant, I can also be unaccountably optimistic in my view of human nature. I can talk a good game—I can bitch and moan with the crankiest of those old geezers down at the barber shop—but deep down, there's still a part of me that wants to believe people are more good than bad. You'd think I'd have grown out of that by now, as much ugliness as I've witnessed over the years, but I haven't. I inherited that piece of my heart from my mama. That's probably the reason I've never been able to ignore it. It's just about all of her I got left.

The thought Earl had been kidnapped flitted across my mind, but I dismissed it out of hand. Kidnappers kidnap for money. Getting a ransom out of Earl's parents would be like trying to squeeze orange juice out of a turnip. I thought that kids write stuff in schoolbooks all the time and it usually doesn't mean anything except that they're bored. Earl was probably sitting in class one day listening to his teacher drone on about photosynthesis or osmosis or whatever and scribbled 'HELP' in his book. As I remember it, kids that age have a horror of being forced to learn about rocks or plants or whatever they teach in seventh-grade science.

Of course, none of that explained the busted latch.

Upon closer examination, I noticed how the 'H' and the 'E' were different from the 'L' and the 'P.' It appeared as if the pencil lead had snapped halfway through writing the 'L.' The 'P' was almost illegible. If there'd been a pencil with a broken tip lying around, I might be able to match it to the handwriting. I dug through in the garbage can, then walked outside and searched the ground around the store. No pencil. I couldn't be sure when or why the word had been written. It did look like it had been written in a hurry, though.

My sanguinity was beginning to be replaced by a queasiness in the pit of my stomach.

I went back into the store and waited while Bonnie rang up a customer. The customer took his change. The bell jingled as he walked out the door. I heard it this time. Bonnie looked at me expectantly.

"Bonnie," I said, "did you hear anyone say anything, or yell or argue when you heard that restroom door slam shut?"

"No, but I didn't hear any voices. Of course, the music was playing, so I probably wouldn't have heard them, anyway. I'm not even one-hundred-percent sure I heard the door slam."

"The latch was broken. It looks like someone bashed in the door. Did that happen recently?"

Those errant hairs were still giving her trouble. She swatted at them like they were gnats. "It wasn't broken when I cleaned up yesterday," she said. "It must've happened today."

"Did you notice if any of the men in those trucks got out at some point? Maybe before you heard the door slam?"

"I don't really know. I couldn't see out the front windows because the blinds were pulled. I didn't even hear them drive off because of the juke box, and Darryl's truck has dual exhausts with Thrush mufflers." She must've divined that I didn't know what a Thrush muffler was. "They're hot rod mufflers," she said. "Very loud."

I nodded like I'd known it all along. "Could your mother have seen if any of them got out and bothered Earl?"

"I doubt it. She left as fast as she could, just as I was coming in. They were still sitting in the trucks."

"But she might've seen where Earl went off to?"

"Maybe," she shrugged. "She might even know those men's names."

Bonnie didn't act like someone who'd easily scare. Still, she was only 15 or 16, which is pretty young to get involved in a police matter. I could ask her to help me find Earl and risk scarring her for life—which seemed unlikely—or let her off the hook and possibly lessen my chances of expeditiously getting to the bottom of this. It seemed possible that the men in the Willys had taken Earl, but I had my doubts. It couldn't have been Darryl; Bonnie saw him drive off as they got off the bus. Why would any of them snatch a twelve-year-old boy whose parents were broke? All things considered, I suspected Earl had probably just gone home with a friend and forgot to call his mother. Still, I needed to track him down, if only for the poor woman's peace of mind.

Bonnie read my thoughts. "You think one of those men might've driven off with Earl?" she asked.

"I doubt it, but I reckon I'd better check."

"Well, I don't know about the men in that Willys, but I do know where Darryl lives."

"Where's that?"

"It's on a road off US 14," she said. "but I'm not sure what it's called. I'm still learning which of these country roads are which. It's better if I show you."

"Think your mama will mind?"

She looked over her shoulder at a Dr. Pepper clock hanging on the wall behind her. It only had three numbers: 10, 2, and 4, leaving us to deduce where the others should be.

"I'd only be closing twenty minutes early," she said. "Business has been terrible, anyway. Mom won't mind." She opened the cash register and stuffed the bills in a brown paper bag. "I'll count this later," she said.

"We'll stop by your house on the way," I said. "I should ask her if it's ok for you to help me with this. I need to talk to her anyway, in case she might've seen where Earl went, or recognized whoever it was in that Willys."

"Suit yourself."

"Think we should call her to let her know we're coming?"

"Phone's broke."

"Right," I said. That's why Ona Ray couldn't get through and why I'd come out there in the first place.

If I had reservations about taking her, Bonnie Hubbard had none. She stomped to the door in those big boots, switched off the light and ceiling fan. I stood like a statue, leaning against the antique stove.

"We going or not?" she asked like I was making her late for an important meeting.

"I guess we are," I said.

CHAPTER FOUR

The late-afternoon sun still beat down hot and bright, as it will in early September. The wind blew and dust devils whirled across fields that had recently been harvested of wheat and were now covered by yellow stubble. A lack of rain made for an ample supply of blowing dirt. Given the choice between baking like a potato with the windows shut (the town council had decided air-conditioning for our new patrol car was an unwarranted expense) and being peppered across the face by dust and assorted flying debris with the windows open, I chose the latter. We paid the price in watery eyes and bugs in our teeth. Even with the windows down, it was as hot as the devil.

I'm not much of a talker at the best of times, but I cannot abide silence when I'm riding in a vehicle with somebody. It just seems rude not to talk in the company of someone just a foot or two away. I'll talk to basically anyone in a moving car, from the officers under my command, to the drunk drivers I transport from my holding cell to the more commodious accommodations of the county jail. A teenage girl who likes to read about psycho killers fits in there somewhere.

"So, Bonnie, how long y'all lived here?"

She looked out the window at the passing parade of wheat fields and windmills and bored-looking cows looking for relief from the sun under whatever shade they could find.

"Since June," she said. "We moved here after my last school got out for the summer."

"Where'd you live before?"

She turned toward me and the wind blew a hunk of long brown hair into her mouth. I imagine having such long hair must be annoying as all get out.

"Wichita," she said, as she spit the hair out of her mouth.

"That's quite a change, moving from a big city like Wichita to a little town like Burr. Or Butcherville."

She turned her attention back to the scenery. "I guess."

I got hold of Cindy on the radio and asked if she'd talked to Earl's friends. She had. None of them had seen him, or had any idea where he was. According to them, Earl didn't have a girlfriend.

Bonnie and I drove some more. I asked her how she liked Butcherville.

"I don't," she said. Short and to the point. I was beginning to like this girl. The road to her house came up. She told me where to turn.

"What made you and your mom move here?" I asked.

"My dad was having an affair with his secretary. My mom wouldn't put up with that and walked out on him. My grandpa said he'd buy her a store if we moved here. So we did. He's rich. My grandpa is, I mean."

She didn't seem to put much stock in being rich.

"Did I hear your grandpa's Clyde Raymer?" I asked.

"I don't know, did you?" she drawled sarcastically. "I'm sorry," she added. "Yes, he's my grandfather."

"I don't know Mr. Raymer all that well," I said. I didn't add that what I did know wasn't exactly positive.

"You're lucky. I know him better than I'd like to."

Maybe she knew the same things about him I did.

"He can't be that bad," I said. "He bought your mama that store, didn't he?"

She frowned. "He's bad," she said, like that was her last word on the subject. I took her cue.

"What do you do for fun?" I asked.

"Photography. My father gave me a nice camera to bribe me into not hating him."

The men in Bonnie's life must be real princes, I thought.

"What do you take pictures of?" I asked.

"Nature, mostly. You ever heard of Ansel Adams?"

"Can't say that I have."

"Well, he's a nature photographer. I like his work."

"You're a reader, too, huh?"

She nodded.

"So am I," I said. "How're you liking *In Cold Blood*? I've been wanting to read that myself."

"You should. I just started it, but so far, it's very interesting. It's like a murder mystery, except that it really happened."

"You like mysteries?"

"They're about all I read. That, and poetry."

She turned and looked at me. I kept my eyes on the road, but I believe she was trying to judge if I could be trusted.

"I'm going to be a policewoman," she said. "I want to be a detective."

"Not many women detectives that I know of. Not in Oklahoma, at least."

"I won't be in Oklahoma. I'm applying to the College of Police Science in New York City when I graduate from high school."

She'll have her work cut out for her wherever she is. Law enforcement is dominated by men who are, by-and-large, not terribly liberal in their views of women, and being a single girl living on her own in New York City is its own kind of challenge. I got the feeling that she knew what she was up against, however. She just didn't care. Bonnie Hubbard had a pair on her, that's for sure.

"I'll tell you what," I said, "if you'd like to come down to the station some time and talk, I'll be happy to have you. I never went to a police college, but I know a little bit about this business."

A smile lit up her face. "That would be great," she said. "Think I could ride around with you when you go out on patrol?"

"That's what you're doing right now."

"I guess I am," she said, still smiling. She straightened up, like she felt the need to adopt a more professional posture.

"Come by any time. We'll show you the ropes."

• • • • • •

Bonnie and her mother lived at the end of a long gravel driveway off County Road 330, a dirt road that crosses Route 14 on the northern edge of Butcherville. Their house was small but neat: a white, one-story wooden farm house with a porch and an awning lined with white pillars on red-brick supports. A white swing was attached by chains to the porch roof. Thick quilted seat cushions looked like they might massage your butt to sleep if you sat on them too long. Potted plants adorned the window boxes, and a welcome mat lay in front of the door. The small front lawn was mowed. In the back, a faded red barn kept watch over a farmyard with an empty chicken coop off to one side. I was reminded of houses kept by widows; even if I didn't know Bonnie lived there alone with her mother, I'd have suspected the place had not enjoyed a male presence in some time.

As I went up the front steps, I heard a piano being played inside. I couldn't identify the piece, although it sounded familiar. It was classical music, the kind they play at Civic Center Music Hall in Oklahoma City. It was pretty while it lasted, which was only as long as it took Bonnie to burst through the door and yell, "Mom!" The music stopped instantly, like when you lift the needle off a record, but without that ripped-corduroy sound it can make if you're not careful.

The living room was as cluttered and unkempt as the outside had been neat and homey. Boxes were stacked against the walls. Some had their top flaps open and looked as if they'd been unpacked only a few items at a time, as needed. The furniture consisted of two metal folding chairs and a new couch wrapped in plastic. A small portable television with long rabbit ears sat atop a taped-up box doubling as a table; the word 'BOOKS' was written on the side in thick black letters. Bedsheets were tacked over the windows.

Bonnie disappeared through a door in the back of the room. She returned a few seconds later, trailed by a brown-eyed, brown-haired woman about my age who, despite being shorter, looked enough like Bonnie to be her sister. She stood with her arms crossed, like she was ready to put up a fight.

"Am I under arrest?" she asked, clearly less than happy to have a cop standing in her front room. "What's the matter? Unlawful piano playing?"

"No ma'am. I'm pretty sure there's no law against playing the piano, especially in Butcherville. Even if there was, I wouldn't arrest you for it. I haven't heard a piano played that well in a long time." I thought of my mama, who played the heck out of Jelly Roll Morton but knew her Mozart, too. "What was that you were playing?"

"It's called the 'Pathetique' Sonata, by Beethoven. Maybe you're familiar with him."

She didn't have much of an Okie accent, possibly because her daddy sent her to some fancy boarding school back east, where they favored the likes of Ludwig van Beethoven over Buck Owens and Conway Twitty.

"I'm more partial to Charlie Parker and Dizzy Gillespie," I replied, "but I give Mr. Beethoven a spin on my record player once in a while."

She dialed back her scorn a notch. "Well, good for you," she said. "I've been known to enjoy some jazz myself."

She held out her hand. For a small woman, she had very long, tapered fingers. The better to play the piano, no doubt. "I'm Grace Hubbard," she said. "Soon to be Grace Raymer. Again."

"Hardy," I said. "Emmett Hardy. I'm chief of police over in Burr. Nice to meet you. I just made the acquaintance of young Bonnie here at your store." We looked over at Bonnie, who seemed to not like being looked at. "She's quite a little gal," I said.

Grace smiled. "She's definitely a horse of a different color, isn't she?"

She was, especially now that she was blushing. She looked down and let her hair form a curtain around her face.

"We could use more like her around here," I said. "I've been talking to her about a boy we're looking for. He was last seen a couple of hours ago getting off the school bus in front of your store. I wanted to ask if you could add anything to what she's told me."

"I was standing at the door when Bonnie got off the bus," she said. "The same boy got off with her who usually does."

"Earl Collins, mom," Bonnie said from underneath all that hair.

"Did you see what he did when he got off?" I asked.

She shook her head. "I was in such a hurry to get home, I wasn't paying much attention. There were some men in the parking lot. Darryl Martin is one, I know that. Drives a fancy blue pickup. I believe there were a couple of others sitting in that red station wagon-like thing. The man behind the wheel has been in the store a few times. I don't know anything about him, except that he drives that red jeep."

Bonnie came out from behind her wall of hair.

"That's a Willys, mom."

Grace Hubbard rolled her eyes.

"Like I care," she said and gave Bonnie a bored look. Bonnie looked bored right back. They broke into smiles, as if they were sharing a private joke.

I asked if she got a look at the other man in the car. She did not. I asked if either had said anything to or approached the boy. She couldn't say for sure, but didn't think so.

"You know anything else about this Darryl Martin?" I asked.

"Just that he drives that truck and works for my father's company. We generally just talk about the weather when he comes in the store. He showed up one day on crutches, with a big cast on his leg. I think he explained why, but I wasn't paying attention. One time he mentioned his wife was a good cook."

"Did he come in today?"

"Yes, he did. Just before Bonnie got there. Bought a bag of flour and a bottle of buttermilk. He was pulling out of the parking lot when I left."

"Did you see if he talked to the men in the Willys?"

"I hardly even looked in their direction, I was in such a rush to get out of there."

"Did you see where Earl went?"

"I'm sorry, Chief Hardy, I just barely noticed him out of the corner of my eye. Bonnie got off that bus at four. By four-oh-one, I was halfway home."

CHAPTER FIVE

I asked Grace's permission for Bonnie to show me where Darryl Martin lived. She said that would be fine.

Bonnie and I chatted some more on the drive over. I couldn't resist poking around the one subject guaranteed to embarrass a teenage girl more than anything.

"Got yourself a boyfriend?" I asked. "Or is that none of my business?"

She blushed again down to the roots of her hair.

"It's none of your business, but I'll tell you anyway: I kind of have one. He's a friend and he's a boy. That's all I'm going to say. Don't ask who it is."

"That's fair enough. I reckon a woman is entitled to her secrets. It does make me curiouser about who it is, though."

"A man is entitled to be curious about a woman's secrets," she said, "but it doesn't mean he has the right to know what they are."

"Can I guess?"

"I wish you wouldn't."

I let the matter drop. Instead of giving her a hard time, I tried to remember how I knew the name Darryl Martin but couldn't come up with it. I thought it might be nice to listen to some music so I turned on the radio. I listened to ten seconds of "These Boots Were Made for Walkin'" and turned it off. Nancy Sinatra sure ain't her dad

The road Bonnie forgot was Windmill Road. That's not the official name— county roads are numbered—but people call it that because some fella who lives out that way has made it his life's work to collect specimens of every type of windmill ever made, and put them on display. There must be over a hundred of them. If Bonnie had said "it's the road with all the old windmills on it," I'd have known what she meant. I suspect she didn't because she wanted to go along for the ride.

The Martin house was a simple, medium-sized one-story brick house set a few dozen feet off the road. It was the same dark reddish-orange color as most of the soil around here, likely because the bricks were forged nearby. Brick manufacturing has always been a thriving business in this county. Gives us something to do with all that red clay.

The house was attractive enough but it seemed like it had been built for a family of Munchkins. The doors seemed shorter than normal, the windows closer to the ground. The garage could've been built to shelter a go-kart. It's like the house had sunk into the ground after it was built.

We parked in the road and I surveilled the scene.

A mailbox painted red, white, and blue sat on a white post at the end of the driveway. "MARTIN" was spelled out in silver and black reflective letters. A dark green Chevrolet Biscayne sedan and a blue and white Chevy C-10 four-by-four pickup were parked in a car port in front of the garage. Someone had written, "Go Patriots!!!" in white shoe polish on the Biscayne's rear window. The front yard was enclosed by a waist-high picket fence painted in alternating red, white, and, blue stripes. Inside the fence, a few yards from the house on a diagonal, was a square concrete slab, about 12-by-12 feet and raised about six inches off the ground. A metal door set in the middle would've led to an underground shelter, designed to protect the home's occupants from tornadoes and atom bombs.

I had Bonnie wait in the car. I got out and looked around for signs of a kidnapped boy. There were none that I could see, not that I expected to find any. I pulled open the gate. The paint was wet. I let go as a reflex and the gate slapped against my thigh, leaving a red-white-and-blue striped pattern on the front of my jeans.

That's not gonna come out, I thought.

I climbed up onto the porch and knocked. A spate of high-pitched barking commenced from inside. A woman's voice hollered at the dog to shut up. Footsteps pounded toward the door. A young lady with a Rosie the Riveter build and a scattering of freckles that complemented her frizzy rust-colored hair greeted me, holding a bowl of dough under one arm and stirring it with the other, while trying to discourage an angry black-and-white terrier the size of a medium-sized rabbit from ripping me to pieces.

I introduced myself.

"I'm Erin Martin, pleased to meet you," she replied, friendly-like, and with notable calm, given that the dog was still barking and showing its teeth. She inspected my newly redecorated trousers and said, "Oh, my. Darryl should've put a 'Wet Paint' sign on that fence. I'm so sorry about that."

I told her not to worry, and asked for the man of the house. She motioned me inside. "I'll go get him. Let me get you a rag first, so you can wash that stuff off your hands."

She started to close the door and noticed Bonnie sitting in the Galaxie. "Is that the girl from the store over yonder? Why don't you bring her in? It must be hot, sitting in that car."

The sun was indeed still high enough in the sky to make things uncomfortable. I called-out to Bonnie and asked if she was ok. She waved and nodded. Mrs. Martin waved back and closed the door. "Ok, then," she said. She led me into the living room without offering me a seat and went to fetch her husband.

I shuffled my feet and looked around. The house was cookie-cutter nice. The furniture looked new, but didn't make much of an impression, which is its own kind of impression, I guess. The requisite portrait of Jesus hung on one wall, meaning the Martins were either God-fearing or wanted folks to think they were. Several water-stained cardboard political signs were stacked against one wall. They were yellow, with the words 'Vote Darryl Martin' above an image of a coiled rattlesnake with its forked tongue darting out of its mouth. Across the bottom it said *Don't Tread on Me*. Of course. That's where I heard of Darryl Martin. He was on the Butcherville city council a while back.

The only thing out of the ordinary were several framed photographs of various long-legged, long-necked, long-beaked birds hanging on the walls.

Erin returned, without the bowl or the dog. I could hear it bark faintly, like it was shut in a room or a closet. "Darryl will be here in a minute," she said. A series of loud, uneven thumping sounds began from somewhere in the rear of the house. Erin paid it no mind.

"Someone around here likes birds," I said, pointing at the photographs.

Erin laughed. "That's Darryl's thing. He's crazy about those strange birds they got at the Salt Flats over by Rose Crest."

Rose Crest is a small township a ways north of Butcherville, about a thirty-minute drive from downtown Burr. The Rose Crest Salt Flats are a miniature version of that place in Utah, where car racers are always setting those world land speed records—a glimmering white pan of salt and rocks, standing water, and scrubby vegetation that attracts wildlife you won't see anywhere else in the state.

"Darryl loves those funny little birds," Erin said. "He goes out there and takes pictures of them with that fancy camera of his whenever he can." The thumping was getting closer. "He's got a shack out there on a little island in the middle of the lake where he goes to be alone," she said. "He doesn't think I know about it, but I do."

"What do I think you don't know about?" A stout young man wearing horned-rim glasses with lenses as thick as the bottom of Coke bottles entered the room. He leaned on a pair of wooden crutches, made necessary by a huge, hip-to-ankle cast on one leg.

The man had a prominent nose, sad eyes, and drooping lips. Except for a small tuft of hair over his forehead, he was completely bald on top, with a bushy but well-combed fringe ringing the sides and back of his head. Imagine if the drummer from The Beatles had gone to sleep one night and woke up the next morning looking like Larry from the Three Stooges.

"I was just saying you like those birds you take pictures of more than me," she said.

"Don't be silly," he said. "I don't love nothing or nobody more than you." He kissed her cheek and put his arm around her in a way I was thought too showy to be affectionate.

"Darryl Martin," he said and offered his hand. "Glad to meet you, Chief Hardy." The delight in his voice was out of proportion with the modest pleasure of making my acquaintance.

"Likewise, Mr. Martin."

Erin wriggled out of his embrace and commenced rummaging around inside the hall closet. She pulled out some old rags and handed them to me. "You can use these to try to get some of that paint off you," she said. "I don't believe we have any turpentine, do we Darryl?"

He shook his head. "We should, but we don't, unfortunately."

I tried to wipe off the paint but only succeeded in combining the colors into a red, white, blue, and purple smudge. The dog had escaped from wherever he'd been, and began gnawing at my pant leg. Erin picked him up and scolded him in baby talk. I like dogs, but prefer larger breeds, like my yellow Labrador retriever, Dizzy. I talk to her, too, but like a grownup.

Darryl looked pained. "Oh, I am sorry about that," he said. "That's all my fault. I should've put a warning sign on that gate, but we weren't expecting company, so I didn't see the point."

"You've been painting your fence with that big ol' cast on your leg?"

"Heck yeh," he said, as if I'd asked if he intended to continue breathing air into his lungs. "The first game of football season only comes once a year. Got to support the team."

"You're a better man than I am," I said.

With some people, it's hard to tell whether they're really eager to be liked or couldn't care less. Darryl was one of those people.

He grinned. "Oh, I'm sure that's not true," he said. "But I'll tell you what, I want to write you a check to replace those pants."

I don't make enough money to be buying a new pair of jeans every time one gets dirty. If Darryl Martin wanted to make an offer, I wasn't going to talk him out of it.

"That'll be fine," I said. His grin faded a tiny bit. "Anyway," I said, "the reason I'm here is to ask if you were at the Butcherville Store a little earlier today. Around four o'clock."

I knew he was but it never hurts to give a man enough rope to hang himself, if he's so inclined.

"I was," he said. "Erin wanted me to pick up some buttermilk and flour." He grinned at Erin. "Didn't you, sweetheart?"

"I did," she said with a smile that aspired to the brilliance of Darryl's, but fell a few kilowatts short. "I needed it to make biscuits."

"Best buttermilk biscuits in the state of Oklahoma, and she's got the blue ribbons from the state fair to prove it," Darryl said. "Whyn't you come back to the kitchen and try one?"

"They ain't ready yet, hon," said Erin.

"That's alright," I said. "Darryl, tell me, were you there at the store by yourself?"

"I didn't go in with nobody, if that's what you mean, although I wish I had someone to help me with this danged cast. It practically weighs more than I do. Getting in and out of the truck with these crutches is a pain, let me tell you."

"Yeh, I reckon it must be hard," I said. I did not want to get into a long, drawn-out conversation about how he broke his leg. "On your way out, did you see a boy outside the store?"

"You know what? I did see a boy get off the bus, about the time I was leaving."

"Did you see where he went?" I asked. "Did he go into the store?"

He shook his head.

"Or around back, to the restroom?"

He shook his head again. "I didn't even know the Butcherville Store had a restroom," he said, then smiled at Erin and pinched her cheek. She pretended not to mind and drew her little dog closer. "Nah, I didn't notice," he said. "I was driving off when he got there."

"I understand there was another truck there at the same time you were."

"Yeh, I noticed that," he said. "That old Willys pickup. Red."

"Do you know who it was? "

"I knew the guy in the driver's seat," he said. He ran a hand through the nonexistent hair on top of his head. "I mean, I don't really know him," he said, "but I know who he is. People at work call him Tyler."

"You work with him?"

"That's right, at the WestOK plant."

"Do you know if that's his first or last name?"

"I believe his last."

"Do you know his first?"

"I might know it if I heard it, but I can't recall."

"You wouldn't know where he lives?"

"I'm sorry, I don't." His facial muscles must've been sore; his smile was now a shadow of its former self. "I reckon he lives around here somewhere," he said, "but I wouldn't know where."

"You said you knew the man in the driver's seat. Was there someone with him?"

"Yeh, there was, but I don't know who. I never saw his face. What's all this about, anyway?"

I explained about Earl Collins's disappearance. I stressed that it was probably no big deal, that the boy would likely find his way home on his own, but I was taking a look around because his mama was worried. Both Darryl and Erin seemed suitably concerned. I asked Darryl who I should talk to at the plant if I wanted to get hold of this Tyler.

"Elmer Kepley is the plant manager," he said. "He could help you, but I'm pretty sure he's out of town. Gone camping and fishing this weekend, is what I heard."

Erin touched Darryl's arm. "What about George Fisher?" she asked.

"What about him?" said Darryl. Erin withdrew her hand.

"Who's George Fisher?" I asked.

"George is the plant personnel manager," Erin explained. "I'm sure he can help you out, Chief Hardy. Darryl, I think his business card is on your desk. At least it was the other day."

Darryl shook his head. "George won't be in the office this late," he said. "I'm sure he's gone home by now."

"You should give me his number anyway," I said. "I might get lucky."

Darryl sighed. "Alright, hold on a second," he said, and began thumping off down the hall. Erin called out, "I'll get it, hon," but Darryl waved her off. She and I waited. I'd still not been invited to sit.

Darryl returned with the card. "You can keep it," he said. "I can get another one. I doubt you'll be able to get hold of him until Monday, though. The office is closed on weekends."

"You wouldn't have his home number, would you?" I asked. "In case I need to talk to him before then."

"Sorry, I don't."

"Think he'll be at the game tonight?"

"Nah, George commutes from Woodward," Darryl said. "I don't think he's much of a football fan."

"Must be a communist," I said. Erin and Darryl chuckled.

I thought I could try Woodward directory assistance for his home number if I needed to.

I thanked them for their time. Erin sat the dog behind a little fence she'd rigged up in the doorway separating the living room from the kitchen. It kept barking while they escorted me out. Erin steadied Darryl's arm as he awkwardly heaved his damaged leg down the front steps using only one of his crutches. Darryl held open the gate for Erin and me, careful not to get wet paint on his hands.

He noticed Bonnie sitting in the truck and struck up a conversation. Most of their talk seemed to be about Darryl's pickup, which Erin and I didn't find very interesting. Darryl and Bonnie might've gabbed all day if I hadn't broken it up.

I got in and started the engine. With some difficulty, Darryl clomped over to my side to say goodbye. Erin stood several yards away truck, chewing on a thumbnail. I noticed a pack of Tareyton cigarettes sticking out of Darryl's shirt pocket.

"You're a fighter, huh?" I said.

"What's that?"

I nodded at the cigarettes. "Those commercials say Tareyton smokers would rather fight than switch."

He smiled. "Oh, that. Nah, I'm a lover, not a fighter. I'd rather switch then take a beating. You'd better believe it." He pulled the pack out of his pocket, shook out a cigarette, and lit it off a matchbook that said *First State Bank of*

Watie Junction. He craned his head around me and winked at Bonnie. "Good to see you," he said, a little too flirtatiously, if you ask me, given that his wife was standing right there. Bonnie smiled back politely.

"I'll write you a check for those pants," Darryl said, without actually making a move to do it.

I shifted into reverse and started to back up. Erin took her thumbnail out of her mouth and waved for me to stop. "Chief Hardy," she called out, "I thought of something."

I braked. "What's that?" I asked.

"Do you know if this Earl Collins is any relation to Merle Collins?"

I switched off the engine. "Merle is Earl's daddy," I said. "Why? Do you know Merle?"

Darryl looked exasperated. "Honey, you need to let Chief Hardy go. He's got work to do."

"I know he does," she said, "but I was just thinking the boy's disappearance could have something to do with everyone at the plant being so mad at Merle Collins."

"Why's everyone at the plant mad at Merle Collins?" I asked.

Erin looked imploringly at her husband, took a couple of steps backward, and resumed munching on her thumbnail. She'd said all she was going to say.

Darryl didn't seem happy she'd brought it up. He leaned against the driver's side door with one hand and placed the other hand on his hip. His mending leg appeared to be causing him some discomfort. "Well, it probably doesn't have nothing to do with anything," he said, "but you probably heard about how WestOK is looking to expand the plant."

"I heard something about it," I said, "but I don't know the details."

"Merle Collins is standing in the way."

"How's he doing that?"

"Listen," he said, leaning in and blowing smoke out of his nose, "I don't like to spread rumors, especially about where I work. Other folks know a lot more about it than I do." The cigarette dangled in one corner of his mouth. Smoke filled the cab. Bonnie coughed quietly.

He pushed himself away from the truck. "That's all I got," he said. He flipped his half-smoked cigarette onto the gravel. "Erin probably shouldn't have brought it up. The boy probably just went home with his friends after school. He'll turn up later, safe and sound."

I agreed he probably would, and asked Erin if she had anything to add. She gave a few quick little shakes of her head. I had one more question.

"What's your position at WestOK, Darryl?"

"Oh, I work in the financial department," he said off-handedly.

"Oh, so you're a big shot, then," I said with a smile, silently wondering why someone working the money side of things wouldn't know more about an expansion of the business. He grinned and shrugged and I grinned and shrugged back. I pointed my vehicle back in the direction of Bonnie's house and drove.

• • • • •

Bonnie told me I could drop her off at the store, but it was just as easy to take her home.

"I don't mind walking from the store," she said. "I do it every day."

"That's quite a hike," I said.

"I like it. Sometimes I ride my bicycle, but it's a dirt road most of the way, and it's not much fun riding a bike on a dirt road. Usually I walk."

"By the way," I said, "when I was in Darryl's house I saw a bunch of pictures of birds on the walls. His wife says Darryl takes them himself, out at the Salt Flats near Rose Crest. Did you know about that?" She shook her head. "I'm no expert, but they looked good to me. You ought to ask him about it. You two might have more in common than a fondness for fancy trucks."

"Mm-hmm," she said. "Maybe I will."

I asked if she knew anything about that plant expansion Darryl mentioned.

"All I know is my grandpa wants to make even more money than he's got, and he's already got way more than he needs."

I figured that was true, but didn't feel it was my place to say.

The sun had resigned its commission for the day. The sky had turned leaden by the time we pulled into the Hubbards' car port. Bonnie's eyes were drawn to the house across the road, where a little girl sat in a porch swing. The girl leaned forward and squinted at us like she was trying to make out who we were.

Bonnie smiled. "There's my little shadow," she said, and waved. The girl jumped out of the swing and hurried to the side of the road. Her gait was wobbly, as if her legs were disinclined to do what she wanted them to do. She waved excitedly at Bonnie.

"Friend of yours?" I asked.

"That's Princess Bellchamber. My best friend, except for my mom," she said. "She's a sweetheart."

She opened her door and started to get out. "Well, thanks for letting me help," she said. "That was fun. Of course, it would've been more fun if you would've let me hear you interrogate the witnesses."

"Maybe next time, if you promise not to hold out on me like you did this time."

"Hold out on you? How'd I do that?"

I gave her a stern look. "C'mon, now, you know what I'm talking about. The way you described Darryl Martin."

She looked puzzled. "I don't remember describing him at all," she said. I kept a straight face as long as I could. "You didn't tell me he had hair like Bozo the Clown."

She leaned back, punched me in the shoulder, and laughed uproariously. "No, dang it, he looks like Allen Ginsberg. The poet. Who, for your information, is really cool."

Maybe I should read up on this Ginsberg fella.

CHAPTER SIX

A couple of hours had passed since Ona Ray Collins first called. What at first seemed to be a case of a thoughtless 12-year-old boy going somewhere without telling his mother now felt more serious. I radioed Cindy, told her what I'd learned, and asked her to pass it on to my officers. I also told her to get on the horn to the Tilghman County Sheriff's Department and let them in on the deal. Usually, I'd rather shovel horseshit with a toothpick than ask for their help, but in a situation like this I can't afford to be stubborn.

That doesn't mean I have to like it, however.

It took me five minutes to get from Bonnie Hubbard's house to the Collins's. The house was a white cracker box with slatted windows that open and shut with a crank from the inside. It looked like it was built from one of those kits from Sears that you can put together yourself if you've got more time than money (I don't), and are handy with a set of tools (I'm not).

A stone's throw to the east, sticking straight up out of the ground, all alone in an empty field, surrounded by overgrown weeds and tall grass, was a door. No building. Just a door. Viewed head-on, you'd think it led nowhere. Viewed at an angle, you'd see it for what it was—the entrance to a root cellar. It had probably also served as a storm shelter, not unlike the one at the Martins's place, although presumably much older and worse for wear.

Rising above the landscape, not more than a quarter-mile behind the house, was the WestOK gas plant: a homely mess of pipes and towers and storage tanks all tangled and connected together in some complicated way that almost looks random but of course isn't. It would be hard to imagine the damn thing getting any bigger and uglier and smellier than it is already, but if

Clyde Raymer has his way, that's what's going to happen. Depending on how good you are at squinting your eyes, most of Tilghman County is fairly scenic. Unfortunately, no amount of squinting can improve the looks of the WestOK monstrosity.

Except for a riding lawnmower parked next to the driveway, the only vehicle in evidence was a broken-down old Chevy coupe, without tires or wheels, propped up on jacks. Whatever functioning vehicle they had must've been with Merle. A skinny Heinz-57 dog tied to the Chevy's front fender barked to wake the dead as I got out the Galaxie.

Ona Ray answered the door with a cigarette held between her fingers and an anxious expression on her face. She wore what must've been one of her husband's T-shirts and a pair of lime-green pedal pushers. Merle's a little taller than Ona Ray, but he's as narrow as a broomstick and she's kind of big, so the shirt fit tighter than it was designed to.

I knew Ona Ray to be in her early-forties or thereabouts. Standing there at the door, she looked old enough to be Earl's grandma. Worry was beating her to a pulp. She'd had Earl late in life, which I'm sure made him all the more precious. One look at her red-rimmed eyes, and I knew he was still AWOL.

"No word?" I asked.

"No, and now his father hasn't come home, either," she said. "He should've been here half an hour ago."

She gazed distractedly at the paint on my pants but thankfully did not comment.

"Could Earl be with his father?" I asked.

"I don't see how, unless he picked him up right after he got off the school bus. I called Merle at work to tell him Earl was late, but his boss said he'd left already. Merle told him he wanted to pick us up to go to the game." She took a drag and blew smoke out through her nose. "He still hasn't shown up, though."

I suggested that maybe Merle had seen Earl walking home from the store and picked him up, and maybe they'd gone straight to the game without bothering to tell her. She wanted to believe that was possible.

"It wouldn't be the first time Merle didn't tell me where he was or when he was coming home," she said.

Sadly, I'm not nearly as good at blowing smoke up my own backside. That word "HELP" written in the textbook preyed on my mind.

"How's Earl and his father get along?"

"They get along good. I reckon sometimes Merle is a little too hard on him, but they're best friends. Merle does have an awful temper, but he almost always gets mad at himself, not me or Earl."

"He ever hit you or the boy?"

That was too much for her to handle. "No," she said, "and I resent you thinking that." I thought she might try to extinguish the cigarette in my eye. "Merle has a temper, but like I said, he mostly gets mad at himself. He never hits."

I backed off real quick. "I'm sorry. I had to ask."

Her chin quivered and her eyes watered. "I know," she said. "You're just trying to help."

We listened to the crickets chirp for a few seconds.

"Did Earl carry anything to school this morning besides his schoolbooks?" I asked.

"He took his football with him, to play with his buddies at recess."

More crickets.

I remembered the cellar door.

"Why's your cellar so far from the house?" I asked

She shrugged. "That ain't ours. There used to be another house on that lot, a long time ago. You can still see the foundation if you look hard, but it got torn down before we moved here. Someone bought the land about a year ago. I don't know who."

"Did you look for Earl down there? Could be he's playing hide and seek."

"I looked everywhere I could think of."

If that were true, he must be somewhere she *couldn't* think of—in which case, there wasn't much more she could do to help.

I asked her about the possibility of Earl having a girlfriend. She said she doubted it, echoing what his friends had told Cindy.

"You're not much of a football fan, are you?" I asked.

She shook her head and flicked her cigarette to the ground near the disabled Chevy. The dog strained on his leash trying to get close enough to sniff it, without any luck. "I can take it or leave it," she said, "but I was going tonight. I always got to the first game of the season."

"Maybe those two boys of yours know how you don't like it that much, and decided to give you the night off."

It sounded lame to my ears, but she nodded like she would at a preacher telling her a bible story she wanted to believe even if common sense told her it was hogwash.

"I tell you what, Ona Ray, I'm on my way there myself," I said. "I'll have them make an announcement asking for Merle and Earl to come to the press box. When they do, I'll give them a good talking-to. How's that sound?"

She forced a smile. "Thank you, Chief Hardy," she said. "I'm sure you're right, but a mother can't help but worry."

My return smile came easier. It's not like my son or husband had gone missing. "I don't blame you," I said, "but there's no point getting all worked up if there's a simple explanation. I'll bet you anything they'll be home just as soon as the game's over. Maybe earlier, if it's a skunking." Burr tends to be on the losing end of such games.

"One more thing," I asked. "What kind of car does Merle drive?"

"Dodge pickup. Light yellow, or off-white, you might say," she said. "It's a 1961 model. There's a red tool chest behind the cab."

I filed that away in my memory, which isn't as good as it once was. Sooner or later I'm going to have to start writing things down.

"If you don't mind, Ona Ray, I'd like to take a look in that cellar myself. Just out of curiosity."

"He ain't there," she said dejectedly, "but you're welcome to look."

I told her I'd see her later and to keep her chin up. I reckon she could've used a hug, but hugging's not my line. Karen does my hugging for me.

She walked back into her house and I searched the Galaxie's backseat, looking for the custom flashlight I always carry. I couldn't find it. I did find a stray cigarette lighter in the back seat and reckoned that would have to do.

I walked across a field covered with rocks and scrub toward the cellar. If there was an old foundation there, I didn't see it. The screws holding the door to the lower hinge had rusted away. The top hinge remained attached, barely, and the wood was rotted through in a couple of places. I opened it carefully, so as not to ruin it completely.

I descended the steps and lit the Zippo. Some root cellars are little more than holes dug into the ground. This one was more elaborate, although weeds had started to grow in places they weren't supposed to. The room was small and rectangular-shaped, with a packed dirt floor, and stone-lined walls. The ceiling was made of red brick, laid in an arching pattern, with a square opening on one end where the steps came down. Overhead clearance was low—less than six-feet—so I had to duck if I didn't want to knock myself silly. A few Brown Derby beer cans and partially-burnt candles stuck in the necks of Coke bottles lay on the floor. I picked up a can and shook it. Something rattled inside. I looked in and saw a couple of cigarette butts, then put it back where I found it. I returned to the surface and headed back to town.

I was a mile down the road before I realized I'd forgotten to ask Ona Ray about what Darryl Martin had said about Merle standing in the way of WestOK's plant expansion. I got to thinking how the best way to make an enemy out of a rich man is to keep him from getting even richer. That seemed to be what Merle was doing to Clyde Raymer. Rich men can be bad enemies to have.

I almost turned around to go back, but I was sure I'd be seeing Ona Ray again before the night was over. I'd ask her the next time.

Earl and Merle were probably together, I told myself. We'd find them.

CHAPTER SEVEN

I hit my emergency lights coming back. Just because I could.

I didn't use the siren, though. No one likes a show-off.

On my way in, I got to thinking how things around here have changed over the years. I reckon some of those changes have been positive, but I'm not sure I could tell you which ones off the top of my head.

Take our movie theater, for example. Burr used to have one. Now it doesn't. The old Broncho still stands at one end of Main Street, but it's been closed a long time. Although it's shed a few letters over the years, the marquee still has the title of the last feature to play there: *The Magnificent Seven*. Unfortunately, the poster's long gone. Someone broke into the display case and stole it not long after the joint shuttered. I never found out who did it, to my everlasting shame. I reckon one of these days I'll walk in someone's house and see it hanging in their living room.

Stagecoach was the first film I ever saw at the Broncho. I was eight or nine at the time. The girl behind the candy counter told me it had been filmed in a place called Monument Valley and that there was a place over near Fairview called Gloss Mountain that looked a lot like it. I nagged my parents into taking me. It wasn't nearly as majestic as Monument Valley, but Gloss Mountain was impressive in its own right. Another time, I saw a newsreel about Niagara Falls. I'd heard about a place here in Oklahoma called Turner Falls, so I made my folks take me there, too. It wasn't as spectacular as Niagara, but it was nothing to sneeze at.

To me, places like Gloss Mountain and Turner Falls held their own kind of magic, not least because they belonged to us. Even after leaving Burr and seeing some of the best the world has to offer, I retained my affection for Oklahoma's modest natural wonders.

I've always liked how our different landscapes butted heads. Drive south out of town on US 14. On one side of the highway there's rough, hilly grassland with gnarled blackjack trees and deep, waterless gullies. The other side might have dark green winter wheat planted as far as the eye could see. A little further down the road, there are red mesas rising two hundred feet into the air, like ancient islands above a dry sea bed. As a young boy, I'd count the stripes of exposed shale and sandstone, and imagine each was its own lost world. A few miles past that, if you know where to look, you can find a lush valley nestled within the walls of a small hidden canyon, worn away over the millennia by a small but persistent creek.

The views of nature are still nice, but not as nice as they used to be. Now, everywhere you look, there's a pump jack or a gas well or storage tanks, or miles and miles of electric and telephone lines. In Butcherville, Clyde Raymer seems determined to foul the environment and blight the landscape until there's no clean air left to breathe and no decent place to live. Oil and gas companies like WestOK put a lot of people to work in this state, and that's a good thing, but the way they can run roughshod over the land makes me sick to my stomach.

Maybe I'm nuts (no maybes about it, I guess), but I can't help feeling there's a place in this world for the kind of beauty that can only survive if you leave it the hell alone. Too many Oklahomans treat their state like it's nothing more than a sea of petroleum inconveniently obscured by a layer of soil and mountains and trees and other things that need to be stripped away as quick as possible, just so a man like Clyde Raymer can make more money than John D. Rockefeller and Jed Clampett combined.

The bottom line: the WestOK plant is an unsightly, reeking mess. Expanding it can only make it worse. I won't pretend the citizens of Butcherville are, as a rule, the most intelligent or industrious you'll ever encounter, but that doesn't mean they should be forced to inhabit the fourth circle of hell just so a millionaire can become a billionaire.

•　　•　　•　　•　　•

Even from miles away, I could see the halo of light over the stadium. Downtown was deserted except for a couple of cars parked in front of Edna's Eats. I turned down a side street toward the high school. As per Bernard's plan, I took the gravel road leading from the bus shed to the south end zone and parked next to the Fury. Bernard leaned lightly against it—not sitting on it, of course, because he might scratch it, and I believe Bernard would commit hari-kari if he accidentally did something to damage that car.

The game was only five-minutes-old and already the Patriots were down 12-zip. Burr hasn't won a state championship since the late '40s, when teams captained by a handsome single-wing tailback named Emmett Hardy won back-to-back titles. Recent squads have struggled, although their fortunes improved a few years ago when they went from 11-man football to the eight-man game. Having to suit up fewer able-bodied boys means they don't have to raid the marching band for players like they did in my day, which, most agree, is best for everyone. That's not to belittle the marching band, of which I was also a proud member, but there's not a lot of overlap between blowing a saxophone and tackling a fullback.

Arriving late has its benefits, one being that people are too busy watching the game to bother with me. The less I have to slap backs and shake hands the more I like it. My position is appointed, not elected. I don't have to fish for votes.

The action was happening right in front of where I'd parked. Carmen was inside the five yard line and threatening to score again. Before I even had a chance to say hello to Bernard, they'd scored another touchdown.

"Looks like it's going to be another long season," I said.

Bernard shrugged and stared straight ahead as the teams lined up for the two-point conversion.

"Could be," he said, and pulled out a crushed pack of Marlboros from his pants pocket. Why he doesn't carry his cigarettes in his shirt pocket like a normal person, I have no idea.

"Carmen's good," he said as he tried straightening a crooked cigarette. "Anyhow, that Truitt kid hasn't even touched the ball yet."

"How is it that the first quarter's almost over, and he still hasn't touched the ball?"

Bernard lit the cigarette, inhaled deep, and choked. "Long story," he said between coughs.

The Burr defense stuffed the conversion. Bernard gave the same half-hearted cheer as everyone else, then turned and looked at me for the first time since I'd arrived.

"What happened?" he said, looking down at my damaged dungarees. I told him the sorrowful tale about my encounter with Darryl Martin's gate. "Should've run him in," he said. He might've been joking, although with him you can't always tell.

"I let him off with a warning," I said. I didn't tell him Darryl had offered to pay, as I had little hope of that ever happening.

We watched downfield as the teams lined up for the kick-off.

"You find Earl Collins?" he asked.

"I did not. Did you make an announcement?"

"I had the public-address announcer call for Merle and Earl Collins to come see me. They haven't shown up, although they made the announcement just as Carmen was scoring their first touchdown, so it's possible nobody heard."

"Stay within listening distance of the radio. I had Cindy call the sheriff about Earl, so they'll be keeping an eye out, too."

"I reckon we'll be seeing a deputy or two out here before the night's over," he said sarcastically, referring to the tendency of Tilghman County deputies to commandeer our speed trap. It's on the road leading into town from the south, behind a billboard advertising the Temple City Motor Inn, and is notorious among cops working the overnight shift for being a good place to catch forty winks on the sly.

I left Bernard and circled around the end zone toward the press box. Carmen had bussed-in its marching band and cheerleaders, and brought a fair number of fans, but, as always, the hometown contingent outnumbered the visitors five or ten to one. I'll be sucking my chicken-fried steak through a soda straw in some old folk's home before I can fathom why a brutish game poorly-played by a bunch of gawky 16-year-olds can be consistently counted on to attract upwards of five-sixths of a town's total population. I reckon it's because there just isn't much else to do besides watch TV, and even that's not much fun. The reception here is terrible.

I walked down the sideline and had just about reached the fifty yard line when a tall, muscular boy wearing number 30 in a blue Burr Patriots jersey chugged past me, breathing heavy and dragging a couple of underfed Carmen players behind him like tin cans tied to a newlywed couple's car. I could almost hear their heads rattling around inside their helmets. Number 30 shook them off at the ten and waltzed into the end zone. The crowd cheered like they'd all won new Cadillacs. Number 30 followed that by bulling through the line and scoring the two-point conversion with half the Carmen team on his back.

It suddenly occurred to me that the adjective "poorly-played" might not apply to the brand of football demonstrated by Marlon Truitt, Jr. The phrase "man among boys" might be a better fit. Maybe this year the townsfolk's faith would be justified.

While young Marlon spent the rest of the first half wreaking havoc on the Carmen Lions, I held my breath and walked around shaking hands, answering questions about my paint-stained pants, and asking folks if they'd seen the Collinses. None had.

At halftime before the bands played, I made another announcement over the loudspeakers, urging anyone who might know where to find Merle and Earl to contact Bernard or Kenny or me. I then went back to my car and had Cindy patch me through to the sheriff department's dispatcher, who informed me they'd issued an all-points bulletin to the deputies on duty. I emphasized that we were taking it seriously and so should they.

After I'd finished doing that—and while Bernard's back was turned—I dug my flask out of the glove compartment. A farmer gave it to me as a gift some months back after I'd returned a tractor some teenagers had taken for a joy ride. Unlike the metal flask I used previously, this one was made of fancy cut glass. I liked that. I could always tell exactly how much bourbon I had left.

I indulged in a surreptitious snort, my first since my afternoon nap. I generally drink Old Grand-Dad 100-proof bonded bourbon, but to tell the truth, any brand will do. I pretend to have a favorite brand just to trick myself into believing I drink it for the taste.

I let my miracle brain juice work its magic, chased it with a couple of spearmint Certs, then strolled over to the parking lot, hoping Officer Harjo and Councilman Chrisco might've seen Merle's yellow or off-white 1961 Dodge pickup.

Jerry had moved to the stands to watch the game, but Kenny was where he was supposed to be, on the edge of the lot where he could see the action on the field. He commented on my pants, so I had to tell that story again. He said he might've seen the Dodge but couldn't swear to it. There were a few hundred vehicles parked closer together than cattle in a feedlot, and he hadn't been looking for a particular car. I started to walk through and take a look-see but I was distracted by a commotion over by the stands. Two drunks were fighting it out over Lord knows what. Bernard and I ran over to sort it out.

We eventually got them separated and handcuffed. One was from Carmen, the other from Burr. We put the Carmen idiot in the Galaxie and the Burr idiot in the Fury. Bernard assured me he could handle them himself and that I should go about my business. I told him to try and cool them off and get them to shake hands so we could release them at the end of the game. Last thing I wanted was for them to press charges against each other so we'd have to haul them both to the county jail.

By that time, the contest was in its final minutes, with the hometown boys three or four touchdowns to the good. While on my way up to the press box, I heard several variations of, "Damn, we got our money's worth with that boy"— referring, of course, to Marlon Truitt, Jr. It looked like Burr fans might've found their pot of gold at the end of the rainbow. At the final gun, young Truitt was carried off the field by teammates and cheerleaders and a few grownups who should've known better than to act that way.

Upstairs, everyone was shaking hands and lighting cigars and congratulating each other for having the collective good sense to recruit Marlon Truitt, Jr. I butted in and asked if anyone had seen or gotten word of the Collinses. No one had.

I left it to my officers to clear the stadium and began making my way down to where the Pep Club was sitting. I picked Karen Dean's auburn hair out of the crowd. She stood facing away from me, talking and laughing it up with a Pep Club sponsor. I snuck up from behind and slipped onto the bench underneath her. I gave her a little nudge. She let out a startled "Oh," and fell in my lap.

"Excuse me miss, this seat is taken," I said. She turned around, put an arm around my neck and gave me a delighted smile. "Aren't you fresh," she said and gave me a peck on the cheek. Fortunately, she stayed put. It might have proved embarrassing if she'd exposed my lap at that moment.

Karen and I have been getting a little more physical in public recently, so I was pretty sure she wouldn't mind my little trick. For years, she and I have had between us what one of those lady authors like Jacqueline Susann might call "sexual tension." It finally found release in a fashion most spectacular this summer following the town's Fourth of July barbeque. Things heated up after that. We kept it under wraps for a while so as to not offend the bluenoses, which Burr has in considerable numbers. Lately, however, we've been caring less about what people think.

"Well, I guess you're happy," I said.

"I guess I am," she said, beaming. "How 'bout Mr. Marlon Truitt, Jr.? He reminds me of someone else who used to play for the Patriots once upon a time."

"Looks to me like he's better than I ever was."

"Well, he hasn't won state yet," she said. Sometimes I think I get more respect for captaining a pair of championship football teams than I do for being police chief.

I asked if she'd heard that Earl Collins had gone missing.

"I heard Cindy talking to Bernard about it on the walkie-talkie before the game," she said. "I also heard the announcements over the public address. Is it serious?"

"It might be," I said. I didn't want to mention the 'HELP' message in the schoolbook just yet. "There's not a lot we can do except to keep an eye out for him. His daddy's missing, too, last I heard, so they might be together."

The stands around us emptied as we talked. She shifted off my lap as young girls stopped and said good-bye. Before long, we were about the only two left in the stands.

"You need a ride?"

"I'd thought you'd never ask," she said, standing up to gather the last of her things. She took notice of the dried paint and opened her mouth to comment. I gave her the evil eye and she shut it. We walked across the field, to where I'd parked the Galaxie. The drunk was no longer in the back seat, and the Fury was nowhere to be seen. I got on the radio and raised Bernard. He said he'd let the two drunks go and resumed his normal duties.

Karen and I got in the car. "My goodness, I know I'm too old for this," she said, wearing the friendly half-smile she wears more often than not, "but I just love football season." She turned sideways, leaned against the door, and draped her arm over the back of the seat. "Tell me the truth," she said, fluttering her eyelashes Scarlett O'Hara-style. "Am I too old for this?"

I thought of what Colonel Butler said to Scarlett in Gone With the Wind: "You need to be kissed often, and by someone who knows how." I did just that. Karen pretended to be outraged at my effrontery, but couldn't keep it up and kissed me back.

There is in general an air of girly contentment about Karen Dean that I've never fully grasped, yet long ago learned to appreciate. Not girl-*ish*, exactly, because, truth be told, she's almost a tomboy in some ways. I guess it's just a way she has of being at peace with her life. You might even say proud. Proud of where she lives and where she's from. Proud to be her own woman. Karen's the kind of person who if she found out she only had six months to live and could spend it doing whatever she wanted, she'd keep doing just what she's been doing, because it's what makes her happy.

I knew I could give a sly answer without getting in too much trouble. "Yes, I believe you are definitely too old for this," I said.

My smart-aleckiness earned me a fake-outraged laugh, and a punch on the shoulder where Bonnie Hubbard had belted me earlier. "Ouch," I said. "Just for that, I'm going to make you go with me while I check the parking lot."

"And waste valuable time when I could be out partying with the girls? You, sir, are no gentleman."

"Never claimed to be," I said, then pulled her close, nuzzled her hair, and kissed her again.

I backed-out carefully and detoured around the bus shed onto a dirt path behind the home grandstand to where the parking lot was. The game had been over for nearly an hour. Kenny had gone home, Bernard was patrolling downtown, and Jeff was out celebrating somewhere.

There were only two cars left in the lot, both parked within ten yards of each other. The first I recognized as the green Corvair belonging to Gene Treadway, who works for Deke Bixby over at the bank. It's a slick car, but Gene's had problems with it from the day he drove it off the lot. I didn't see him around, so I reckoned it must've broke down on him again.

I also recognized the second vehicle. It had been described to me in some detail a couple of hours earlier.

It was a yellow or off-white Dodge pickup. A 1961 model, if I wasn't mistaken. With a red metal tool chest behind the cab.

CHAPTER EIGHT

The pickup sat there without saying a word. Not that I expected it to, but it would've been nice.

I parked at a judicious distance. No sign of Earl and Merle. I peered in the windows. It was too dark to see, but the driver's side door was unlocked. I opened it and the dome light came on. I saw what you might see in the cab of any pickup: an overflowing ashtray and half a pack of Marlboros; a brown paper bag made nearly transparent by a leaky can of brake fluid; assorted paper cups and beer cans. A couple of rifles in a rack across the rear window. Nothing suspicious.

I looked at the bed. All that was there was the tool box, which appeared to be padlocked.

"I'm not seeing anything except a truck," I said to Karen. "How about you?"

"I don't see any dismembered limbs or anything, if that's what you're asking."

I realized she wouldn't be so flip if she knew the full story. I related the part about the broken restroom latch and the 'HELP' message written in Earl's textbook, which cast the situation in a darker light.

"My Lord, Emmett," she said, "we've got to do something."

I told her Cindy had notified the sheriff, who by now would've called in the Highway Patrol.

"We should make sure this is Merle's truck," she said. I had no doubt that it was, but she radioed Cindy anyway and asked her to have the sheriff's office check the license plate records, just to be sure. They promised to get back to us as soon as they knew something. Karen also asked if Ona Ray had called, or if anyone else had come up with a line on the Collinses. Cindy said no on both counts and then asked if she could go home. She had an early shift at the telephone company the next morning and needed her sleep. I thanked her and said she could go.

"I guess Merle could've gotten a ride with someone else," Karen said. "Left this here intending to pick it up later. Hopefully, he has his boy with him."

I wanted to believe that but couldn't think of a single reason I should.

A pair of headlights flashed across the parking lot and a green Chevy tow truck pulled in. Wes Harmon was behind the wheel with Gene Treadway in the passenger seat. Wes owns the Sinclair station and garage south of town. He pulled up alongside the Corvair, a few yards away from the Dodge and Karen and me.

"That transmission giving you problems again, Gene?" I called out. Gene's shiny bald scalp reflected the stadium lights from underneath a few long strands of hair he combs over his scalp. No person with at least one functioning eyeball would confuse Gene for anything but what he is—a good-natured, paunchy, middle-aged man, trying to keep his gut sucked in and the top of his head covered by any means necessary. That doesn't stop him from doing whatever he can to look skinnier and younger and generally more attractive to the opposite sex. As of yet, he hasn't taken to wearing a toupee.

He's had a hard time since his wife died a few years ago. I expect his desire to find a girlfriend also explains the sporty automobile, never mind that it spends more time in Wes's repair bay than on the road. I can't blame Gene, really. Folks can do strange things when they're lonely, including making fools of themselves. I know from personal experience.

"Not the transmission this time," Gene said, grinning despite his predicament. "I left the damn lights on and the battery ran down and I didn't have any jumper cables." He glanced at my jeans without mentioning the paint, which I appreciated.

"Hell, Gene, I would've given you a jump," I said.

"Didn't want to bother you. I figured you had your hands full, being a game night and all. I suppose Wes here can use the trade, anyway."

Wes jerked open the hood of his truck. It made a mighty screech and I thought he should take the time to oil the hinges. "Ain't going to get rich giving jumps," he grumbled as he walked around to the front of the Corvair and raised its hood. I reckoned he probably went home after the game expecting to drink beer and watch TV, but instead got a call from Gene and had to go back to work. I'm sure that vexed him, but as the only wrecker service in town, he understands he holds a civic responsibility.

Wes got everything hooked up and signaled Gene to turn the ignition. Both of the clips popped off the Corvair's battery. Wes barked a profanity and moved to hook it back up. While he huffed and puffed, I asked Gene if he saw anyone get in or out of the Dodge earlier.

"I believe I did see someone out of the corner of my eye, right after I drove in," he said. "A couple fellas, actually. Parked in that spot just as I got out of my car. Another car pulled up behind them and just left his engine running, like he was there to pick up the other two."

Wes got the cables reattached and stood glaring at Gene and me. "While we're young, boys," he shouted, but I made him wait because I needed to hear what Gene had to say. I asked if he knew the men. He didn't. I asked if he'd recognize Merle if he saw him. He said he would not. I asked if they had a boy with them. He said he didn't think so, but couldn't say for sure.

I let Gene try to start the car. The engine turned over. Gene revved it a few times. Everything seemed to be in order. He stuck his head out the window. "Now that I think of it, Emmett," he said, "those fellas in the car were talking pretty loud to each other, like they might've been arguing. Can't say for sure."

"You know the model of that car?" I asked.

"It was one of those new Ford sports cars," he said. "A Mustang, fixed up like a hot rod. It had wide tires with white lettering and the engine was loud, like it had Thrush mufflers."

Before today I'd never heard of a Thrush muffler. I reckon I'm behind the times when it comes to cars.

"What color?" I asked.

"Dark blue or black. Hard to tell. I didn't look too close."

Wes coiled the jumper cables and got ready to go. I asked him if he knew anyone around here who drove a Mustang like Gene described. Wes said no, he didn't.

"Understand now," Gene said, "I can't be completely sure about any of this. I didn't pay much attention. It's what I think I saw, is all."

"Understood," I said. I plied him some more, but he'd given me all he had and couldn't wait to get home. I said 'thank you' and left him to settle up with Wes.

"We should call Ona Ray," I said to Karen while Gene and Wes were talking. "Just in case someone gave her boys a ride home. Could be that Merle's truck broke down, and they figured they'd pick it up later. Who knows? They may pull into this lot any minute."

But they didn't. Wes was about to follow Gene out of the parking lot when I flagged him down. I wanted to ask him if he'd ever worked on Merle's pickup. He said no, he hadn't. I asked him give me a ring if he heard from the Collinses, and he said he would.

Wes took off, but didn't drive more than ten feet before I stopped him again. I had an idea. A gruesome idea. But I figured I needed to act on it.

"What now?" Wes asked, so aggravated, the smoke from the cigarette in the corner of his mouth might have been coming out his ears. If I wasn't the law, I think Wes might've run me over and been done with it.

I asked him to cut off the lock on the Dodge's tool chest.

"Do I have to?" he asked.

"I'd appreciate it."

He switched off his engine and jumped down off the truck. "I ain't replacing that lock," he warned. I told him I'd take full responsibility.

He fumbled around in his tool box for a set of bolt cutters, then trudged over to the Dodge. He took one look at the padlock, gave me a disgusted look, and pulled it off with his bare hand. He tossed it to me. "It was already broke," he said and tramped back to his truck.

They'd turned off the stadium lights and I still didn't have a flashlight, but I could shine my headlights on the truck well enough to see. I heaved open the lid. Mostly, I saw what you'd expect to see—wrenches, clamps, pliers, assorted loose nuts and bolts.

There was one thing that didn't belong. It was about a foot long, several inches around, and wrapped in red oil rags. Judging by the shape, it could've been a loaf of bread, or a bomb, or a loaf of bread with a bomb stuffed inside it. I reckoned it could also be something you couldn't eat or that wouldn't blow up, but I wouldn't know until I unwrapped it, so that's what I did.

It was a football, with Earl Collins's name written on it in black magic marker.

I remember being glad it wasn't a bomb.

CHAPTER NINE

I had Karen radio the Tilghman County Sheriff's Department. She's a lot better at that kind of thing than I am. She's even good at the 10-4s and stuff that we don't use much but which the county and state boys love. More than once, I've tried to explain something on the phone or over the radio and the person on the other end will ask me to put on her on because they don't know what the hell I'm talking about.

She explained to her opposite number how Earl was still missing and that now his father was, too. She described how we'd found Earl's football but not Earl, and related what Gene had told us: that a man matching Merle's description had last been seen with two other men in a dark-colored Mustang with loud mufflers and wide tires. She also told them not to bother sending a tow truck to impound the Dodge, since Wes was already here and would take care of it. Wes moaned when he heard that.

After Karen finished with the sheriff's department, she radioed Bernard with the same information. I told her to not to bother Kenny, since he had to wake up early and was likely asleep. I said she could try Jeff but shouldn't expect him to answer. I reckoned he'd be out getting drunk off his ass.

Wes and I turned off our ignitions and our headlights went dark. The entire parking lot was without light except for the moon and a streetlamp fifty yards away. A dog barked in the distance. I thought it sounded like Dizzy. I hadn't seen her since I'd left for work around 4:30 that afternoon. I assumed she was out making her rounds.

It was our good luck that the deputy who answered the call was Undersheriff Keith Belcher. Keith's about the only one of Sheriff Burton

Murray's boys I have any use for. Officially, he's Burt's second-in-command, but in reality, he does most of the actual sheriff-ing in Tilghman County, leaving Burt to shake hands and run for re-election, which is what he likes and what he's good at. Keith and I see eye-to-eye on most things, not least politics; we're both unapologetic LBJ-voters in a county that in '64 backed Goldwater two to one.

"Late night, huh?" Keith said as he got out of his car. Like mine, Keith's vehicle was a Ford Galaxie. Unlike mine, which is painted a respectable black and white, the sheriff department's cars are painted a hideous shade of green. The deputies' uniforms are green, too, although they're considerably less gaudy than the cruisers, which look like they should have a parade of clowns crawling out of them.

"Yeh, we're working late," I said. "Didn't expect to be, but here we are."

He said hello to Karen and Wes, both of whom he knew. "The forensic unit should be here in a minute," he said. "Maybe you can fill me in while we wait."

I explained the situation as succinctly as I could.

"Yeh, I heard you were looking for a yellow or off-white Dodge pickup," he said. "I guess you found it."

"I guess we did." I showed him the football and told him Earl carried it to school with him that morning.

"That should mean father and son met up at some time during the day," he said, "in which case they might be together, wherever they are. Unless I'm missing something."

"Except we got a sighting of the father with a couple of other men. The son wasn't with them."

"So you don't think they're together?"

I didn't know what to think, to be honest. I was so tired, I felt like I was swimming through quicksand. I advised Keith of that fact.

He slapped me on the shoulder. "You should go home and get some rest," he said.

"Nah, I still got things to do."

"Maybe this is all nothing," he said. "Maybe both of them will show up safe and sound."

"Lord, I hope so," said Karen.

"On top of everything else, I got to go tell the wife we found her husband's truck, but not him or the boy."

Keith frowned and said, "I don't envy you there."

"I'm taking her with me." I gestured at Karen. "She's my secret weapon."

Keith took off his Smokey the Bear hat and ran his fingers through his hair. "You ain't going to make her do it, are you?"

"No, I reckon not, although I am sorely tempted. That girl's got charms that can soothe the savage beast."

"I think you mean the savage breast," Keith said, "and I believe music is what's supposed to do that."

"You're pretty damned literate for a cop. I never met a savage breast, myself. I've generally found them pretty easy to get along with."

"You watch yourself, Emmett," Karen warned.

"On the other hand," I added, "I sure as hell have met some savage beasts."

We had time to kill before the crime scene investigators arrived, so I told a story about visiting relatives in Louisiana and almost getting my rear end chewed off by a razorback hog. Karen's heard the story a million times and looked bored. Keith found it entertaining, but insisted it was savage breast and that Shakespeare said it. Karen took Keith's side, only she said it wasn't Shakespeare, but some fella named William Congreve. We pretended to argue, but I knew if she said it was William Congreve, it was William Congreve. Whoever William Congreve was.

Wes looked at the three of us like we were out of our minds.

The forensic van drove up. Folks got out and started doing whatever it is they do. I gave them the same info I'd given Keith. I asked one of the them to go over the area around the car, just in case.

"That's what we do, Chief," the man said.

"I know, I'm sorry. I'm just worn out."

"Don't worry about it."

I asked Keith if my continued presence was required.

"I reckon not, Emmett. If this is a kidnapping—which is what it looks like to me—you might as well hand it over to us. We'll probably just bring in the OSBI, anyway. You told me all we need to know. Y'all should call it a night."

First, I meant to keep my promise to Ona Ray, drive out there and give her an update, even if it meant telling her something she didn't want to hear.

•　　•　　•　　•　　•

Downtown, the celebration was still in full swing. Cars with red, white, and blue streamers waving from their antennas cruised from one end of Main Street to the other. Music blared from car radios. Most were tuned to KOMA out of Oklahoma City, which after sundown has a signal that can be heard as far away as Los Angeles. We tailed an old Chevy with "Darlin' Marlon" painted on the rear window in white shoe polish. The car was occupied by more young girls than was safe, all of them leaning out the windows and chanting our new star tailback's name. If I were a betting man, I'd wager young Marlon would not lack for female companionship.

Every stall at the new Sonic drive-in on the northern edge of town was filled with carloads of honking, happy teenagers. Enjoy it while you can, I thought. It's a long season.

As is my habit when I come across too many teenagers and automobiles congregated in one place, I slowed down to take a closer look. I noticed a small dark-colored car parked near the back. I hit my lights and jerked the car hard to the right, into the driveway.

The abrupt turn caused Karen to slide across the seat and ram up against me. "Dang it, Emmett," she said, "you're the law, you're supposed to be able to drive better than that."

"Sorry, ma'am, but we're about to rope ourselves a Mustang."

"Ha-ha, very funny, but that's not a Mustang."

She was right. It was another Corvair like Gene's, except it was dark blue. I checked the kid's license so as to not look foolish. A couple of greasy-haired boys in the back seat looked to be close to Earl's age, so I asked if they knew him. They said they did, but hadn't seen him since school got out that afternoon. I left them to eat their hamburgers and fries in peace.

I got back in the Galaxie. I said to Karen, "I got to work on my car recognition skills."

"It is truly a blight on your manhood."

We headed toward Butcherville. We'd gotten about a mile out of town when our headlights fell on a man walking along the side of the road. Actually, stumbling might be a better description. He staggered from one side of the road to the other, with his arms hanging limp at his sides and his knees buckling like he'd gone a few rounds with Cassius Clay.

I eased up behind, hit my emergency flashers, and trained my searchlight on him. He turned back to look, his hands in front of his eyes. I thought I recognized him.

"Is that who I think it is?" I asked Karen, who knows just about everybody in the county on sight.

"That's Merle, alright."

"You see my flashclub? I been looking for it all day."

"Flashclub" is what we call my special flashlight. A few years ago, I had a local handyman make me a combination flashlight and nightstick. The first time Kenny saw it, he called it a "flashclub" and the name stuck. It's basically a length of steel pipe about a foot-and-a-half long with a lightbulb on one end. It fits in the slot on my fancy gun belt (which I seldom use) where a nightstick is supposed to go. It's the perfect tool for situations like this, when you might need a weapon, but a gun is too much. I could use it to shine in Merle's face and bust him over the head with it if he got cantankerous.

It took Karen exactly two seconds to find it. It had been jammed between the seat cushions. A seatbelt and one of Dizzy's Milk Bones came out at the same time.

"Snacking on the job?" she asked.

"You're a regular Phyllis Diller."

Merle stood there, peering at us like we were from outer space. I approached him with some care. You never know how a drunk's going to act, and he seemed like he'd had a few. When I got near, however, I could tell being inebriated wasn't his only problem. Not only was he drunk, he'd also had the shit kicked out of him by someone with very bad intentions.

Merle is tall but so skinny he looks like a stiff wind might blow him halfway to Kansas. And that's when he hasn't been beaten to within an inch of his life.

His head was caked with blood, his face was smashed-in, his hands were swollen and twisted. He wears his hair in a crewcut, so it was easy to see most of the blood came from a mean-looking gash on the back of his head—the result, I surmised, of having it being slammed repeatedly against a surface with no give to it whatsoever.

Thinking I was out to arrest him, I guess, he tried to run away, but his legs would not cooperate. I caught up to him easily, took him by the upper arm and guided him back to the Galaxie. He mumbled incoherently. I asked him to repeat what it was he said. He did, but I still couldn't understand him. I helped him into the back seat and got in beside him.

Karen turned around and looked at Merle. "My Lord," she gasped, "what happened to you, Mr. Collins?"

He made roughly the same unintelligible sounds as before.

"Hopefully, that's what we're fixing to find out," I said.

I switched on the dome light. He didn't look any prettier. "Merle, what happened?" I asked.

He slobbered and slurred, "Tha' sumbish doan tell me whuddado."

That, I understood.

"Who doesn't tell you what to do, Merle?"

His head wobbled backwards and banged against the top of the backseat.

"Ow, goddam. Jesus Christ tha' hur's."

He needed medical care. The fastest thing was to drive him to the hospital myself, so I backtracked through town and drove toward Temple City, twenty miles away. State Road 43 from Burr to Temple City is as straight as a string and lightly traveled, especially at night. I didn't hesitate to go upwards of 90 mph with my lights flashing. Merle's perfume of sweat and beer and vomit and piss made him a lousy traveling companion. All we could do was open the car windows and hope for the best.

While I drove, Karen tried to wheedle information out of him.

"What do you mean 'that so-and-so don't tell you what to do'?"

"He *don't*."

"Alright, alright," she said. "Who's he?"

"They beat the shit out of me 'cuz I won' take their money," he sobbed. It was obvious Merle was in no condition to interrogate. However, one question couldn't wait.

"Merle, have you seen your boy?"

"Seen my wha'?"

"Your boy, Earl. Have you seen him?"

He leaned forward, his head resting on the backrest between Karen and me. "Earl?" he said. Vomit and slobber dribbled down his chin. "Oh, no, no, no, did they get Earl?" he said, then fell backwards onto the seat and laid there, bawling.

He passed out before I could ask him anything else.

CHAPTER TEN

Karen radioed ahead to the hospital, told them we'd found Merle Collins beaten all to hell, and that we'd be there as fast as we could. Then she called the sheriff and filled him in. Finally, she sent Bernard out to tell Ona Ray we'd found her husband in poor condition, and told him to offer her a ride to the hospital if she wanted to go.

Bernard radioed back just as we pulled up to the hospital. Ona Ray wanted to know if Merle was going to die. I said he was hurt pretty bad and hadn't seen a doctor yet but we were confident he'd pull through. In that case, she said, she'd rather stay home and wait for Earl. She told us to call if Merle took a turn for the worse.

Karen ran into the building and came with a couple of medics. They brushed past me and carried the still-unconscious Merle into the emergency room. Karen and I tried to follow but a nurse stopped us at the door.

From behind a plate glass window, we watched them run a vial of smelling salts under Merle's nose. It got his attention; he made a face like he'd been offered a plate of raw mountain oysters and thrashed around so hard the nurse had to summon an orderly to restrain him.

A tall, curly-haired young man wearing a white lab coat over a flannel shirt and a stiff new pair of Levi's entered the room. He bent over Merle and said something that seemed to calm him. Merle revived enough to talk and they had a little back and forth. The young man shined a small flashlight in each of Merle's eyes, then turned him over and looked at the back of his head. He ran his hands over his arms and legs, listened to his chest with a stethoscope and generally acted so much like a doctor, I assumed that's what he was. They talked some more and the man smiled and gave Merle a thumbs-up sign.

A nurse asked Karen and me a few questions about how he sustained his injuries. We didn't know, of course. The doctor joined us after he finished with Merle. He introduced himself as Dr. Gibbons and apologized for being dressed like a chicken farmer, said he'd only been called in at the last minute, when they got notice we were on the way. He said Merle's injuries weren't as bad as they looked. Other than a broken nose, and that nasty cut on his head, most were superficial. The nose would need setting; the cut, stitches.

I asked a few questions. The answers comprised long strings of complicated words that, for all I knew, the doctor could've been making up on the spot. From what I was able to understand, Merle would probably be fine, but they wanted to keep him under observation overnight. We had little choice but to leave matters in their hands. The doctor seemed to know his stuff, notwithstanding his hayseed wardrobe.

Keith Belcher arrived shortly thereafter, accompanied by a fuzzy-cheeked deputy who had the uncommonly good sense to be seen and not heard. I told Keith what had happened and asked if they minded handling it from here, as I wanted to continue looking for Earl a little while longer. I mentioned it would be a good idea to ask Merle how he got separated from his truck and how Earl's football ended up in the toolbox. Keith said he planned to ask those very things. I left him to it.

Karen and I headed back to Burr.

"It didn't seem like Merle knew Earl went missing," she said.

"He didn't," I said. "I doubt he had anything to do with the boy's disappearance one way or the other."

"Where're we going now?" she asked.

"Drive around and look for him, I guess. That, or leave it to Keith and the Highway Patrol, and go home and try to sleep. I know I'm not going to able to do that. If you want, I'll take you home, but I'm going to keep looking."

She yawned and cuddled up next to me.

"No need. I won't be able to sleep, either. Might as well do something constructive."

Her face was so close, I could feel her warm breath on my cheek and smell the cinnamon from the Dentyne she chews. I tried keeping my eyes on the road but I could feel her looking up at me with a fondness I don't feel like I deserve.

She squeezed my arm.

"I'll keep you company, if you don't mind," she said.

• • • • •

It was midnight or later by the time we got back to Burr. The sidewalks had been rolled up. The post-game celebrations had ended or moved inside. A couple of pickups were still parked in front of Edna's. Karen stayed in the car while I ran in and asked if anybody'd seen Earl. No one had.

We rode up and down every street in town twice, which took all of ten minutes. We branched out to the surrounding county roads. I kept my speed under twenty-miles-per-hour and shined my searchlight over every square inch of roadside. No sign of Earl.

The lateness of the hour discouraged conversation, leaving us to our own thoughts. That's seldom a good thing, in my case. Excessive personal reflection tends to have a less than salutary effect on my mental health. Not too good for my liver, either, since at such times I am liable to find comfort in the soothing properties of alcohol.

Indeed, I was silently ruminating on bourbon's potent allure when we came upon an old Pontiac parked on the side of a dirt road in the middle of nowhere.

If I could've been sure it was just a couple of horny teenagers wanting some privacy, I might have given them some time to put their clothes on. Given that Earl Collins had been missing for seven or eight hours, however, I was disinclined to give whoever it was the benefit of the doubt.

I hit my emergency lights and aimed my searchlight at the car. Through the rear window, I saw a couple of heads bouncing around and realized I was dealing with a couple of kids after all. I grabbed the flashclub and approached the car. The driver's side window was already rolled down. I shined a light on my unfortunate victims.

The boy was Joe Don Harp. Just a few hours earlier, I'd watched him play quarterback for the Burr Patriots. Presently, I watched him struggle to pull up his trousers and buckle his belt. Next to him was a cute little brunette wearing a pink brassiere and the bottom half of a cheerleader uniform. She was struggling to get the top half back on and didn't realize it was inside out. I didn't say anything, not wanting to embarrass her any more than she already was.

Joe Don gave me a song and dance about his car breaking down. I'd heard the same story from other young men in the same situation. I told him what I told them: I might've been born yesterday, but I stayed up all night studying. I said he needed to take the girl home, and I meant right now. I knew where he lived and I'd be around in a little while to check and make sure he did.

Before I let them go, I asked if they'd seen Earl. They didn't understand why I'd ask and insisted they didn't even know who he was, which I believed, since they were several grades ahead of him. I clicked off the flashclub and let them get situated. Joe Don's car trouble disappeared like magic and they drove off. I didn't like giving them a hard time, but it was my civic duty, even if I hadn't been looking for Earl. Burr's had an epidemic of shotgun marriages recently.

I watched their taillights recede into the distance, and thought of all those times I'd gone parking with a pretty girl after a football game when I was their age. The way the moonlight peeked through the arthritic black jack trees seemed familiar. I wondered if I might have parked in this very spot. For a second, I had a mind to try and finagle an old-fashioned necking session with Karen—that is, before my lust was curbed by imagining her reaction to such a request. 'Appalled' would not begin to describe it. I was somewhat comforted that I'd caught myself in time. There's no law against having racy thoughts, but it's often best to keep them to yourself.

What I craved more than carnal gratification was a drink—another thing I wasn't going to get with Karen in the car. The flask of Old Grand-Dad stashed in my glove compartment might as well have been locked in a safe at the bottom of the ocean, for all the good it was doing me.

Karen thinks I stopped drinking. I let her think it, but I haven't. I just don't do it around her. I also keep a ready supply of Certs in my pockets and Listerine in my medicine cabinet.

I tried to put all that out of my mind. I would check in with Ona Ray, then take Karen home and call it a night. That's when I'd have my drink, after my services were no longer required. Exhaustion had caught up and passed me like I was standing still. That didn't necessarily mean I'd be able to sleep, but I had to try, or tomorrow morning Butcherville wasn't going to have Emmett Hardy to kick around anymore.

Maybe we'd arrive at the Collins place and find Earl home, safe and sound. Maybe then I'll go home and find Raquel Welch waiting for me in that skintight outfit she wore in *Fantastic Voyage*. Karen wouldn't like that very much.

I turned off the road onto the Collins's driveway. I caught Ona Ray in my headlights, sitting on a cinderblock step in front of her house with her legs crossed at the ankles, wearing the same too-snug T-shirt and bright green pedal pushers as before. She bit her nails and smoked a cigarette. I cut my lights. Other than a sliver of moon and the dome of light coming from gas plant rising up behind the house, we were in darkness.

The dog was still tied to the Chevy, but he only barked a couple of times, then laid down, too tired and disinterested to raise much hell. It had been a long day for him, too.

I got out of the car and immediately banged my shin against the sharp edge of something large and immobile. Too late, I remembered the riding mower parked next to the driveway. I managed not to cuss out loud, in deference to Ona Ray's distress.

Matters had not righted themselves. Ona Ray's hands shook and her face was even more tear-streaked than before. She stood and hurried toward me, only the orange tip of her cigarette warning of her advance.

"Chief Hardy, what in the world is going on?" she cried. Up close I could see her hands shake. "First, Earl goes missing, and now Merle is in the hospital." She flipped her cigarette onto the driveway. It glowed like a downed lightning bug with a broken 'off' switch. "What in the world is going on?" Her voice quivered, like when you talk into the blades of an electric fan.

The three of us went in the house. Karen switched on some lights and put on a pot of coffee. I sat Ona Ray down at her kitchen table, then looked around for her phone. I found it in the living room. I called the hospital and managed to get Keith on the line. He echoed what the young curly-haired doctor had told us earlier; other than a broken nose, a gash on the back of his head, and some cuts and bruises, Merle was fine. They'd set and bandaged the nose and closed the gash with stitches. They wanted to keep him a while before sending him home, to be on the safe side.

As far as answering questions, however, Merle was still insensible. More deputies and patrolmen had been assigned to the search for Earl. The OSBI had also been brought in to investigate. I asked Keith if they were going to send anyone to the Collins's, and he said Highway Patrol troopers would be there shortly.

I passed the news to Ona Ray. She seemed relieved about her husband, but was still frantic about her son. Karen got her to drink some water, then poured her a cup of coffee, which seemed to help her settle down. Her crying subsided to a rasping, hiccupping moan.

Once we got her quieted down, I asked if she knew of anyone who'd want to hurt her family. That got her going again. "Where in hell you been?" she bawled, her voice rising to a hysterical pitch. "The whole town is against us!" I thought that sounded unreasonably pessimistic, but I withheld comment.

She got to crying again. Karen said pretty words and patted her hand. I pondered why Ona Ray would think the entire town of Butcherville was out to get her family. The Collinses seemed pretty harmless. They were nice enough, if not particularly ambitious or industrious, which put them smack dab in the mainstream of Butcherville culture. That barking mongrel of theirs might be as annoying as hell, but I couldn't imagine it would inspire a kidnapping, or an ass-whipping like Merle got. I suspected Ona Ray was just being paranoid.

I motioned for Karen to follow me into the living room. Ona Ray was too distracted to notice.

"What do you think?" I whispered.

She whispered back, "I think that woman is beside herself with worry about her son, is what I think."

"I'm thinking it might not be a good idea for her to be alone tonight."

"I'd be glad to stay with her. You weren't planning on staying at my place tonight anyway, were you?" I do that sometimes when we're sure no one's looking. She never stays at my place, due to my utter lack of even the most rudimentary housekeeping skills.

"Won't hurt for me to sleep in my own bed," I said.

"Or your own chair," she said, referring to my La-Z-Boy, where I usually end up.

We returned to the kitchen and she got back to comforting Ona Ray. I went outside to take another look around. I didn't really expect to find anything. Earl had disappeared from the store, not his home, but it wouldn't hurt to check out the area around the house again. You never know.

I switched on the porch light and retrieved the flashclub from the Galaxie. I circled the house, looking for what, I did not know. There wasn't much to see: scattered nails of various sizes half-buried in the red dirt, a couple of empty Valvoline oil cans, a broken bicycle, a rusty kid's swing set without any swings. As far as I could see, the only evidence of a crime having been committed on the premises was littering. I reckoned the OSBI would do their own search. Maybe they'd have better luck.

As I rounded the last corner of the house, Karen burst out the front door.

"Emmett, come here, you need to hear this," she said, sounding concerned yet strangely amused. I followed her into the kitchen.

"Ona Ray," she said, "tell Emmett why everyone in Butcherville is against you."

Ona Ray looked from Karen to me, then back to Karen, then to me again, puzzlement written all over her face.

"You mean about Merle being the mayor?" she said. "Don't tell me you didn't know that?"

CHAPTER ELEVEN

Butcherville is the way it is today because someone kept setting its brothels on fire.

Folks don't talk about it much these days, but right before it became an official town, Butcherville was home to a booming flesh trade. The opening of the WestOK plant in the wake of World War II brought a workforce of young, single men, most of them just out of the service.

As young single men will do, many enjoyed spending their nights drinking and whoring.

Given how Tilghman County is proudly American and America is proudly capitalist—and understanding that in a capitalist society few needs go unfulfilled when there's money to be made—it makes logical sense that, with an influx of horny young men, a number of bars and whorehouses sprang up around the new plant. Butcherville's lack of local law enforcement didn't hurt, either, nor did the county sheriff's willingness to turn a blind eye toward the situation, provided, of course, he was adequately compensated.

Butcherville's golden age of fornication lasted only five or six years. Eventually, plant workers got older and less hellbent. Many ventured into nearby towns and snared respectable girls. Coincident to the increased domesticity was a community-wide counterattack against sin, culminating in a literal incineration of the town's dens of iniquity.

The fires were presumably set by some Carrie Nation-like crusader for the betterment of public morals. We'll probably never know who it was for sure. The sheriff never apprehended a culprit. To the arsonist's credit, he or she was careful to set the fires when the establishments were empty, so no one was ever hurt. However, since the houses were so flimsily constructed, and the only folks prepared to fight the fires were a few off-duty prostitutes wielding garden hoses, every building set afire burned to the ground.

After the first few fires, a coalition of local business owners, consisting mainly of bootleggers and pimps, met to consider their options. Unable or unwilling to see that the fires were a symptom—not the cause—of their problems, they decided to establish a fire department. One naïve soul proposed that the whoremongers and bootleggers start their own private firefighting organization. He was ridiculed, of course, the prevailing wisdom being there was no reason they should pay for it, when, in the tradition of great American businessmen from Rockefeller to Capone, they could shift the monetary burden to their customers in the form of taxes.

The trouble was, Butcherville was unincorporated. It wasn't officially a town. There was no mechanism in place to collect taxes. If they wanted to do that, they would have to incorporate.

Somehow, through a process I don't pretend to understand, the movers and shakers fulfilled the legal requirements and put incorporation up for a vote. Needless to say, seeing how your average Butchervillian is as ornery as an atheist at a Saturday night prayer meeting, they had to promise things would remain mostly the same; the only thing to change would be that frequenting prostitutes and smoking in bed wouldn't be quite so dangerous.

(While all this was going on, the town of Burr sensed an opportunity to expand its own tax base and tried to annex Butcherville. The attempt failed miserably. Someone spread the rumor that Burr intended to make Butchervillians pay for garbage collection, whereas before they'd always just burn it or let it accumulate in big piles behind their houses. The rumor had no basis in fact. Burr didn't even have trash collection for itself. Still doesn't. We burn it in barrels. Butchervillians saw no need to let truth get in the way of their ambition, however. The rumor had the desired effect. Butcherville would not be a part of Burr.)

The new government's plan was to institute a one-percent tax covering certain commercial transactions, with all accrued funds used strictly for establishing and maintaining a fire department. 'Certain commercial transactions' comprised a beverage tax, which applied to the sale of all thirst-quenching and/or intoxicating liquids; and a hotel tax, which covered the many microscopically short-term stays in the upstairs rooms of Butcherville's many drinking establishments. Since there wasn't hardly any other kind of business in town except for the Butcherville Store, you could call Butcherville "The Town Boozing and Whoring Built."

In the beginning, thanks to all the boozing and whoring, tax collections accrued beyond expectations—so much, that Butcherville was able to build the grandest fire department in the state of Oklahoma, if not the entire country. It had the best equipment: the most expensive and technologically-advanced firetrucks, hoses, slickers, helmets, and whatnot. The town council hired a fancy architect from Little Rock and an interior designer from Dallas to design the firehouse, and told them price was no object. They took it literally. The building's outer walls were made of imported Italian marble. The garage doors were made of the finest polished walnut, and adorned with polished brass fittings. The upstairs sleeping area had full-sized beds with Serta Perfect-Sleeper mattresses. The kitchen featured something called a Radar Range, which I'm told is an oven that can cook a steak in less time than it takes to chop an onion. A photographer and reporter from Look magazine actually came to Butcherville and did a story on "America's Taj Mahal of Firehouses."

The fire department would become the pride of Butcherville. It appeared the vice industry was saved.

It *was* saved, from fire, or at least it would have been. But the sin merchants were too late. Time marches in only one direction. It left the old Butcherville behind.

The pimps and bootleggers had misread the situation. The fires weren't the cause of their problems, but a symptom. They didn't realize sentiment against them had been growing in all quarters. In fact, by the time the firehouse was completed, the backlash was almost complete.

Butcherville's new town government had acquired a taste for passing laws. Not many, but a few. The town council sensed which way the wind was blowing and resolved to legislate sin out of existence. They passed an ordinance outlawing the sale of all alcohol except 3.2 beer, which aligned with state law, but in Butcherville that had never mattered before. They pretty much banned hotels completely, which put the brothels out of business. The county sheriff at the time had been augmenting his salary with kickbacks, so he couldn't have been happy when the town government pressured him to tamp down illicit commerce. Enough voters lived in Butcherville to make a difference in getting him elected, however, so if he wanted to keep his job, he had little choice. Enforcement of the new laws was confusing and inconsistent (I stayed as far away from the mess as I could), but in the end, the Deadwood of western Oklahoma became the hardest place in the state to procure a hooker or buy a stiff drink.

The town fathers' success in regulating sin soon went their heads. They began doing things town governments typically do, such as provide basic amenities. A sewage treatment plant replaced cesspools and septic tanks and outhouses. The town piped water into people's houses, so they didn't have to drill their own wells.

And Butcherville continued to have a fire department second to none.

All that stuff cost money, but the local government wasn't greedy. They kept taxes low. For a while, the luxury of being able to crap in flush toilets and drink fresh water delivered by underground pipes overrode economic concerns.

Until someone convinced them the whole thing was a communist plot.

●　　　●　　　●　　　●　　　●

I'm not the only person who as a kid remembers being told, "You can't have your cake and eat it, too." I'm probably also not the only one who thought it didn't make a lick of sense.

It wasn't until years later, in witnessing the Butcherville de-annexation crisis, that I understood what it meant.

It wasn't long before Butchervillians started taking indoor plumbing and hot and cold running water for granted. They forgot what it was like to have to pump drinking water by hand or visit the outhouse in their pajamas on a cold winter night. The town's sordid past became a foggy memory.

They stopped being satisfied with how pretty their cake looked. Now they wanted to eat it.

And it was Clyde Raymer who served it up.

Clyde's father, Armbrister "Army" Raymer, staked a claim during one of the land runs. Like many of the men who later ended up running the state, Army bought up the quarter-sections from neighbors who couldn't make a go of it. He ranched a little bit, but made his big money in oil and natural gas, much of it drilled on those lands he bought on the cheap.

Army soon realized there was still more money to be made by processing the gas once he got it out of the ground. He founded WestOK in his late middle-age, and ran it until he was too old to get out of bed in the morning, at which point he turned it over to his oldest son, Clyde's brother, Beauregard.

Beau Raymer had no interest in, and even less talent for the oil and gas business. Within a couple of years, he'd run the company into the ground and absconded to Florida, taking with him with what was left of the company funds. There, he changed his name to Drew Brewster and found his true calling: selling swamp land to gullible Yankees looking to buy a piece of paradise.

With Beau out of the picture, and as the son next in line, Clyde took over the tattered remnants of WestOK. Unlike his older brother, Clyde had a passion for the business, and built it up even bigger than before. Clyde wasn't satisfied with being rich; he wanted to be John D. Rockefeller-When-He-Owned-Every-Drop-of-Oil-in-America rich. To get there, he conceived a plan that would triple the size of his Butcherville operation. That required the acquisition of large sections of property adjacent to the plant. Clyde would have to buy-out his neighbors.

Like father, like son.

Things went smooth, at first. Most folks who owned land around the plant were only too happy to sell their land to Clyde at the inflated price he was offering. Unfortunately for Clyde, when the time came to start construction, a newly-emboldened town government threw him a curve, and did something no one thought a Butcherville town council would ever do: passed a zoning ordinance. Essentially, they thanked Clyde for being a fine, upstanding Butchervillian—and a great American, besides—but shook a finger in his face and told him his plant was plenty big enough as it is.

Clyde Raymer didn't get where he was by taking 'no' for an answer from the auto mechanics, chicken farmers, and school teachers who comprised the Butcherville town council. He aimed to get what he wanted, one way or the other.

Ultimately, he got most of it, not by presenting a reasoned argument in favor of having a natural gas plant billow toxic fumes a few yards from where kids play, but by convincing natives that their sovereign rights as citizens were being violated by an out-of-control local government. He funded a publicity campaign built on the premise that the mayor and town council were essentially undercover agents from Moscow sent to undermine everything that's good about Butcherville, and, by extension, the United States of America.

His crusade focused on the beverage and hotel taxes, as well as an annual property levy the council had recently passed. Taken together, the taxes didn't amount to hardly anything; Butcherville residents paid the lowest taxes in Tilghman County, if not the state. Before Clyde started making a stink, folks hardly thought about paying them. Afterwards, however, you'd have thought they were being asked to surrender a child—not their first-born, mind you, just one they wouldn't miss *too* much.

In the next election, Clyde underwrote a slate of so-called "reform" candidates for mayor and city council. Given that Tilghman County's unofficial motto is "Money Talks, Bullshit Walks," it came as no surprise when Clyde's people won every seat. The kicker was their promise to give individual landowners the right to de-annex from the town, thus freeing them from the unspeakable tyranny of having to pay for water and sewage. An added side benefit would be that secessionists could sell their property to Clyde, no strings attached.

First thing the new council did was pass the law allowing de-annexation, which they were as hot-and-heavy for as the people who voted them into office. Right away, John Birch Society-types and folks who wanted to re-fight the Civil War quit the town. The sane minority (a.k.a. those who grasp the value of having running water and indoor plumbing and a luxury fire department) remained. As a result, a checkerboard of properties was created across the map—some part of Butcherville, others not.

Poorer folks suffered the most. Many rented from de-annexing landowners who either couldn't wait to sell to Clyde or were too cheap to provide for sewage and water. Those people were suddenly without services or, in many cases, a roof over their head. Their homes were de-annexed and sold to Clyde out from under their feet.

What's surprising is how many of them went along with it without a peep of protest. Clyde bet the house that the old Okie inclination to tell the government to go screw itself would triumph over common sense. And he won.

Initially, people were smug in the knowledge they'd done the right thing and outsmarted the eggheads determined to steal their hard-earned one-penny-per-dollar-spent. Then reality set in. Even from my distant and admittedly detached perspective, I became aware things were falling apart in our liberty-loving neighbor to the north.

People soon got tired of the attendant inconveniences that resulted from having cut off their town-supplied water and sewage. Those who couldn't remember the hardships of the Dust Bowl and Great Depression realized, too late, how difficult and expensive it was to dig their own wells, and dispose of their own waste. The stink coming from dozens of new outhouses provided the rotten cherry on top of the stench already coming from the gas plant.

The saddest development was how de-annexation affected the fire department. Right after it happened, two houses next door to one another caught fire. One was still part of the town, the other, seceded. The firemen did their job according to the new lay of the land. They saved the Butcherville house and let the other burn.

At that point, you might've thought the new town government had targets on the tops of their shoes, the way they kept shooting themselves in the feet. But there was more to come.

The freak show finally reached its pitiful climax when the mayor and every member of the council hypnotized themselves into believing the fantasy they'd been peddling and de-annexed their own properties, either forgetting or not understanding that by seceding, they were no longer residents of Butcherville. As plenty of people were happy to point out, if they weren't residents, they couldn't serve on the town government. The damn fools tried to run the town anyway, until a tax-paying resident finally took them to court. Somehow the judge managed not to laugh as he ordered the mayor to resign and the council to disband. Afterwards, a group of concerned citizens petitioned the governor and asked him to appoint a new mayor to clean up the mess.

That's the last I heard about it.

Until now.

CHAPTER TWELVE

"Merle is the mayor?" I asked, sure that I'd misheard and that a lack of sleep and/or an excess of alcohol had finally caught up with me.

"You didn't hear about that?" said Ona Ray. "He got appointed by the governor."

"When did this happen?"

"A few weeks ago. It was in *The Butcherville News*," she said, like she was talking about *The New York Times* and not six pages of farm reports and editorials about how the world's going to hell because of Jews and negroes and Earl Warren. I can't read it without getting a headache.

"We were excited at first, but it turned out to be the worst thing to happen to us since—" She screwed up her face in deep thought and tapped the table with her fingernails. "I guess since that time Merle ran over my foot with the lawn mower."

I snuck a peek at her bare feet. One was a couple of toes short. She caught me looking and raised it up so I could see better.

"Cost us an arm and a leg in doctor bills."

I bit my tongue. "Did you know about this?" I asked Karen.

"I'm embarrassed to say, I did not." Karen prides herself in knowing something about everything that goes on in Burr, but maybe her interest in local news doesn't always extend past the city limits.

I asked Ona Ray how it happened. She explained that Butcherville's fire chief, Harry Cuthbert, and our current governor are old friends, having served in the same tank platoon in the Pacific during WWII. When the Butcherville mess landed on his plate, the governor tried to appoint Harry mayor. Harry begged him not to, so the governor asked him to recommend someone. Harry wrote out a list. Merle's name was down toward the bottom, but he ended up being the first to accept.

"No offense, Ona Ray, but why would Merle be on that list at all?"

"I know," she said. "We were as surprised as anyone. I reckon it's because Harry and Merle go rattlesnake hunting together. Harry told Merle, 'Hunting rattlesnakes with a man is almost like trusting him with your life. If I can almost trust you with my life, I can almost trust you to be mayor.' He laughed when he said it, but I think it's true."

"I'll tell you what," said Karen, "I don't know Merle very well, but I do know politics is a dirty business. Even if you're a good person, it can put a target on your back."

Especially if you're a good person, I thought.

"I'm sure he's an improvement on the last mayor y'all had," Karen added.

"Dang right he is," Ona Ray said. "Merle has a backbone, which is what gets him in trouble."

"How has having a backbone caused him trouble?" I asked.

"Chief Hardy," Ona Ray said, exasperated by the evident stupidity of my question, "don't you pay no attention at all to what happens in Butcherville?"

Before I could answer, she launched on a colorful and detailed explanation of the pile of excrement her husband had stepped in upon being named Butcherville's chief executive. "You do know that Clyde Raymer's been trying to get the town council to let him expand the gas plant, right?" she asked.

I said that I did, whereupon she told me something else as obvious as the wart on a witch's chin—namely, that Clyde spent a lot of money to get his puppets elected so he could change the zoning to suit himself.

"It took him years, but he finally got most of his ducks in a row to make it happen," she said. I already knew that part of the story, but the telling seemed to do her good. "That was before that whole mess with the councilmen and the mayor de-annexing themselves and ruining the town government, you know?" She seemed to want a reaction, so I nodded. "Clyde needed all that land surrounding the plant," she said. "A lot had houses on it—houses that were rented to poor working folks. Clyde was willing to pay twice what that land was worth, so of course the landlords were happy to sell, even if it meant those people wouldn't have nowhere to live."

What I didn't know for sure, but had by now surmised, was that Clyde had secured every parcel he needed ... except for one little plot owned by a certain married couple—Merle and Ona Ray Collins—who'd built their own house on it and didn't want to sell at any price.

Ona Ray looked wistfully out her kitchen window. The gas plant seemed so close you could almost reach out and touch it. Lord knows why they'd want to stay here, I thought.

I let her talk some more. I couldn't have stopped her even if I'd wanted to.

"It was bad enough when we just refused to sell him our land," she said, "but once Merle got named mayor, things got worse and worse. Right now, Merle is the only government Butcherville's got, and he's not going to roll over for Clyde Raymer. Clyde's offered us five times what this property is worth. Merle hates bullies so much, he won't sell. We built this house. It ain't much, but we put it together ourselves and we're proud of it and we love it and we ain't going to move because some millionaire decides we're in his way."

"No reason you should," Karen said.

"Tell that to the folks who stand to make money on this deal," Ona Ray said. "They hate us, and they've tried to make everyone else hate us, too— even folks you'd think would be on our side. We get calls in the middle of the night from people threatening to burn down our house. They say we're keeping them from getting rich. The town charter says that to change zoning, there has to be unanimous consent from the zoning committee. Well, there ain't a zoning committee. There's Merle. Merle says: Over his dead body. He means it."

Judging by the events of the last few hours, it appeared as though somebody might be ready to take him up on that.

●　　●　　●　　●　　●

A team of sheriff's deputies and a couple of plainclothes types who I correctly assumed were OSBI showed up after a while. I was glad—if surprised—to see so many of them working so late. I hung around a while longer, answered their questions and tried to pry new information from the deputies. They still hadn't been able to talk to Merle, but were confident his beating and Earl's disappearance were related. They hadn't received a ransom request, but to a man they thought Earl had been kidnapped.

It was two o'clock before Karen and I got patted on the head and sent on our way. I ordinarily don't like getting treated like I just fell off the cow chip wagon, but bone-weariness trumped my wounded pride. I couldn't get away fast enough. The Highway Patrol promised they were bringing in a female trooper to stay with Ona Ray. I was kind of surprised they had one. Karen was free to accompany me back to town.

Before we left, I asked Ona Ray for a recent picture of Earl. She hunted around in a kitchen drawer and pulled out his school picture from the year before.

"He looks the same," she said. The picture showed a tow-headed, blue-eyed boy with freckles and a gap between his front teeth, smiling slyly at the camera, like he knew something we didn't.

Young Earl looked a lot like the image of Tom Sawyer I've always had in my mind.

Karen hugged Ona Ray and wiped away both of their tears. We headed home.

"What do you think?" Karen asked after we'd gotten underway.

"You know me. I always look on the bright side."

She scoffed. "Yeh, the eternal optimist. That's you all over."

I picked up the radio handset but she pried it out of my hand before I could use it.

"Who do you want to call?"

"Bernard's working overnight. I just wanted to tell him to spend as much time as he could looking for Earl."

"I'll do it. As tired as you are, I don't trust you to do one thing at a time, never mind two."

She had her conversation with Bernard, then we lapsed into silence.

After a spell, she asked, "What now?"

I need a drink, that's what now, I thought, although these days it seems like all drinking does is keep me sober. There's not a damn bit of fun in that.

"It's time we get you home," I said.

"It's time you get yourself home," Karen said. She was right. Tomorrow was shaping up to be a long day. We'd need to get an early start. Naturally, she'd get to work before me, because that's the way she is.

I drove her to the little white frame house she used to share with her mother before she passed. It was on the same block and about one-hundred feet behind the First Baptist Church, which Karen attends faithfully. I kissed her in the car, in case we were being spied on. I watched her unlock her door and go inside, then headed home.

Dizzy met me in my driveway. Diz is to Burr what Cyclops the Cat is to Butcherville. Queen of all she surveys.

"Come on, girl," I said, not that she needed my encouragement. She bounced up and down like a kangaroo and barked like she was glad to see me. I knew better. She just wanted me to feed her. Spending all day roaming around town and snacking out of people's garbage is no substitute for the evening meal. I'd missed mine, too, but my dinner would be of the liquid variety.

I was in as big a hurry to drink as Dizzy was to eat. Only a pair of achy knees kept me from hopping around, myself.

CHAPTER THIRTEEN

I woke up well before daylight, feeling like hell and forgetting where I was. Someone had evidently plucked out my eyes while I was asleep, soaked them in pickle brine, and jammed them back in my head without regard to which eye went into which socket. Knocking back half of a fifth of bourbon before bedtime doesn't exactly brighten the morning after. The booze had knocked me out, but after an hour or two I was awake again, and that was it. I sat in my La-Z-Boy another hour trying to get back to sleep before finally giving up.

Instead of wasting energy trying to sleep, I unpacked my old Conn Wonder alto saxophone, stuck a rag in the bell so as not to wake the neighbors, and worked on a song I've been trying to learn for twenty years. "Parker's Mood" was first recorded back in the '40s by a great saxophone player from Kansas City named Charlie Parker. I bought the 78-rpm version when I was in the Marines and wore the dang thing out. I've gone through multiple copies over the years but never learned it all the way through. Some of it I can play, but not all.

I actually got to meet Parker right after I got my discharge. I'd decided to try living in New York City, figuring that after Korea, it should be a piece of cake (I was wrong, but that's another story). I heard Parker play at a joint in Greenwich Village called The Open Door. Afterwards, I screwed up my courage and went up to talk to him. People say he was a depraved drug addict, but he was nice to me.

I doubt I'll ever stop playing the saxophone, if only for my own enjoyment. I'll never give up on "Parker's Mood," either. One of these days I'll get it.

Not tonight, though. I was too distracted by the Collins mess to play worth a damn. On the bright side, the alcohol clouded my perceptions to where I thought I sounded better than I probably did. I put away the horn at some point and tried sitting outside and looking at the stars. It was a good night for listening to the toads blow their trumpets and the cicadas shake their maracas, but I was too restless to do it for long.

Given my state of semi-inebriation, driving around aimlessly wasn't the best idea in the world, but that's what I did.

On the other hand, I expect I've driven more miles under the influence than most people have sober, and never had a serious wreck. So there's that.

I retraced every inch of road I traversed earlier, stopping to shine my searchlight across a field, or peek in the window of a parked car I didn't recognize. I didn't find anything that would lead me to Earl. By dawn I was about ready to start yelling his name at the top of my lungs. I'd tried everything else.

I went home as the sun came up.

•　　•　　•　　•　　•

A shower cleared my head. I forced down a pack of mini powdered doughnuts and a glass of orange juice. I felt marginally better.

I loaded Dizzy into the car and drove to the station. Once there, we went our separate ways. Diz spends the daytime begging food from her human friends, who all seem to believe they're the last thing standing between her and starvation. I don't know how they can think that, she's so danged fat, but there you go.

I got to work at seven o'clock, an hour earlier than is typical. Of course, Karen was already at her desk. Bernard had arrived, as well. Both were drinking coffee. Karen had a cup ready for me when I walked in the door.

"My Lord, Emmett," Karen said, "why don't you go back to your coffin and try to get some sleep."

"I don't look that bad, do I?"

"I'd stay away from mirrors, if I were you."

"I do that as a matter of course."

I leaned on the counter separating her space from the reception area. I started doodling on a small scratch pad with the Oklahoma Gas & Electric logo printed on it. I drew a hairy wart on Reddy Kilowatt's nose.

Karen clapped her hands sharply. "Let me have your attention," she said. "I have an announcement. Guess what today is." There were only two of us in the office besides Karen. Bernard didn't seem inclined to answer but was content to smile, smoke, and sip his coffee.

"Saturday," I said, not feeling up to cracking wise.

"It is Saturday," said Karen, "but this is something else. Something more important." She gave me a knowing wink and inclined her head in Bernard's direction.

"If it's his birthday, just give him some money out of petty cash."

Bernard got up from his folding chair, walked over to the percolator and poured himself another cup of coffee.

"Nah, it ain't my birthday," he said. "I'm getting my braces off."

As a child, Bernard suffered the slings and arrows of outrageous dentition—he had bucked teeth—but his parents couldn't afford braces. Not until he was in his twenties, when he got the job as my second-in-command, was he finally able to see an orthodontist.

"Congratulations, son," I said. "Now all you need is a pair of contact lenses, and you'll be all set."

"Set for what?"

"Everything. You'll get fewer cases of resisting arrest, I can guarantee you that."

Hard case types like to test Bernard, based on the fact that in uniform he's about as physically imposing as the Scarecrow from the Wizard of Oz. He'd look tougher without the braces. Not that he needs to. More than one self-styled tough guy has discovered over the years what a genuine hard ass Bernard Cousins is. Bullies pick a fight with him at their own risk. It seldom works out well for them.

Bernard enjoys being underestimated. "I hope I still have a few," he said.

"I'm sure you will, hon," Karen said. "You'll always be tougher than you look."

She meant it as a compliment, but I'm not sure he accepted it in the spirit in which it was intended.

"The doctor's going to see you on a Saturday?" I said.

I'd turned Reddy Kilowatt into a buck-toothed winged dinosaur with blood coming out of his eyes. And a hairy wart on his nose. I ripped the drawing out of the pad and rolled it into a tight little ball.

"The dentist made arrangements to accommodate Bernard's work schedule," Karen said.

"You realize you're not allowed to take special favors," I said.

"I'm paying him regular price, Chief."

I chuckled and threw my paper ball at him. I missed by a foot.

"I'm just kidding you, son. There's no law against people being nice to us, as long as they don't expect anything in return."

Bernard retrieved the ball and gently tossed it into the trash can from across the room.

"I'll remember that, Chief."

"It's not like folks are going out of their way to help y'all," said Karen.

She was right about that. I insist my officers treat people with respect. It's mostly reciprocated, but we catch our share of hostility.

"Any word on Earl?" I asked.

"No, but it's early," Karen said.

"I don't suppose you noticed anything overnight," I asked Bernard.

"No, except for you playing the saxophone when you should've been asleep."

I thought I was playing soft and said so.

"Sound carries that time of night," he said.

"No wonder you look so awful," Karen said. "What've you got against sleep?"

"I highly recommend it for other folks. It just doesn't always work for me."

Thinking about it made me yawn. Watching me made Bernard yawn.

"It's not like I don't try," I said.

I went behind the counter and set myself down on the corner of Karen's desk. I've sat on that same spot so many times over the years my butt's worn it shiny.

"So, there's no sign of Earl, and the sheriff hasn't called with an update on Merle," I said.

Karen shook her head. "No Earl. No call from the sheriff."

"Let's call over there and see if Earl turned up in the night."

"I'm pretty sure they would've called if they had," said Bernard.

"Maybe, but let's check and make sure."

Karen picked up the phone. "It might also be nice to hear if they got a line on whoever beat up Merle," she said, and dialed.

Bernard yawned again and edged toward the door. "Chief, I'm going home to get a couple hours of sleep before my appointment."

"Alright, son. Next time we see you, you're going to look like Rock Hudson."

"I just hope I don't look like Bugs Bunny," he said on his way out the door.

Karen and I laughed out of surprise more than anything. Bernard doesn't crack many jokes.

Karen got through directly to Sheriff Murray, a miracle on the order of me giving up bourbon. Burt never gets to work before ten o'clock, and never ever works weekends.

She asked him to hold and handed me the phone. "What're you doing there on a Saturday morning, Burt?"

"A fella from channel 9 in Oklahoma City is coming down to do a story about the new statue of Stand Watie being unveiled in Watie Junction this morning. I figured I needed to be there to make things official."

I should have known it would involve getting his name in the news or his mug on TV. Burt's long-range political aspirations extend beyond being county sheriff.

"So they're finally giving old Stand a statue, huh?"

Burt chuckled. "Might as well. They already named the town after him." He cleared his throat. "Don't forget now, Emmett. Stand was a Confederate general." He said this last in such a way that you'd think Mr. Watie had cured cancer and invented sliced bread and discovered the Northwest Passage all on the same day. I doubt he'd have a town named after him in this state if he'd fought for the other side.

I asked Burt if his people had learned anything by talking to Merle Collins.

"I didn't interrogate him myself, but I believe Undersheriff Belcher and the OSBI were able to question him during the night. Keith said he'd write me a report and put it on my desk. I'm looking for it right now and ain't finding it."

I heard papers rustling over the phone. Burt likes to make people think he's working harder than he really is.

"I'll tell you what," he said, "I understand they're ready to cut Mr. Collins loose. How 'bout you pick him up and give him a ride home? I'm stretched thin right now, with the unveiling and all. That way you can question him yourself."

He was trying to have me do something he should've been taking care of himself, but I welcomed the opportunity to question Merle in person, so I agreed to do it. "I'd also appreciate any information you or the OSBI might have about the son's disappearance. He's the one we're worried about right now."

"Emmett, I got to git, but I'll give you Keith's home phone number and you can talk to him about that, too." More papers rustling. He gave me a number I already had, but I wrote it down anyway. We said our goodbyes.

"Nothing, huh?" said Karen.

I shook my head and looked out the front window. An actual tumbleweed rolled down the middle of Main Street. I had to laugh, it was so corny. That's just Burr all over, I thought. I half expected Wyatt Earp to stick his head in the door and say hello.

Karen didn't know or care about what I was looking at. "Hey," she said and snapped her fingers. "Pay attention. What did the sheriff say?"

"Basically: 'Ask Keith.' He also asked me to give Merle a ride home. I said I would."

She made a disgusted sound. "That man is allergic to anything that won't get him votes. You going there now?"

"Maybe you could call and make sure Merle's ready to go home."

"I'll do that right now."

She did. He was ready.

"I wonder what they're doing about finding Earl," she said.

"Keith'll know. He's the one running that department anyway. Remind me to go through him next time something important comes up."

"I'll do that."

I said I'd give a Keith a call, and retired to the cramped little room that serves as my office. Without getting up, Karen rolled her chair through the door, up close to my desk. I dialed Keith's number. I had to let it ring awhile before he answered.

"H'llo?" He sounded like he was speaking from the bottom of a well.

"Keith, buddy, it's Emmett. I'm sorry about waking you up at this hour, but I need to know what you got out of Merle Collins, if anything. I was also wondering if y'all had made any progress on finding the boy."

"That's ok, Emmett, hold on a second."

I heard the phone being put down, then, a few seconds later, a toilet flush. He came back on the line.

"Okay, sorry about that. Yeh, I did finally manage to talk to Collins just before my shift ended, which seems like it was about five minutes ago. He's in some deep shit, sounds like. Did you know he was mayor of Butcherville?"

We expressed our mutual amazement. I told him I was going to pick up Merle from the hospital, and reiterated my desire to know what he'd told Keith.

"He didn't tell me a danged thing, but he did talk to a couple of OSBI agents."

"What'd he tell them?"

"You heard about how Clyde Raymer wants to expand his business down there in Butcherville, right?"

I briefly related what I knew, up to and including the harassment directed at the Collinses. "I'm surprised when anyone has the balls to stand up to Clyde," I said. "He usually just pays off whoever he needs to pay off."

"Yeh, well, he tried that with Merle, but Merle likes where he lives and doesn't like being pushed around."

"I'm starting to think Merle's my kind of guy."

"Yeh, he's got guts, sounds like. Anyway, he told those OSBI agents he made a pitstop at Leave it to Bever's on his way home from work. You know the place?"

I knew the place.

Leave it to Bever's is the only former brothel that managed to weather Butcherville's vice cleanup. It owes its survival to an inspired interpretation of the United States Constitution.

On the verge of being forced to close with all the rest of the sin palaces, the owner—Orville Bever—got the idea of building a stage, stocking some reading material, and reinventing his whorehouse as a combination strip joint and bookstore. Brothels were illegal, but once in a while even a respectable married man wants to look at a naked lady who's not his wife. A few outraged locals called the owner's bluff and took him to court, but the judge ruled that, as a bookstore, Bever's was protected by the First Amendment. As you would expect, a few folks raised hell. It got set on fire—not once, but twice. However, Leave it to Bever's weathered every storm. People say it has more lives than Cyclops the cat.

"I know it by reputation only," I said.

"I'll bet," Keith said, his smile coming over loud and clear.

The last time I'd been there was to remove an intoxicated farmer who refused to vacate upon request. He'd come in smelling like chicken shit and was a little too free with unsolicited religious advice, but his money was green. They gave him table dances as long as he dished out five-dollar bills. When his money ran out, so did his welcome. He did not take rejection well. Management called me. When I got there, he was sitting quietly by himself at the far end of the bar, reading a pornographic novel called *Catch 'er in the Raw*. I brandished my flashclub in a threatening manner. He did not resist my entreaty, although I still had a helluva time getting him home; he was so drunk, he couldn't remember where he lived.

"So, what happened at Leave it to Bever's?" I said.

"Merle says he went in there to drink a quick beer or two before he went home to pick up his son. A couple of guys started buying him rounds."

"I'm guessing Merle isn't one to look a gift beer in the mouth."

"I guess not," said Keith. "They kept buying and he kept drinking. At some point he realized he needed to leave if he was going to get to the game on time, but by then he was too drunk to drive. The two fellas offered him a ride. One of them drove his truck to the football field, while the other one drove the car they came in."

"Let me guess: a black Mustang."

"Yes indeed. Merle thought they were all going to the game, but when they got to the football field they just parked his truck and forced him into the Mustang. He was too sloshed to do much about it. All of a sudden, they quit being friendly. They took him to some old barn—Merle isn't sure where—and beat the hell out of him. Told him that if he didn't sell to Clyde Raymer, he and his family wouldn't live long enough to regret it. He thinks they wanted him to sign something, but they didn't have it with them. Forgot to bring it, looks like."

"Was there a weapon or did they just use their fists?"

"Merle said one of them had a black jack or a tied-off sock filled with BBs. Something like that. They flashed a gun but didn't use it. I guess we can be thankful for that."

"What about the football in his tool box?"

"He doesn't know how that football got there. He left for work before the boy got out of bed yesterday morning, and didn't see him all day. I suspect he's telling the truth."

"So, I guess that means we're looking at Earl's disappearance as an abduction."

"Yeh, that's how the OSBI is treating it. They've mobilized every agent they got, trying to find Earl. We're searching and asking questions ourselves. Obviously, it ain't for ransom. The Collins's hardly got a pot to piss in."

We fell silent. I imagine both of us were thinking the same thing, although we might have different reasons for not bringing it up. But one of us had to.

"We need to consider whether Clyde Raymer has something to do with this," I said.

There was a sigh on the other end. "Yeh, I know. He's the one who has the most to gain. I don't like our chances of us pinning it on him, though. He's got every politician in the county in his pocket. Not to mention my boss," meaning Burt Murray. "I think we'd best find the boy first and worry about who to blame later."

He was right, but only up to a point. "We'll still need to talk to him," I said. "I understand it's unlikely, but we have to go out there if we think there's even a slight possibility he's got the boy."

"Burt'll never stand for it," Keith said, "and I can't go out there without telling him."

The last thing I wanted to do was get Keith fired. "Don't worry about it, I'll do it. Burt can't do anything to me. I'll go out there after I take Merle home."

"I appreciate it, buddy," he said. "I'm so exhausted, I'm sure I'd just make a mess of it."

I told him to go back to bed and that I'd call after I talked to Clyde. We said our goodbyes.

"Y'all think it was an abduction and that Clyde Raymer was behind it," Karen said as a statement of fact.

"It'd take a really stupid crook to think he could wring any money out of those folks for ransom," I said. "I don't think any crook's that stupid, to tell you the truth, which must mean Earl was taken for another reason."

"Clyde needs Merle's cooperation if he's going to expand his business," she said.

"That's a motive, right there," I said.

"A lot of other people stand to make money if Merle gets out of Clyde's way," she said.

"Count 'em all up, that's a lot of motives," I said.

"I guess we'd better sort it out, don't you think?"

"Yup," I said. "I reckon so."

CHAPTER FOURTEEN

Some people think that just because I don't always carry a sidearm, I must be prejudiced against guns. They're wrong. I'm against bad guys having them, of course, but generally I'm pretty fond of guns. It goes back to my relationship with my father. He and I have always gone shooting together, going back to my seventh birthday when he gave me my first Winchester .22. Dad's mind has been failing for some time now, but on his good days, when my other duties aren't too pressing, he and I will drive out to the old airport and shoot at paper targets pinned against hay bales, just for the hell of it.

I don't hate guns. It's just that I prefer to shoot at inanimate objects. I had enough of killing when I was in the Marines. These days, if something draws a breath, I leave it alone. Until recently, in all my time as police chief, I never had reason to fire a shot in anger. Burr's generally an agreeable place. I do everything in my power to keep it that way.

The main reason I tend not to carry is to avoid inciting some shit-for-brains redneck with a chip on his shoulder into reenacting the Shootout at the OK Corral on the streets of my town. I don't doubt that any man so inclined would end up second-best in a confrontation, but I'd rather do what I can to discourage such things from happening in the first place.

That said, there are times when common sense dictates I wear my service weapon. With Merle coming to physical harm, his son missing, and the culprits still at large, now was such a time.

Old-timers in my business say semi-automatic handguns are unsuitable for the job because they're likely to jam in a crisis. I took that as gospel and carried a revolver as my service weapon, until about a year ago, when I switched to the same Colt .45 semi-auto I used in Korea. If it's good enough for the Marines, it's good enough for the Burr Police Department.

I always keep a round in the chamber, just in case.

•   •   •   •   •

I arrived at the hospital in time to catch a tall, overfed country boy with frizzy hair and a peach-fuzz mustache pushing Merle out the front door in a wheelchair. Merle was dressed in jeans and a red flannel shirt, and held a large wax-coated brown paper bag on his lap. The boy pushing him had on those green fatigues or scrubs or whatever they call those baggy uniforms hospital orderlies wear. Saying he looked bored to death would unjustly malign cadavers.

I hurried out of the car to lend a hand. I caught my leg in the door when I was closing it—the same shin I'd dinged on the Collins's riding lawn mower the night before. Combine that with my achy knees and I might as well have had barbed wire wrapped around my legs.

I limped over to the wheelchair. "I'm that man's chauffeur, orderly," I said. The kid's expression said I don't give a shit just as clear as a bell. He let me take over. I helped Merle into the car. He went along with it without saying a word. Someone from the sheriff's office must've told him I was coming.

It took me a minute to fish the seat belts out from between the cushions and buckle him in. He laid the bag he'd been carrying on the floorboard between his knees. I navigated around a parked ambulance to exit the parking lot, then waited for a dirty red Peterbilt to pass before I could turn onto the highway in the direction of Burr.

We drove a minute or two in silence, past the Dairy Queen and the Western Auto and Temple City's other spectacular sights. The car was hot and muggy. I considered asking Merle to open his window, but his head was resting up against it and his eyes were closed, so I cranked down my own and hoped for the best.

He seemed in decent condition, considering the battered mess he'd been a few hours before. However, it was still clear he'd been through the wringer. The puffy white bandage on his nose was big, almost like something you'd put on a broken arm. Both eyes were black and blue, and cuts of varying size and depth decorated his face.

I asked what was in the bag. "My clothes," he said through puffy lips. "Ones I 'uz wearing last night. All bloody. Ruint."

I hit a big pothole. Merle winced. I apologized. "That's ok," he said. "You didn't do it on purpose."

He held an arm out in front of him and examined the shirtsleeve, like he was looking at it for the first time. He then rubbed a hand up and down one leg of his jeans, as if trying to remind himself what denim felt like. His lips thinned in something like a smile. "Undersheriff Belcher loaned me some of his stuff to wear home," he said.

"He's a nice man," I said.

"Yup, he is."

I let a respectful interval pass before getting to the point. "Ona Ray told me about the problems you're having with being mayor, Merle," I said.

"Yeh, well, it ain't been a walk in the park."

"I'll tell you, I admire the hell out of what you're doing. It takes brass balls to stand up against a whole town."

He snorted. "Butcherville ain't much of a town."

I agreed, but that wasn't really the point. "Don't shortchange yourself. A man as rich and powerful as Clyde Raymer is used to getting what he wants. I reckon he doesn't know what to make of someone like you."

He laughed bitterly. "A man like me? What kind of man is that, Chief? A man so gol' dang stupid, he don't know enough to take a bag full of money when someone tries give it to him? I guess I'd rather get my ass whipped and have my boy kidnapped and whatever else. Pro'bly get my house burned down. That's the way they do things in Butcherville."

We passed the last of Temple City's traffic lights. I accelerated to 50 mph and left it there. "You think your boy missing has something to do with all this?"

Merle gave me one of those "is the pope Catholic" looks. "Hell yes," he said, so forcefully, it seemed to cause him physical pain. He grimaced and voice turned strained and weak. "I don't see how it couldn't, do you?"

"I got to admit, it sure looks like it." I almost added, "it's too early to tell," but decided there was no need insult his intelligence. He knew what was what.

I looked at him as best I could out of the corner of my eye. He didn't fit any common idea of how a hero should look. He wasn't big or strong or mean-looking. The opposite, in fact. He was thin-faced and scrawny and had a kind face. Recent events had had the same effect on him as on his wife; he looked at least ten years older than the 40-something I knew him to be. Partly he seemed sad and scared. Overall, however, he seemed like the kind of man whose daddy used to tell him to avoid fighting if he could, but if conflict was inevitable, be sure and get in the first punch. His face wore the same look of frightened determination that I reckon David must've had before going up against Goliath. Real courage is facing down someone who's a sure bet to kick your ass. Merle resembled a skinned rabbit after the beating he'd taken, but I wouldn't have bet against him going forward.

"All I know is what those two sons-of-bitches told me last night," he said, "about how I'd better give Clyde Raymer what he wants or else. Alright," he nodded, "that's fine. If he wants to come after me, let him. But he'd better stay the goddam hell away from my family. I'll kill any man tries to hurt them." He realized what he'd said and who he'd said it to. "I guess I shouldn't be telling you that," he said, "but you know what I mean, don't you?"

"I do, Merle. I'd feel the same way if I was in your shoes."

He touched one of the of the cuts on his face and examined his fingers, as if to look for fresh blood. There wasn't any but he was clearly in pain. "I'll take a bullet for em," he said. "I don't care. It'll take more than one of them to put me down, I promise you that." I believed him.

"Ona Ray says people have been calling on the phone and threatening y'all. You know who's doing it?"

"Hell, no. Gutless bastards. Calling in the middle of the night, raising their voices high so I can't recognize them, telling me what they're going to do if I don't give Clyde what he wants. I went to Clyde and told him about it. Of course, he says he don't know who's doing it but that he'll look into it. He didn't, though. Now this happens."

He closed his eyes tight and pressed both hands over his ears like he was trying to shut out something he didn't want to hear. He stayed that way for a few seconds, then opened his eyes and leaned forward so his forehead rested lightly on the dashboard.

The road back to Burr was straight and lonely. Way in the distance, a car rose over the horizon, coming toward us. I tried to think of something comforting to say, but I was afraid anything I'd come up with would just make things worse, so I just kept my mouth shut and drove.

The car coming at us was closing the gap faster than it should. At a distance it was apparent it was some kind of hot rod, probably being driven by some reckless kid. For a moment, I considered hitting my lights and pulling him over, but I had other priorities.

Merle was still leaning forward against the dashboard with his eyes closed. He didn't see the car as it sped past us.

But he heard it.

He jerked up his head and watched the car speeding away from us in the opposite direction. I looked in the rear view and realized what it was. A black Mustang.

"That's them, chief," he said. "That's the car."

I guess I would be pulling them over after all.

I jerked to a stop and spun into a U-turn. Merle's head whiplashed. He smacked his head against the window and his mangled nose against the dash. He yelled in rage or pain or both. I hit the lights. My tires skidded on the shoulder. We fishtailed, spraying gravel. By the time I got straightened-out and going full tilt, the Mustang had a big head start. I closed on it fast, though. Mustangs are quick little cars, but they're like little wind-up toys compared to my Galaxie Police Interceptor.

Maybe the other driver knew that, because he didn't try very hard to get away. Once he'd realized I was after him, he pulled off to the side of the road, alongside what used to be, a long time ago, the Greater Burr Golf and Country Club. These days, it's an open pasture with a pump jack where the first tee used to be.

I felt sure I'd spooked our suspect into surrendering without a fight. I was wrong about that.

Wronger than I've ever been about anything.

CHAPTER FIFTEEN

Dad and I have a history of arguing and fighting over pretty much anything and everything, even if we know that, down deep, we agree about what's most important.

One thing we've never even pretended to disagree about, though, is our love of shooting. Give us couple of guns and something to blast away at, and we're as thick as thieves. Target shooting and reloading shells and looking for a good deal on a Sears Roebuck Colt .45 Cow Boy Special are things we can enjoy together. Talking about guns gets us to open up about other things. I learned a lot about life talking to my dad when we were out on some friendly farmer's land taking turns trying to put holes in an empty Coors can.

Dad can flat out shoot.

Doesn't matter what kind of gun it is. A shotgun. A rifle. A handgun. He's the best I've ever seen at all of them. I was never as good—at least, not when it came to doing things his way. When it came to doing things my way ... well, that's another story.

I used to see a lot of westerns at the Broncho Theater when I was a boy. At some point in nearly all of them, the hero would face-down the villain in a gunfight. Those scenes were always my favorites. So much so, that I decided I'd like to learn to shoot like that.

Dad was always a stickler. It could be tying my shoes, changing the oil in his pickup, or scrubbing a toilet: Whatever it was, there was a right way and a wrong way. Shooting from the hip was not the right way. I should've known better than to tell him I wanted to try, but I did anyway.

He went off like an atom bomb. All that quick-draw stuff in movies was horseshit, he said; there wasn't hardly any gunfighting at all in the Old West, and there wasn't any way in hell I was going to shoot that way when I went out with him. I was going to be taught how to shoot correctly, meaning from a stance, using both hands.

I took his abuse quietly and did it his way when I was around him. When I wasn't, I did it my way. I snuck out of the house with the old Colt double-action revolver Dad had inherited from my grandfather, rode my bicycle far enough from the house that I wouldn't be heard, and practiced being John Wayne. Strictly speaking, I didn't shoot from the hip; I just got good at pulling, aiming, and firing really fast. I might not have been quite as fast as those fellas in the movies, but I was accurate. The point is to hit what you're shooting at. Anybody can be quick on the draw, but if you can't hit the broad side of a barn, there's not much point.

When I got really good, I got up my nerve and showed Dad what I'd been up to. I couldn't shoot Thomas Jefferson's pony tail off a dime at one-hundred yards the way he could, but I could use that old Colt of his to put six shots in a group no bigger around than a teacup from twenty paces, in less time than it takes to swat a mosquito. Which ain't too shabby, as my high school football coach used to say. Didn't keep Dad from complaining, mind you. But I could see how proud he was. From then on, he let me do it my way.

•　　　•　　　•　　　•　　　•

I can't say I was thinking about any of that while sitting in the Galaxie, twenty yards to the rear of the Mustang, watching its turn signal blink and its exhaust pipes belch smoke. It did occur to me that I was smart to have strapped on my gun before leaving the house that morning.

Ford hasn't been making those Mustangs for more than a year or two, so this had to have been new or almost new. It's owner must not have liked how it came off the showroom floor, however. It had been modified to look less like a street-legal sports car, and more like something you'd see at the drag race track. Big fat tires had been mounted in the back, with little tires in the front, mounted on slot mag wheels. The rear end was jacked up, while the front end lay close to the ground. The hood had a bug-catcher intake scoop. A spoiler was mounted across the rear. It was one of those cars that look like they're going fast even while they're standing still. Seeing it up-close, I thought it suspicious that the driver didn't try to outrun me. It was a safe bet he had at least as much under the hood as I did.

I saw the backs of two heads through the Mustang's rear window. They were having an animated conversation. Every few seconds, the driver would look up at me in his overhead rear-view mirror. The hairs on the back of my neck stood up. I didn't know who exactly I was dealing with, but I knew they were armed. Don't ask me how. I just knew.

Merle was breathing fast now. Sweat poured off him like he'd run a marathon in a fur coat. He wiped his face with his shirtsleeve, careful to avoid his damaged nose.

"You sure that's them?" I asked.

"It's them," he said, squinting and rubbing his eyes, which must've burned from the sweat. His voice was calmer than you'd expect. "I'm sure."

I picked up the radio handset and hailed Karen. "Red, I'm with Merle Collins on State Road 43 out by Burr Golf and Country Club. I just pulled over a black Ford Mustang that Merle says belongs to the men who assaulted him." I gave her the license plate number and told her to run a check. I then asked if Kenny was on duty.

"No, hon, he's working at the hardware store till noon," she said. Kenny lugs boxes and runs the register at the Oklahoma Tire & Supply to make extra money.

"The thing is," I said, "I'm about to approach the driver of the car and I might need some backup. Contact the sheriff's department and have them send someone over. The sooner they can get here, the better."

She said something but the radio crackled and I couldn't be sure what it was. We were at the furthest extreme of its range. "Did you hear that, Red?" I asked.

She said, "I'll do that," before being cut off by another burst of static.

"Come again?" I said.

She spoke louder, which only served to distort her voice. "I said, are you going to wait for them before you approach the car?"

"I don't think so," I said. "There's only two of them. I think I can handle it."

"Alright hon, you be careful." She sounded concerned, but not especially frightened. God bless her, she thinks highly enough of me to believe the odds are always in my favor.

We signed off.

"Merle, I need you to stay in the car," I said. "I don't know if that fella knows it's you—"

"I sure as hell hope he does know it's me," he said, his voice quivering with fear and rage, which is always a dangerous combination. "Let's see if them sons o' bitches can take me when I ain't drunk off my ass."

He made to grab the door handle but I ripped his hand away and pushed him back in his seat. Touching him was like grabbing an electric fence.

"Wait, now," I said, "just listen to me, dang it. I need you to calm down. Take some deep breaths." He did, or at least pretended to.

"Alright now, that's better. I think it's best if you don't show yourself. Let them think I pulled them over for speeding."

His face went slack. I couldn't read what he was thinking. I chose to believe he was listening to what I had to say.

I looked around the back seat for my bullhorn, then remembered I'd given it to Kenny to use at the football game. I'd have to exercise my strong lungs. I gave Merle a last look meant to warn him against doing anything stupid. Maybe I should've given that look to myself.

I unholstered my Colt, checked to make sure there was a round in the chamber, then put it back.

I got out of the car and stood next to it. I usually approach the driver's window during traffic stops, but whoever this was had shown himself to be a physical threat. I thought it wise to keep my distance. My right hand rested lightly on my gun.

"Step out of the car," I said in a loud voice, taking care not to let it get too high-pitched, as sometimes happens when I shout. "Make it slow, and keep your hands where I can see them."

I saw the driver looking at me in his rear view. He raised his hand in a wave. My heart pounded, but not from fear. I was alert. Extremely alert. So alert, you wouldn't believe it.

The engine shut off and the blinker stopped blinking. The driver's side door opened. A man slowly got out of the car and turned to face me. He was tall and pale-skinned. His hair was black or dark brown, slicked back like Elvis's before he went in the army.

This is 1966, I thought. Not even Elvis wears his hair like that anymore.

He wore a black leather jacket, black square-toed boots, and black jeans. Both hands were stuck in the jacket pockets.

"Chief Hardy," he said. "Long time."

He looked vaguely familiar but I couldn't place him.

"We know each other?"

"C'mon, Chief Hardy," he said. He acted friendly, but sometimes a mad dog acts friendly just before it rips out your throat. "Don't tell me you forgot me," he said, smiling. His teeth would've shamed a hobo, they were so rotten. "Thomas Drury. Rachel Drury's son."

Dammit to hell. Tommy Drury. The evilest child I ever met. All grown up.

"It has been a long time," I said. "I haven't seen you since you went away."

"Yup. Ten years, in case you forgot."

I hadn't. 12-year-old boys who try to kill their mother tend to stick in your mind.

Ten years. They'd flown by. Just seeing him took me back to a place and time I had no desire to revisit.

"How long you been out, Tommy?"

"Oh hell, I been out a while now," he said cheerfully. "They cut me loose soon as I turned 21. Been free as a bird ever since." He grinned and winked. "More or less."

The wink pissed me off, but the smile is what made me want to put my fist through his face. He had a mouth like a channel catfish. His crusty green teeth gapped and overlapped willy-nilly, like roof shingles after a tornado. Maybe the State of Oklahoma cuts corners on dental care for wards of its juvenile justice system.

His eyes were no treat to look at, either. Dark and bloodshot, they did a piss-poor job of hiding that the person behind them had more screws loose than a junked Edsel.

"Tommy," I said slowly and deliberately, so as to avoid any chance of miscommunication, "before we go any further, I need you to take your hands out of your pockets."

My own right hand stayed on the Colt's grip. My index finger curled inside the trigger guard.

"I don't know, Chief," he said, still smiling that loathsome smile. "It's damn cold out."

Grasshoppers clicked and clattered in the weeds. The air smelled of dust and sage brush, which often makes me sneeze, but hadn't so far. A scissor-tail flycatcher sat on a strand of wire on the fence by the road, its squeaky call sounding like fingers rubbing on a wet balloon. It was 80 degrees on its way to being 90 or higher. We'd soon be seeing waves of heat rise off the blacktop.

A typical late summer day in western Oklahoma.

The boy was full of shit or dangerous. Probably both.

"Tommy, you'd best take those hands out where I can see them, or we're going to rumble."

He shifted his weight from one leg to the other, keeping his hands in his pockets and that hideous smile on his face. He looked out the corner of his eye at the person still in the Mustang, who was leaning over and watching us in his side mirror. The few hairs on my neck that weren't already standing up snapped to attention.

"Who's your passenger, Tommy?" I was nervous, but a good kind of nervous. A productive kind. The kind where my senses are as sharp as cut glass.

It was fight-or-flight time, and I ain't got wings.

I flashed back to what Tommy had done to his mother and how much I hated him that night. That hate returned like a blast of cold air, coursing through my entire body, from my brain to my limbs to my trigger finger.

I wasn't going to be the one to start this fight, but part of me wanted it to happen.

The bird stood on that wire, his head flicking from side to side. He looked at me, hopped one last time, and flew away. I saw the pink underside of its wings and thought how pretty it was.

Things went fast after that.

Tommy jerked his right hand in his jacket pocket. At the same instant, the passenger door slammed open. Tommy was trying to dislodge what looked to be a large revolver; the other man raised something small and shiny. I pulled on Tommy first. His gun's six-inch barrel was about four inches too long and got hung up in the lining of his jacket. The delay gave me time to put a round in his eye. He dropped like a bag of cement. I got off my second shot at the other fella at almost the precise moment he got off his first. He missed me. I hit him in the chest. He dropped his pistol and it spun in circles on the blacktop. The gunman fell flat on his rear end and gawked at me like an ape at the zoo—slumped, open-jawed, wondering what it was that made him so interesting to look at. His eyes rolled back in his head after a few seconds and he fell over backwards. His head thunked on the asphalt.

That was it for him.

Two shots. Two kills. Two seconds, more or less. John Wayne, eat your heart out, I thought.

Then I threw up all over my boots.

Oh well, I needed a new pair anyway.

My knees buckled and I shook uncontrollably. "Holy shit, Merle, did you—"

I turned around. Merle lay face-down on the blacktop, blood spreading in a pool around his head.

CHAPTER SIXTEEN

Whatever charge I'd felt had exhausted itself. I'd blown a fuse. I felt tired and old and sick.

I half-ran and half-staggered over to where Merle lay. I dropped to my knees harder and faster than I should, scraping the hell out of them. The rough asphalt ripped holes in my uniform pants. He lay on his stomach with his face to the pavement. The bandage on the back of his head was intact. To my great relief, he was breathing and even moved around a little bit. There was a lot of blood coming from his face. He turned himself over, saving me the trouble. Both of his cheeks were perforated. By some miracle, the bullet had gone in one and out the other, chipping a few teeth, maybe, but missing anything vital.

Fortunate man, at least as far as getting shot is concerned.

"Goddam, Merle, why'd you get out of the car?" He tried to answer, but it just made the blood flow more freely, so I gently shushed him and gave him a clean handkerchief to hold over his wounds. "Never mind, just keep quiet," I said. "An ambulance is on its way." It wasn't, but soon would be.

I rose to my feet, leaned over and picked pieces of gravel out of my bloody knees, then hobbled over to Tommy. I knew he was dead, but I had to make sure. He lay on his back with both legs twisted awkwardly to one side. One eye stared blindly into space, and the other was a gory mess. His hand had fallen away from the gun, which was still connected to his jacket pocket by the world's stubbornest length of thread. He never did get the damn thing pulled. Pieces of brain had sprayed out behind him in tiny pink and red fragments. Some of it was splattered across the hood of the Mustang.

You don't walk away from getting shot in the eye by a Colt .45.

The other man lay a few feet away on the opposite side of the car. I knew I'd hit him in the upper chest, but thought I might've missed his vital organs. I didn't. He lay on his back, eyes glassy, a small, cheap-looking snub-nose revolver with brown plastic grips lying on the ground next to his right hand. Hitting Merle with that little piece of shit had to have been one of the all-time lucky shots (although maybe not as lucky as having the bullet go in one cheek and out the other). I kicked it away from his hand because that's what you're supposed to do, but it was clear that he no longer presented a threat. His chest rose in fits and starts and made rattling sounds. Merle could be helped, but this guy was finished. I went back to my car to call it in.

My knees screamed as I got behind the wheel. My head felt like it had been banging around inside a cement mixer. I tried to remember if I'd had anything to drink that morning. I couldn't be sure. Lately, I'd been having trouble keeping track.

Jesus Christ, I thought, is this how it feels to get old?

I pulled the door shut. The stench of vomit on my boots in the enclosed space almost made me puke all over again, so I shoved the door back open—hard, so that it bounced on its hinges. I shifted sideways, stuck my feet outside the car, and let them rest on the pavement. The smell wasn't quite as bad that way.

I picked up the radio handset.

"Karen, you there?"

"I'm here, Emmett," her static-y voice called back. "How'd it go?"

"Not too good. I'm going to need a couple of ambulances."

"Are you ok?" she asked, with some urgency.

"I'm alright. I'm not the one who needs an ambulance. We've got one dead and two more who need medical attention."

For the better part of a minute the radio made nothing but white noise.

She finally came back. "Ok, Emmett, ambulances are coming. A sheriff's deputy should be there any minute." She said something else but it was garbled. I asked her to repeat it. "What happened?" she said with so much force, I might've been able to hear her without the radio if I tried.

"I'm not going to say over the air. I'll tell you later."

She said she was coming out. I told her not to and that I needed her to stay where she was at, but I knew she'd come anyway. A county car with emergency lights flashing approached from far away. I told Karen to send out either Kenny or Bernard if he was back from the dentist, and we signed off.

I went back over to Merle, who looked like he'd tried to scrub the road clean with his face. The big bandage had come off his nose and he was bleeding from both cheeks, but he was conscious and his breathing was regular. I retrieved the paper bag containing his bloody clothes and put it under his head as a pillow, then got an Army blanket out of the trunk and laid it over him. I went to check on the other fella, only to find he had expired in my absence. I regretted not getting to ask who he was, and who put him and Tommy up to this.

I sat down on the asphalt next to Merle. My mind unspooled to a time I'd been in a similar situation, in a frozen hell called the Battle of Chosin Reservoir during the Korean War. I did then what I'd done today, only I had to do it over and over, more times than I could count, to Chinese soldiers so close, I could smell on their breaths what they'd had for breakfast. It scarred me, but scars heal over and get hard. I've lived with those memories for a long time. I could live with this.

Still, it's one thing to be handy with a gun and another to kill someone, which might explain why I threw up all over myself. I did my share of throwing up in Korea when I first got there. For someone who drinks as much as I do, I have a weak stomach.

Keith was the deputy who answered the call. If I was a believer in a higher power, I might've thought God had sent Keith to make up for putting me in that situation to begin with. Unlike the interchangeable bullnecked deputies Burt Murray seems to order straight out of the Sears catalog, Keith's a real lawman, someone I can respect and trust. He parked his car on the other side of the road, opposite mine.

I remembered the flask of bourbon in my glove compartment. As good as it would've tasted just then, I realized it might prove to be a problem if someone decided to search my car. I scuttled back to the Galaxie while Keith was talking on his radio. I stuffed the flask under a flap of carpet beneath the front seat.

Keith reminds me of that fella who plays Rowdy Yates on Rawhide, only Keith's a bit older. He's older than me, too, by ten years at least, although you couldn't tell it by looking at him. He's tall and handsome and has more hair than any middle-aged man has a right to have, not a strand of it gray. I'd probably have a crush on him if I was a woman. He's never been married. To tell the truth, I'm not sure he likes women that much, although they sure do like him. He's better looking than me. Not by much, but some.

I'll admit this: He sure as hell looked better than me right then.

Keith finished his call and walked over to where I crouched next to Merle. Another siren moaned in the distance. An ambulance, I reckoned.

Keith stood with his hands on his hips and surveyed the scene.

He whistled silently. "I never figured you for no Marshal Dillon, Emmett."

"Me neither," I said. "It's funny how in my old age I'm constantly discovering new things about myself."

He bent over Merle. "How're you doing, Mr. Collins?" he asked.

Merle nodded slightly and blinked a time or two. Keith slapped him lightly on the upper arm and told him help would be there before he knew it.

"Shot through both cheeks," I said. "In one and out the other. Can you believe that?" Merle made a sound that might've been a laugh.

"Didn't get hit anywhere else?" asked Keith.

"Nah, that's it," I said. "The guy just got off one shot."

"You're a lucky man, Mr. Collins," he said.

"I don't reckon he's feeling very lucky," I said. Merle looked up at us with glazed eyes.

I followed Keith over to where the others lay. He stood over them, hands on hips and shaking his head. "These boys won't be waking up any time soon," he said. He bent over Tommy. A look of recognition passed over his face. He turned back to me.

"Is this who I think it is?" he asked.

"Yup," I said. "Thomas Drury's back in town."

He closed Tommy's mouth, which had been hanging open.

"*Was* back in town," Keith said, then whistled again. "Tommy Drury. Good Lord."

"Little SOB drew on me but he couldn't get the gun out of his pocket. I reckon his buddy was shooting at me but missed and got Merle instead. Hitting Merle in the mouth with that little snub-nose was one shot in a million." I paused. "Of course, he was aiming at me."

"That was his mistake," Keith said, rising to his feet. "You ain't going to shoot me, are you?"

"Not if you don't give me any reason to."

He smiled faintly. "How're you feeling?" he asked.

"Well, I smell pretty bad, seeing as I puked all over myself, and I scraped the hell out of my knees. But other than that, I appear to have emerged from this shitstorm unscathed."

Pate Funeral Home's big combination ambulance/hearse arrived. A couple of attendants dashed over to the dead men.

"Don't bother with them," I said. "They're finished. Mr. Collins here is the one who needs help."

Keith and I stepped aside and let them do their jobs. We stood on a gravel driveway that led to the weather-beaten lean-to that had sheltered a practice tee back when the place had been a golf course.

"They got you out of bed for this, huh?" I asked him.

He took off his greenish-gray county-issue cowboy hat and ran a hand through his thick, scrubby hair.

"Yeh, well, I got up after you called," he said. "I was still wearing my uniform. Slept in it. I was drinking coffee when it came over the scanner and figured I'd best be the one to respond. You're not exactly beloved by most of the Sheriff's Department. I don't know if you realize that."

"I thought Burt liked me," I said.

"Oh, Burt does, but he and I are about the only ones."

I turned my attention back to the medics tending to Merle. "Oh well," I said. "Can't please everyone."

We listened to the small sounds the attendants made, and the chirring of insects. They'd shut down at the sound of gunshots, but had now restarted, which I found comforting somehow.

"Are you going to tell me what happened here or do I have to guess?"

"I reckoned I'd wait for you to guess. To be honest, I'm not all that sure myself, it happened so fast."

I went over it step-by-step, as much for my benefit as his. I talked and he scribbled it all down in a little leather-bound notebook. More company arrived: two more deputies and a highway patrolman; Kenny and Bernard in the Fury (Bernard had skipped out on his orthodontist appointment when he got word what had happened); and another combination ambulance/hearse from a funeral home in Watie City. Its two attendants hovered, waiting for the go-ahead to load the bodies. A couple of the same crime scene technicians who'd gone over Merle's truck the night before also showed up.

"Refresh my memory about Tommy Drury," said Keith.

"I don't know what to tell, other than he's about as close to being pure evil as anyone I've ever met."

"He's the one beat his mama half to death when she wouldn't let him take her car to the movies, right?"

"Yeh. Beat her up and took it anyway. Somehow, she managed to call me. I drove out to Butcherville, took her to the hospital, then went back to their house and waited for Tommy to come home. He strolled in like nothing had happened. Called out for his mama, but got me instead. He was convicted and got sent away. I reckon they had to let him go once he turned 21."

"What about the other fella?" he said, nodding at Drury's accomplice.

"Him, I don't know. He looks a little familiar, but I can't place him."

"Well, let's see what we can find out."

We walked over to where he lay. Keith felt around in the pants pockets. He found a black leather billfold and rifled through it. He extracted a laminated card. "Here we go," he said. "It's a WestOK ID card for someone named Dennis Tyler."

Holy Christ, I didn't want to hear that.

He pulled out another card. "Driver's license says the same thing," he said.

"God damn it to hell," I said.

"What's wrong? He a friend of yours?"

"No, he ain't a friend. I never met the sorry son of a bitch, but if he's who I think, I'm afraid I might've just killed the only person in the world who knew where Earl Collins is."

CHAPTER SEVENTEEN

Keith caught on quick.

"You think Tyler had something to do with Earl Collins' disappearance?"

"I do."

"Mind telling me why?"

I explained how Darryl Martin fingered Tyler as the driver of the Willys parked in front of the Butcherville Store when Earl was last seen. I related what Merle's abductors had told him about playing ball with Clyde, and how, on top of everything, Tyler works—worked—at WestOK, meaning Clyde was his boss.

"And Clyde might be behind this whole thing," Keith said.

I let that hang in the air.

"Tyler had another fella with him," I said. "Darryl couldn't see who it was, but it must've been Tommy Drury. Those two had to have been the ones who snatched Earl."

"Makes sense," Keith said. "I don't see them as the brains behind this, though. I didn't know Tyler, of course, but if he's hanging around with Drury, I don't reckon he's Nobel Prize material."

I laughed despite myself. "Clyde could be the brains, but there's no way he gets his hands dirty on this. He's too wily. There's got to be someone else."

"Stands to reason," said Keith. "You wouldn't think they'd hurt the boy, seeing that they're trying to blackmail his daddy into selling his property."

"Tyler and Drury must've handed Earl off to someone before they went after Merle," I said.

We just don't know who it is.

I didn't have time to think about it too much. The little spot on the highway had become overcrowded with Highway Patrol and sheriff's deputies, although Burt Murray was notably absent. That statue dedication must've gone into overtime.

There was no keeping Karen away. She'd called-in Jeff to mind the store, then paged Bernard at the orthodontist and shanghaied Kenny at the Oklahoma Tire & Supply. I will confess to being glad to see her pull up in that little turquoise-blue Ford Falcon of hers. She walked right up to me without saying a word and gave me a big hug. She smelled good and felt nice in my arms.

Those medics from Pate's know their stuff. You'd never even guess they work for a business that specializes in burying its customers. They did whatever on-the-spot doctoring they could, then loaded Merle into the combination ambulance/hearse. One of them offered to bandage up my knees. I thanked him but declined, told them I'd be taking a shower soon, which meant I'd have to do it all over again. They said they thought Merle would be fine, but he'd more than likely be taken to Baptist Hospital in Oklahoma City, which was better equipped to treat gunshot wounds.

After a few minutes of gentle interrogation, I was allowed to go about my business. Given that this was the first time I'd shot someone in the line of duty, I was a little foggy on the chain of command— specifically, whether the sheriff or the OSBI or Highway Patrol had the right to take my gun or suspend me or maybe feed me to a pack of wolves. Nobody seemed to know. Eventually, Keith took charge of my Colt. I didn't resist, but I did ask if it would be alright if I carried my off-duty revolver. He said he saw no reason why not.

I had another favor to ask. I took him off to the side. "You mind letting me have Dennis Tyler's WestOK ID card?"

He hesitated. "I don't know Emmett. I might be needing it myself. What do you want it for?"

"I'd like to have a picture of him to show folks when I'm asking questions."

He scratched his chin. "I will if you promise to get it back to me by the end of the day."

"You got a deal," I said.

He asked what I planned on doing about Ona Ray. I said I was going out there to tell her what happened and give her a ride to the hospital.

"Sounds like a plan," he said. "Let's keep in touch. You find anything at all, get a hold of me. I'll do the same with you."

"You got any idea what the state boys are going to do?" I asked.

"Not yet, but whatever it is, it'll take them a while to get started. They got a lot more hoops to jump through than we do."

"Yeh, well, I'm gone, then," I said. "I'll take advantage of my lighting speed and get a jump on things."

Keith strode over to the scrum of highway patrolmen gathered over the bodies, now covered in sheets. I corralled Kenny and Bernard, asked them to hang around and be my eyes and ears. I let them know Karen was going back with me, and asked if one of them could drive her car. Kenny was happy to do it.

Karen and I got in the Galaxie and drove away. She didn't grill me on what happened. She'd heard enough in bits and pieces to know. Instead, she said, "Poor Ona Ray," which is what I'd been thinking for the better part of 24 hours.

"I tell you what," I said, "if I have to face that woman with more bad news, my head's liable to explode."

"Don't worry about it," she said. "You've been through enough. I'll tell her."

"You sure?" I said.

She linked her arm in mine and snuggled up next to me. Sometimes it seems like the bigger my troubles, the more affectionate Karen gets. "I'm sure," she said.

I had second thoughts about leaving Bernard and Kenny behind. I radioed Kenny and asked him and Bernard to drive back to town as soon as possible. I needed to go home and take care of myself and I didn't want to leave the town unattended. He said they would.

Jeff was behind Karen's desk upon our return. I filled him in on what had happened. Kenny and Bernard showed up not long after. I tossed Kenny the keys, told him to go out to the Galaxie and bring me back my flashclub, then drive Karen out to the Collins place. Bernard drove me home.

"I apologize for taking you away from your appointment," I said. "I know how much you were looking forward to getting those braces taken off."

"Aw, that's ok, sir. We made another appointment for Monday. I'm sorry I wasn't there to help."

"Only one thing for you to be sorry about."

"What's that?"

"If that boy'd been a better shot, you'd be in line for a promotion."

He looked hurt, like he wasn't sure if I was kidding or not. I grinned. "I'm just pulling your leg, son."

"That's good," he said, laughing, "because I like being Deputy Chief just fine."

I tossed the flashclub on the couch and started stripping off my uniform the second I got through the front door. It smelled like it had been laundered in skunk piss and felt like a straitjacket or a jail cell or something else I needed to escape from. I left a trail of dirty clothes on my way to the bathroom, turned up the shower as hot as I could stand, and stayed under it until the urgency of finding Earl Collins began to override the trauma of what I'd been through.

After I dried myself off, I dug out a first aid kit and wrapped up my knees as best I could. The skin had been scraped almost to my kneecap. The wound was angry and red and getting stickier as the blood dried. My knees feel like hell at the best of times. Now, if a doctor had wanted to amputate, I might not've argued.

Like I told Keith, I was sure Tyler and Drury had taken Earl, and that the plan was to scare Merle into selling his land and changing the zoning so Clyde could have his plant expansion and everyone concerned would get their money. I was also sure there was at least one more person involved—maybe two, if we counted Clyde, who after all had the most to gain. If we found the other person, we'd find Earl. Clyde is smart and greedy enough to pull this off without getting caught.

On the other hand, it was as likely to be some landholder who stood to profit from selling to Clyde. Someone who resented Merle for ruining his big payday. I thought it wise to visit Darryl Martin again and show him the picture ID of Dennis Tyler, Hopefully, he'll tell us one way or the other if it was Tyler he saw in the truck outside the Butcherville Store. He might also have some thoughts on who our third man was. Darryl's a politician. Politicians know things.

I'd run out of clean uniforms—I typically do laundry on Saturdays—so I put on a plaid short-sleeved shirt and a pair of non-paint-stained Levi's, which I pulled gingerly over my bandaged knees. I went outside and used the garden hose to wash the vomit off my boots. It was dry and some of it had to be scraped off with a kitchen knife.

By this point, I'd sooner leave the house bare-assed than without a gun. I delved through the bottom drawer of my bureau and retrieved my off-duty weapon, a hammerless Smith & Wesson .38 Special. It used to be my service weapon, before I switched to my Colt .45. Now, it's buried beneath a bunch of shirts that don't fit me anymore, but which I keep, hoping that one of these days I'll lose ten pounds.

I loaded the S&W from a box of shells I keep hidden in my underwear drawer and tried to remember where I stashed my old gun belt. I couldn't find it, but I did locate a clip-on holster at the bottom of my underwear drawer. I shoved it into my pants at the small of my back. It was probably best I couldn't find the belt. I'd recently become addicted to the fried pickles and tater tots from the new drive-in. I'm sure I would've had to let it out a couple of notches.

I clipped my badge to my shirt pocket, retrieved the flashclub from where I'd tossed it, and walked out the door. Bernard and Kenny had custody of the patrol cars, so my pickup was my only mode of transportation. I shoved the flashclub under the seat and checked the Winchester .30-30 I keep in a gun rack over the rear window to make sure it was loaded. It was. Armed to the teeth, I headed for Butcherville.

It took me ten minutes to get to the Martin place. Next door, an elderly man mowed the lawn with a small tractor. Darryl was outside in his yard, sitting in one lawn chair and resting his broken leg on another. In one hand, he held a mug of what I reckoned was coffee. The other gripped the handle of one of his crutches, which he'd jammed upright into the ground like a wooden stake. The other lay beside him. He watched the old boy on the lawn mower, and seemed to find him entertaining. I tend to read when I sit in my yard, but that's me.

I took extra care getting out of the pickup in deference to my own damaged knees. "Long time, no see, Chief," he said with a wan smile. "How's the world treating you?"

I held the gate open and passed through. I saw Darryl hadn't fixed the section that had defiled my jeans. There was another spot of smeared paint I hadn't noticed before. Evidently, I wasn't the only one who got snagged. You should always put up a warning sign. Just out of common decency.

"Well, Darryl," I said, "the world's not treating me all that great, actually, although it's treating other folks worse."

He said he heard about the shooting, the boys down at the barbershop were talking about it. "My Lord," he said. "We should just be thankful you're alright."

"I'm thankful enough for all of us." I reached into my back pocket for my billfold and pulled out Dennis Tyler's WestOK ID. "I'm here because I wanted to confirm this is the fella in the red Willys you saw outside the Butcherville Store yesterday."

"That's him. That's definitely the man." He sneezed.

"Bless you. You coming down with something?"

"No, it's the sun. Makes me sneeze sometimes." He sneezed again. This time I didn't say 'bless you.' Only one to a customer.

"You think Tyler has something to do with the missing boy?" he said.

"He's the most likely person to have last seen Earl Collins."

"I saw him," he said.

"Yeh, but Tyler was there after you left. A witness saw you drive off before Earl disappeared."

"Bonnie?"

"Yeh, she says you drove off as she got off the bus, before Earl was taken. That puts you in the clear."

He smiled. "That's good to hear."

We made small talk for a minute—remarking on how hot it was, swapping opinions on the footballing skills of Marlon Truitt, Jr. I complimented his new-looking storm cellar. He said he recently got a raise, so he had it built. I asked about his wife. He said she was visiting her mother in Waynoka and that he was a bachelor this weekend. I couldn't hear the dog, so I asked if she'd taken it with her. He said she did, and that the dog was hers, and that sometimes she carries it around in a little bag, which is one of the strangest things I've ever heard, although I didn't say so.

"Alright, then," I said, "I guess I'll be going."

"You let me know if there's anything I can do to help."

"Will do." I opened the gate and limped toward the car. "Oh," I said. "One other thing."

"What's that?"

"You ever heard of someone named Thomas Drury? Drives a Mustang?"

He tossed the contents of his cup into the grass beside him. "Can't make a decent cup of coffee to save my life. I think that's what I miss most when Erin's gone."

"If it wasn't for Karen at work, I'd never have a good cup of coffee," I said. "So, do you know this Drury character?"

He frowned and shook his head. "No, I don't believe so."

"Not a name you've heard around the plant, huh?"

"Can't say I have. Why do you ask?"

"Well, for one thing, he's the other fella I shot. He was working with Tyler."

"Ah."

"The boys down at the barbershop didn't mention his name?"

"Not that I recall," he said.

The boys down at the barbershop must've lost a step.

"Be seeing you, Darryl."

"Be seeing you, Chief. Good luck with finding the boy. Let me know how it turns out."

"I'll do that, Darryl. Say hi to the missus."

And her spoiled little dog.

CHAPTER EIGHTEEN

I had no clear plan of action upon leaving Darryl except to question Clyde Raymer, who I didn't want to face without knowing everything there was to know about Tyler and Drury and their relationship to WestOK. I figured I'd go back to the station and try to get hold of George Fisher, the personnel man at the plant. Maybe he could shed some light.

I say I didn't feel guilty about shooting those two and that's the truth, but it doesn't mean I could easily put it out of my mind. I was reminded of the only time my dad took me hunting. I guess was about eight or nine. We'd been out for hours and hadn't shot at anything more threatening than an empty Coke bottle or two, but we had a lot of fun doing it. Eventually, it started getting dark and we decided to call it a day. We'd just put away our rifles when dad saw a squirrel sitting on a telephone line munching on an acorn. He pulled out a little Colt target pistol he was carrying and nailed the poor little fella through the eye, just like I got Tommy. I'm sure Dad did it on impulse. I tried not to cry, but I did anyway. I know Dad felt bad, even if he didn't say so. He collected the dead squirrel in a paper bag and we took it home with us. He skinned it and my mama tossed the little bit of meat into the stew she was cooking on the stove. As I remember, none of us ate much that night.

Dad felt worse about killing that squirrel than I did about shooting Tommy Drury and Dennis Tyler. That bothered me, made me wonder if I'd become too hard for my own good.

On the other hand, it consoled me somewhat to know that squirrel didn't aim a gun at my dad and me, and I'm sure it never hurt another living creature the way Tommy hurt his mother. That's not to say I felt like throwing a party, but at least I could justify my actions to myself. When it came right down to it, the worst thing was how shooting those two hoods made it even more difficult to find Earl Collins.

I made a brief pit stop at Miller's Drug when I got back to town. The blast of air-conditioning felt nice on my skin but had the effect of worsening an already bad headache, which was the reason I was there in the first place. I bought a Dr. Pepper and a packet of BC Powder, mixed them together, and drank it down.

Kenny and Karen were still at Ona Ray's when I got back to the station. Jeff and Bernard were present, however, as was Cindy Bartlett. Jeff had decided to ask her to come in when her shift at the phone company ended, which surprised me, since Jeff is seldom inclined to take the initiative on anything having to do with work.

I went back to my office and dialed the number on the business card Darryl had given me. I didn't hold out much hope that anyone would answer, but I had to try. I was so surprised when a man's voice answered, for a split second I couldn't remember who I was calling.

"WestOK Petroleum, how can we help you?"

"I'm looking for George Fisher in personnel."

"Speaking," the voice answered.

I must be living right, I thought.

I identified myself and asked if he could give me some information about a Mr. Dennis Tyler. I chose not to mention Mr. Tyler's recent demise. George Fisher gave no indication that he knew.

"Hmmm," he said. "We don't generally like to give out that kind of information over the phone, but I reckon since you're the law, it'd be ok." Thank goodness George Fisher was a trusting soul. I could've just been pretending to be who I said I was.

"Mr. Tyler is the plant's Chief of Security," he said. "He answers directly to Mr. Raymer." Is there a difference between something giving you goosebumps and making your skin crawl? I believe at that moment I experienced both.

I asked him for Tyler's address and phone number. Mr. Fisher asked me to hold on. He came back after several seconds and gave me Tyler's Butcherville address and phone number. I took a flyer and asked if anyone named Tommy Drury worked at the plant. Mr. Fisher said no, he'd never heard of him. I said I hadn't expected he would and thanked him for his time.

I stepped out from behind my desk and ventured into the front office. I hadn't told Jeff and Cindy about the shooting, but it was apparent they knew; the three of them looked at me like my cat had just died.

"What's the latest?" Jeff asked.

"I got Dennis Tyler's address from WestOK, believe it or not, because I'm not sure I do. Bernard, I want you to come with me and check it out. Even if Earl's not there, we might find something that'll tell us where he is."

Jeff raised his hand like a well-behaved 8-year-old in geography class. I called on him.

"Um, Chief, I knew Dennis Tyler a little bit. I went out drinking with him a few times."

Jeff must think I don't know he has a barstool at Edna's with his name engraved on it in gold letters. "Alright," I said, "you're drafted to come along, too."

I asked Cindy if she'd be okay until Karen got back. "It may be a while," I added.

"That's fine," she said primly. "I can use the extra money."

I asked her to try to find out where Tommy Drury lived while we checked Tyler's, then pulled a five dollar bill out of my billfold and dropped it on the desk. "Call over to the drive-in and order yourself something to eat."

She made like she didn't want to take my money, but she was just being polite. I pushed it on her and she finally accepted.

The noon whistle blasted overhead just as we walked out the door and nearly caused me to jump out of my boots. I'd lost track of time.

We started to pile into the Fury, but Bernard suggested that the road to Tyler's was probably rough and it might be a good idea to take my pickup. It was a trick for the three of us to fit in my old F-1, but we managed to squeeze in.

Dennis Tyler lived about as far away from civilization as you can get without leaving Tilghman County. It took us a good half hour to find the turn-off. We located it at the end of an oil lease road where no one should've been living but where Dennis Tyler had nevertheless parked his rusty house trailer.

My first impression was that Chief of Security at WestOk must not be an executive position. Either that, or Clyde pays his people in beer, because empty cans were scattered everywhere. Most of the trailer's windows were broken and repaired with cardboard and duct tape. The trailer had no skirt around the bottom. The wheels were exposed and the space underneath was used to stow all kinds of useless junk—empty bottles, dented wheel rims, brown paper sacks full of garbage. One tire had gone flat, causing the trailer to tilt to one side. There was a small plastic kiddie pool sitting at the rear of the lot, and for a second, I worried that Tyler might've been raising a child in this hell hole. Upon closer inspection, however, I saw it was filled with used motor oil.

The red Willys jeep station wagon was nowhere to be seen.

"Let's go in," I said, half-expecting Bernard to point out we didn't have a search warrant. He can be a stickler. But not this time.

A couple of rotted wooden steps led to the front door. Both were split down the middle, like someone had purposely stomped on them until they broke. The front door was unlocked, which made me nervous. I've found that folks who live in filthy dumps can be unreasonably leery about getting their homes broken into, and tend to keep them locked tight.

I slowly stuck my head in the door, afraid Tyler might have a crazy girlfriend with a shotgun and I might get it blown off. "Anyone home?" I said.

No one was. I stepped inside and was immediately assaulted by an odor that defies adequate description, but definitely included a clogged toilet, dirty underwear, stale beer, and cigarettes. I also thought I detected the scent of Lemon Pledge, which was strange, since the only furniture was an orange couch with most of its stuffing ripped out, and a battered three-legged coffee table that no amount of polish could make attractive or useful. For the most part, the living room was littered knee-deep in garbage: empty Pabst Blue Ribbon cans and Guy's potato chip bags, unspooled rolls of toilet paper, a bowl of something green and black and furry, copies of *Stag* and *Guns and Ammo* magazines. The carpet might've been brown or it might've just been very, very dirty. Hard to tell. It only showed through in a couple places, anyway.

"Quite the housekeeper, ain't he?" said Jeff.

"This is what your place would look like if you weren't married," said Bernard. Jeff flipped him the bird.

"Bernard, do me a favor and take a look in the back rooms," I said. "I don't want to get my church shoes dirty." I was still wearing my previously vomited-upon boots and I don't go to church, but I do enjoy exercising the prerogatives of command.

Bernard ventured down the hall, stepping over what he could. "Try to leave things the way they are, if you can," I said. "We're just looking for something that might help us find Earl. I don't want to piss-off the state and county boys." They'd be doing their own investigation, I knew. I didn't want to compromise it or give them any reason to come down on us.

While Bernard banged around in the back, Jeff and I rummaged around the living room and kitchen. We found nothing of note, other than an impressive collection of girly magazines from the '50s hidden underneath an overturned metal washtub, and a new Magnavox color television, which stood out like a diamond in a pile of cow manure. We did not find anything connected to Earl Collins.

I swiveled around and took in the scene. "What do you think? Any signs of violence?" I said.

"This whole goddam trailer is a sign of violence," Jeff said.

Bernard tripped on something coming out one of the bedroom doors and fell against the wall in the hallway. His head made a dent in the cheap paneling. "There's some guns," he said.

We started back to take a look. Bernard stumbled again, this time over a deflated basketball. "You say you're friends with this guy?" he said to Jeff.

"I didn't say we were friends," said Jeff. "I said I drank with him. I drink with a lot of people who ain't my friends. I'd drink with you if you drank anything besides 7-Up."

The back bedroom was the only space in the house that didn't look like an indoor junkyard, presumably because it was being used as a gun closet. Spread out on a bare mattress were four shotguns, a M-1 Garand rifle, a Winchester .30-30, and one of those mail-order Mannlicher-Carcanos like the one Oswald used to kill Kennedy.

"Looks like Mr. Tyler was fixing to fight a war," I said.

"He's got all these good guns, I wonder why he was carrying that cheap little snub-nosed?" asked Jeff.

"Probably not very smart," said Bernard. I leaned toward his assessment.

The presence of so many firearms wasn't all that unusual—this is Oklahoma, after all—except that the owner had tried to kill me, which I figured was justification for suspecting criminal intent. We might never know whether Tyler intended to fight the second Civil War or just had an unhealthy fascination with guns.

We waded through the trash back to the front room. I tried to be careful not to bang my mangled knees against the broken lawn chairs and dog kennels and wheelbarrows and whatever else littered the premises.

"Where's that Willys?" said Jeff.

"Where Drury was living," said Bernard. "Wherever that is."

"Makes sense to me," I said. "I think I'll try raising Cindy and ask if she found an address for Mr. Drury."

We escaped the trailer and gorged ourselves on fresh air. I tried to hail Cindy on my truck's police-band and got Karen instead. She'd returned from her errand at Ona Ray's.

I asked her how it went.

"You don't want to know," she said. "Horrible."

"I reckon it was. Did you take her to the hospital?"

"We did. They stitched up Merle's cheeks and had to re-stitch the wound on the back of his head. He's woozy, but he'll survive. Mostly, the two of them are sick to death over their son."

She said the state police had met them at the hospital and seemed to have things in hand. I asked if she'd gotten an address for Tommy Drury. "Cindy tried, but hardly anyone even knew he was back in town. You might check his mama's old house. Wouldn't surprise me if he was staying out there."

"She's been gone almost as long as Tommy."

"Yeh, but I don't think she ever sold it. I remember her folks owned it free and clear."

I didn't need directions to Rachel Drury's house. I remembered all too well where it was. I did ask her to contact the sheriff and Highway Patrol and tell them about the guns we found. I also asked her to find out the legal owner of the Willys.

"It probably belongs to Tyler," I said, "but you never know."

"Will do, hon," she said. "You feeling alright?"

"I've been worse. Don't worry about me."

Aside from my battered knees, I felt pretty good. Hadn't craved a drink all day, at least that I could remember. I still half-expected—even hoped—remorse at having killed two men would land on me like a ton of bricks, but it hadn't yet.

"You take care," Karen said.

I said I would.

The three of us piled into the truck. We followed the maze of dirt roads back to the highway. I thought we might run into a sheriff's deputy or a highway patrolman, but we saw no sign of either.

It appeared we were at the forefront of this particular investigation.

CHAPTER NINETEEN

Rachel Drury's place was at the opposite end of Butcherville, closer to Burr than Tyler's trailer was, but still a long ways off the main highway. The road leading up to it was little more than a couple of deep ruts. The tall grass between the ruts was noticeably bent this way and that, as if it had been driven-over recently.

Jeff had lost the coin flip and sat in the middle between Bernard and me with his legs straddling the gear shift. I drove faster than was safe under the conditions, resulting in Jeff's head being banged against the roof repeatedly. Bernard managed to escape that fate by having something to hold onto; he used his arms to brace himself between the dashboard and door. My suspension was shot to hell anyway, and not in any condition to handle the abuse I was dishing out. Lord knows the beating that road was giving my exhaust system.

The weeds around what had been Rachel Drury's house were even taller than the ones clogging the road in. A rusty mailbox at the head of the driveway was bent downward at a 45-degree angle and shot full of holes from a high-powered rifle. Vines nearly swallowed the white clapboard walls, as if Mother Nature was using every means at her disposal to reclaim it for herself. Someone had recently used a machete or a scythe to hack a hole in the vegetation growing thick around the front door. The lock was broken.

I had some hope we'd find a safe-and-sound Earl Collins inside. I also hope I'll get a Cadillac Eldorado for Christmas.

I reckoned the odds for both were about the same.

"I never seen someone park their truck inside their house," said Bernard.

"Me neither," said Jeff.

Some engineering genius had decided to compensate for the house's lack of a garage by cutting or sawing or otherwise hacking a giant hole in a back wall and parking a red Willys Jeep station wagon in what had once been Rachel Drury's living room.

Sawdust and splintered wood littered the floor where it hadn't been muddied or ripped to pieces by the jeep's tires. The rough edges around the hole looked to have been chopped with an axe in some places, and carved with a chain saw in others. Evidently, Tommy and Tyler had needed a place to hide the Willys, and decided busting a huge gash in the wall and parking on what was left of Rachel's wall-to-wall carpet was their best option.

"Who in the world would want to do that?" asked Bernard, wonder in his voice, perhaps forgetting for a minute how someone as mean and stupid as Tommy can be capable of doing all manner of destructive and nonsensical things.

"Someone looking to hide a vehicle where it wouldn't be found," I said.

Except for the sawdust and splinters, there wasn't much manmade trash or clutter, although there were plenty of rotten leaves covering the floor around the Willys. Compared to Dennis Tyler's trailer, the place was almost spic and span, if you could overlook the jeep in the living room. I thought letting Mother Nature take over might not be a bad idea. She keeps house better than your average murdering psychopath, that seems clear.

There was a small kitchen/dining room attached to the living room. Doors off the living room led to a couple of bedrooms. Weeds had sprung up through cracks in the foundation. Ivy crept in through broken windowpanes and spread across the ceiling, which in several places dipped toward the floor and looked ready to collapse. Water-stained blue-and-silver-colored wallpaper had lost its stick and hung like drooping curtains. There wasn't any furniture unless you count the Willys.

One bedroom had a few modest signs of life: a charcoal blue Westinghouse transistor radio, a well-thumbed *Playboy* magazine, and an empty Royal Crown Cola bottle on the floor, next to a green army surplus sleeping bag lying in one corner of the room.

Jeff was in a big rush to read the interview with Sidney Poitier in the *Playboy* and didn't notice when an envelope and a couple sheets of paper fell from its pages. I picked them up.

The envelope had been ripped open on one end. Inside was a check made out to Thomas Drury for five hundred dollars by Elmer Kepley, dated the day before. It took me second to recall what that Elmer Kepley was the WestOK manager.

One of the papers was a bill of sale for the Collins's property. Merle was listed as the seller, WestOK as the buyer. The document had been notarized by the aforementioned Mr. Kepley, which was a little bit fishy, considering neither buyer nor seller had signed it.

The other paper was written in some kind of legal mumbo jumbo, the essence being Merle Collins in his role as Duly appointed Mayor of Butcherville in the County of Tilghman in the State of Oklahoma hereby decrees that Clyde Raymer and WestOK Petroleum has permission to expand their venture with no rules or strings attached, hallelujah Jesus and God Bless America.

I pocketed the documents, being reasonably sure they'd come in handy at some juncture. I showed my young officers the check but kept the existence of the other two documents to myself.

A search of the rest of the house was anticlimactic. We did not find anything interesting or relevant. In addition to my aching knees, I'd started to feel like a cement mixer had dumped its contents onto my chest. Anxiety, worry, call it what you want. I'd about gone my limit without having a drink.

I ordered Jeff and Bernard to go over the Willys with a fine-toothed comb. That gave me time to go outside and cadge a snort of Old Grand-Dad from my flask, which I'd managed to refill at some point. I couldn't remember when. That was worrisome, but I pushed it out of my mind.

I drank half of it down in one gulp. It eased the pressure on my chest and made me forget about my sore knees and dulled a little bit of the disquiet. I chomped on a couple of spearmint Certs and rejoined the boys.

Aside from the vehicle identification and license plate numbers, the Willys delivered no good information—certainly nothing that might give us a clue to Earl's disappearance. I stood pressed up against one of the remaining walls alongside my officers and mulled over what to do next.

"Seems to me we should talk to Clyde Raymer," Bernard said. "We know Tyler worked for him, and we know what Tyler and Drury did to Merle. The personnel guy says Drury doesn't work for WestOK. Maybe this Kepley character hired him off the books."

"That would be my guess," I said. "Someone didn't want Drury traced back to WestOK."

I hated to take time away from looking for Earl, but visiting Clyde was necessary, especially now that I'd found documents connecting him to Tyler and Drury. He wouldn't admit being involved—that wasn't going to happen—but maybe we'd get lucky and he'd let slip something helpful.

"I don't know Clyde well enough to know whether or not he'd be mixed up in something like this," I said without adding that what I did know led me to suspect he would.

"I know him," said Jeff. "He's President of the Burr Football Booster club, so I've talked to him quite a bit. Helped pay for the high school's new football uniforms last year. He treats me fine, is all I can say. Little full of himself, is all, but a lot of them rich fellas are like that."

Bernard lit a cigarette. I reminded him not to leave ashes, since the crime scene examiners would likely need to go over the place, then realized how silly that sounded, given the mess that trailer was in. A few cigarette ashes on the ground outside wasn't going hurt anything. Still, being my obedient servant, Bernard acknowledged my request and tapped them into his palm. "What I'd like to know," he said, "is how'd they have time to kidnap Earl then meet up with Merle at Leave it to Bever's?"

"There you go," said Jeff. "There's got to be a third person involved. Got to be."

"That's assuming Drury was with Tyler when Earl got snatched," Bernard said. "We don't know for sure."

"We got a couple of witnesses who saw two men in the Willys," I said. "I think it's safe to assume the other one was Drury."

"So, who'd it be?" mused Jeff.

"Kepley?" said Bernard.

"Raymer?" said Jeff.

"Kepley makes more sense than Raymer," I said, believing that even if he was behind it, there was no way Clyde would be an active participant.

Jeff picked up some gravel and started chucking pieces at the ruined mailbox from about ten feet away. "Of course, Tyler and Drury could've just killed Earl and dumped him somewhere," he said, tossing a pebble and missing badly. "That would've given them all the time they needed to whip up on Merle."

Bernard rolled his eyes. "That don't make sense," he said. "The only reason to kidnap him in the first place is to use him as leverage against Merle."

"Could've been an accident," said Jeff.

I picked up some gravel myself, tossed a pebble at the mailbox, and missed.

"Yeh, I think it's unlikely they'd have hurt the boy," I said. "At least until they'd gotten what they wanted."

I threw another pebble and missed, then said a mental "to hell with it," picked up a rock the size of a coconut, and threw it as hard as I could. Direct hit. The mailbox spun sideways off its support and clattered to the ground.

"Lucky shot," said Jeff.

"Right tool for the right job," I said.

Bernard leaned into the pickup's open passenger window and dumped his handful of ashes in the ashtray. "One way or the other," he said, "we got to talk to Mr. Raymer, don't you think?"

I did and said so. My head was itching something fierce, so I took off my hat and scratched my head. I've been using this shampoo that looks like blue Pepto-Bismol. It's supposed to get rid of dandruff, but as far as I can tell, it doesn't do a goddam thing. Judging by the hair accumulating around my shower drain, dandruff won't be a problem for much longer.

"Alright, let's go talk to Clyde," I said, then thought better of it. "Nope," I said. "Scratch that. I'll do it myself. I'm taking you two back into town." Bernard asked why. I said I didn't want to leave Burr unprotected.

"Oh yeh," said Jeff. "Someone might jaywalk."

In reality, I didn't see any reason for them to get crossways with Clyde. Putting my own job on the line was one thing. Putting theirs at risk was another.

Bernard licked his index finger and tapped it to the end of his half-smoked cigarette. It hissed and went black. He put it back into the crumpled pack, and stuffed the pack in his pants pocket. "You should at least take one of us," he said. "Just to be safe."

The idea of pudgy little Clyde Raymer trying to do me physical harm was the first genuinely funny thing I'd heard that day. "I wouldn't worry about it," I said. "Clyde might try to get me fired, but I don't think he'll pull a gun."

Jeff laughed. "He better not, if knows what's good for him," he said.

CHAPTER TWENTY

I dropped off Jeff and Bernard at the station. I told them to keep their eyes on things and get Karen's help in tracking down Elmer Kepley. If they found him, they should ask about that check to Tommy and what Tommy had done to earn it.

I headed out to Clyde Raymer's house, hoping he wouldn't be out playing golf or sailing the seven seas or whatever it is rich men do on weekends.

I thought about what I knew and what I didn't, and how to fill in the blanks.

I had to assume Dennis Tyler—and almost certainly Tommy Drury—had taken Earl. The question was: What did they do with him?

We knew they went to the Drury house to hide the Willys and pick up the Mustang.

There was no sign of Earl at the Drury house. That didn't mean he'd never been. It just meant he wasn't there now.

How and where could they have stashed him between the time they left the Butcherville Store and arrived at Drury's?

There was no evidence Earl had been to Tyler's trailer, either, although it was so messy, it was hard to tell. Again, all we knew for sure is that he wasn't there when we checked.

Was it possible they didn't take the boy? Doubtful. If they did, though, there almost had to be a third person involved.

That check Elmer Kepley wrote to Drury and the notarized-but-unsigned bill of sale made him the prime suspect.

Of course, the person who had the most to gain by extorting Merle Collins was Clyde Raymer.

Clyde might be mean, but he's not stupid.

It also could be that Tyler and Drury killed the boy and dumped the body, but I couldn't see what purpose that would serve.

No, I had to believe the boy was alive and hidden away somewhere.

Unfortunately, Tyler and Drury were not in a position to tell.

I drove by a big sculpture of a spider made out of a black Volkswagen body with googly eyes and twenty-foot-long legs, standing out in a pasture all by itself.

Only in Butcherville.

I cussed and took swig of bourbon.

•　　•　　•　　•　　•

I've already called the Butcherville fire station the Taj Mahal of firehouses, so I guess I should find something even grander to call Clyde Raymer's place up in northern Tilghman County. I'm not smart enough or well-read enough to do that, so I'll just describe it as I go and hope that does the trick. I reckon the palace where the Queen of England lives is fancier, but probably not by a whole lot.

I've been out to Clyde's for the parties and receptions he holds for Republican bigwigs. During election season, our current governor practically lives at the Raymer Mansion. I shook hands with Richard Nixon at one of Clyde's shindigs. It was like grabbing hold of a frog.

Clyde went to Burr High School about ten years ahead of me, too old for me to have known him, although my daddy has none-too-fond memories of his father and older brother. Clyde and I nod at one another when we run into each other on the street, but I doubt we've exchanged a dozen words over the years. I'd be happy to keep it that way, given that I'm among the last in a line of die-hard Democrats who look askance at the kind of ostentatious greed Clyde so proudly represents.

Unlike a lot of wealthy farmers who dump a layer of chat on the dirt road leading up to their house and call it good, Clyde Raymer paved his with coal-black asphalt, as smooth as glass. The road is lined on both sides by rows of pine trees not native to these parts, but tall- and wide-enough to occupy the Jolly Green Giant's living room at Christmas time.

Clyde's house is a gigantic, rectangular, three-story building constructed out of polished granite. In front of the staircase was a fountain with a statue of a naked lady in the middle, holding a jug that spewed an endless supply of water. The staircase itself was twenty-feet wide and had more steps than are healthy for a man in my condition to climb. It led to a set of twin front doors made of polished oak. Carved into the door on the left was a scene of a cowboy riding a bucking bronco; the door on the right featured another roping a bull. The huge, immaculately maintained lawn was crisscrossed by neatly-trimmed hedges arranged in geometrical shapes. A circular driveway ran under the large staircase. From there, a shorter flight of steps led up to the front door. I took those.

I expected to be met at the door by an Englishman in a tuxedo or a cute little French maid, so I was surprised when Clyde's wife Clara pulled open the massive doors herself. "Chief Hardy, what a surprise," she said. She wore white high heels and a light summer dress with a floral pattern. Around her neck she wore two or three strands of tiny, irregularly-shaped pearls. Her eyes smiled behind a small pair of wire-framed glasses. She invited me in.

I stepped into a large hall with a twenty-foot ceiling and paintings covering every wall. I've been to the Cowboy Hall of Fame in Oklahoma City enough times to have gotten my fill of western painting—Indians chasing stagecoaches, cavalrymen chasing Indians, cavalrymen chasing Indians chasing stagecoaches. The Raymer's had plenty of those, but there were also a couple by artists who clearly looked at the world in a different way. One in particular caught my eye: a six-foot-tall portrait of a family of four that could've come right out of the *Grapes of Wrath*, except the details of their clothes and facial features were blurred, like you were looking at them through pebbled glass.

"You like that one?" Clara asked. I said I did. "Clyde hates it," she said. "Thinks it's too modern. When I was a child my father would take us to The Museum of Fine Arts in Boston. That's where I saw my first Picasso. This one reminds me a little bit of that."

Clara hails from Maine, which would explain her childhood trips to Boston. I have no idea how she ended up with Clyde.

"What brings you out to our neck of the woods?" she asked. She may be a Yankee but she speaks Okie like a native.

"I'm hoping your husband can help me with a matter I'm investigating, is all. I'm looking for some information on one of his employees."

"Well, I'm sure he'll be happy to help," she said. "Let's go find him. I think he's in his study."

Her heels made clicking sounds on the polished wood floor. She led me through a set of swinging doors made of thick glass, similar to the kind you see in banks and other businesses, except these were decorated with etchings that resembled what you might see carved on an expensive leather saddle.

We walked through a maze of rooms. Most were dominated by some combination of heavy wooden tables and plush chairs. On the walls, black and white photographs of constipated-looking men and women in beehive hairdos competed for space with framed certificates and awards folks have given Clyde over the years for being rich.

Our final destination was a huge room lined with hundreds of books covering every square inch of wall space. Clyde sat at a large wooden desk talking on the telephone. Behind him was a huge, multipaned window. The sun cast long shadows of his head and shoulders across the room. He saw us and shielded his mouth with his hand, like he didn't want us to hear what he was saying. He growled a few choice words then slammed down the phone. He glared at Clara like he would a puppy that'd piddled on the rug. "What's this about?" he said. "I'm busy."

"Chief Hardy needs to ask you something important about someone who works for you, Clyde," she said, her tone challenging Clyde's high-handedness. "I'm sure he wouldn't have come if it wasn't important."

Clyde mumbled something I couldn't understand except for the last word: "Alright." He said, "You can go," just as Clara started to leave. She stopped in her tracks and stared him down before apparently deciding that now was neither the time nor place to give him a verbal ass-kicking.

Instead, she turned to me and smiled. "Would you like some iced tea?"

"Thanks, but I don't think I'll be here long enough."

"You give me a shout if you change your mind." She gave Clyde a furious look on her way out. I wondered if maybe they'd been fighting before I'd arrived.

Clyde got up out of his chair, strode across the room, and locked the door. He gave the knob a twist and a tug to make sure, then stomped back to his desk and sat down.

"What do you want?" he said irritably.

"I need to ask you about a couple of men in your employ. Dennis Tyler and Elmer Kepley."

"You mean the Dennis Tyler you shot?" he said. "I've been dealing with that all morning. I assume you came here to apologize." He spoke rapidly, with barely a hint of an Okie accent.

"I don't think I need to apologize for shooting someone who was trying to shoot me." I said. "No, I'm investigating Tyler for the beating of Merle Collins and the abduction of Merle's son, Earl. I also have reason to believe Mr. Kepley was involved."

Clyde looked at me like I was a piece of chewed-up bubble gum he'd scraped from underneath his chair.. "Elmer Kepley is 64 years-old and has emphysema," he said. "He can barely walk from his desk to the men's room without stopping for a rest." Flying drops of spit decorated the sheets of paper on his desk like tiny wet polka dots. "If he's a kidnapper, I'm the King of France. As for Tyler, I'm not responsible for what he does on his time off. I barely knew him, anyway."

"I was told Tyler answered directly to you."

"You were told wrong. I got a plant manager who deals directly with the employees."

"That'd be Elmer Kepley."

"That is correct. You want information about Tyler, talk to him. Only you're going to have to wait until Monday. I heard he's gone fishing over the weekend."

Maybe he took Earl with him, I thought. "You got a phone number where I can get in touch with him?"

"No, I don't got a phone number," he barked. "All I know is he went fishing. I do not know where. What exactly is he supposed to have done?"

"I found a check he'd written on his personal account to Tommy Drury. Last night, Drury and Tyler beat the hell out of Merle Collins and threatened his family if he didn't play ball with you. You know Tommy Drury?"

"Just that he's the other man you shot this morning. I'd never heard of him before today. If Elmer's writing him checks from his personal account, that's his business. Maybe Drury mowed his lawn or something."

Five-hundred bucks is a lot to pay someone for mowing your lawn, but I didn't bother saying so. I knew Clyde was peddling a line of crap, and he knew I knew. I told him I thought he'd want to clear this up, that it didn't look good, his plant manager and chief of security being involved in a kidnapping.

"There's nothing to clear up. I'm not involved in any of this. Now, if you don't mind, I've got work to do." He made a big show out of picking up and reading a document. I noticed it was upside-down before he did, but I didn't let on.

"I know you're busy, Clyde, and I thank you for your patience. Just a couple more questions, if I may. I know Merle Collins has been a bother to you recently. I heard all that about him being mayor, and refusing to sign-off on the rezoning so you can expand your plant. That's got to be a huge pain in the ass for you. Nobody'd blame you for being mad." I clasped my hands behind my back and looked down bashfully, like I was intimidated by his presence. "Merle said that last night Tyler and Drury made it sound like you'd told them to threaten the Collinses. I know you wouldn't've done that. I was just hoping you might have some idea why they'd try to make it look like you did."

Clyde didn't get to be Clyde by falling for the likes of that. "If there was a question somewhere in that load of horseshit, I didn't hear it," he said. "I know what you're trying to do, Hardy. Just know that if you accuse me of having Merle Collins abducted or having anything to do with his son's disappearance, I'll have your badge so fast your head will spin." He seemed to be getting a kick out of being so mad. "I might have it anyway. You better believe I can."

I felt like telling him he could have it right then, but didn't. "Mr. Raymer, I'm not accusing you of anything," I said. That wasn't strictly true, but owning up to it would cause me more trouble I didn't need. "I'm just thinking Dennis Tyler and Tommy Drury beat up Merle last night as a way of trying to get on your good side."

"Merle Collins was standing in the way of a *lot* of people making a *lot* of money," he said, his mouth constricting like a drawstring bag pulled tight. "Not just me. Maybe Tyler and Drury stood to lose, too, you ever think of that?"

He stood up too quick, so that his chair fell back and thudded against the windowsill behind the desk. Clyde grabbed the chair and clumsily set it upright. "You need to leave, Hardy," he seethed. "And let me tell you, just as soon as you walk out that door, I'll be back on the line to Sheriff Murray and tell him what went on here."

"Is that how you heard about the shooting? A call from Burt Murray?"

"That was him I was talking to when you came in. I don't expect he'll be too happy to hear that you've been accusing me of murder and kidnapping."

"Clyde, I'm just looking for answers. If I can't get them from you, I'll get them from someone else. Someone who might not have your best interests at heart. I reckon you better be straight with me, or it's you who might regret it."

That was as close as I normally get to threatening anyone, never mind someone who has the political pull to run my jockey shorts up a flagpole while I'm still wearing them. I realized I'd caused more problems for myself, even if I didn't exactly know what they might turn out to be.

"That's enough of this," he said calmly, which I thought was scarier than when he was about to blow his stack. "You can find your own way out."

He sat back down, picked up the phone again, and started dialing.

I reckon that as far as he was concerned, I'd already left.

I had a terrible time finding my way out. I finally entered a room with vases of flowers in every corner and paintings of flowers on every wall. Clara sat on a couch with her legs folded underneath her. She saw my predicament and showed me to the front door. "I hope you got what you needed," she said.

"Some of it," I said.

She held the door open. I started out, then thought of something. "Clara," I said, "have you by any chance seen a boy around the age of 12 skulking around the last day or so?"

"Would this be the boy who's missing?" she asked.

"Yes, ma'am. His name's Earl Collins. We're asking everybody if they've seen him." I didn't want her to think we were singling her out.

"No, Chief, I sure haven't, but if I do I'll give you a call."

"I'd appreciate that."

"Glad to."

I thanked her for her hospitality and stepped onto the porch.

"I hope everything turns out for the best," she added.

"It usually does," I lied.

•　　　•　　　•　　　•　　　•

I didn't even try to raise Karen on the radio until I was halfway back to town. I felt it best to put some distance between Clyde and me before I said anything against him, even if I was just talking to my dispatcher. Rich men have big ears.

It ain't that I'm paranoid, it's just that everyone's out to get me.

Once I did get through to Karen, I asked her if she'd found Kepley's address. She said she had. He lived in town—town being in this case being Burr, not Butcherville. Jeff and Bernard had gone to investigate. I told her I'd see her in a minute.

The most innocent explanation for Burt calling Clyde was as a courtesy—informing him of his employee's death. Burt may even have asked Clyde some of the same questions I did.

Knowing how Sheriff Murray's mind works, however, I had to believe the reason was politically motivated. Raymer's got deep pockets and Burt's going to need plenty of gold to fund his next campaign. Helping Clyde stay out of trouble would be in Burt's best interest.

I'd just reached the Burr city limits when I noticed in my rearview a county sheriff's vehicle coming up fast behind me. Whoever it was hit his flashing lights. I pulled over. I looked in my side mirror and saw it was Keith Belcher.

He looked like he might be upset, although those Dr. Strangelove sunglasses he wears makes it hard to tell.

He approached my window, which was already rolled down. I smiled. He didn't.

"What's going on, deputy?" I said.

"Emmett, it hurts like hell to say this," he said, "but you're under arrest."

I did not see that coming.

CHAPTER TWENTY ONE

Keith followed me into town. We dropped off my pickup at the station. I stuck my head in the door and told Karen what was going on. She wasn't a bit happy about me being unjustly detained. I thought she might vent her pissedoffedness on Keith, but I calmed her down, and he and I took off for Temple City.

You'd have thought that the poor bastard had run over my dog, the way he wouldn't stop apologizing.

"Emmett, I swear to Christ I don't have any idea what this is about," he said, driving with one hand and loading a pinch of snuff into his bottom lip with the other. "As far as I'm concerned—hell, as far as anyone with half a brain is concerned—that was a good shoot. But ten minutes ago I picked up an APB from Burt that said you're wanted for negligent homicide or some other such bullshit. I told them I'll do it. Better me than one of them other assholes."

"That's not a nice way to talk about your fellow deputies."

"Yeh, well, them being assholes ain't exactly a secret," he said, then lifted a Dixie cup from between his legs and spit tobacco juice into it.

"Don't worry about it, brother," I said. "This is coming from on high."

"Meaning higher than Burt?"

"Meaning someone who pays Burt's campaign bills."

"Meaning Clyde Raymer, is what you're saying."

"That's what I'm saying."

"Got it," he said. He spit again. "But that don't make it right. Far from it."

Burt was on the phone when Keith and I entered his office, just like Clyde had been when I walked in on him an hour earlier. In contrast to Clyde, Burt was laughing it up good-old-boy-style with the person on the other end. He gave me a look and said his goodbyes.

I strode right up to the front of his desk. "What's this about, Burt?" I asked.

He leaned back in his chair and folded a pair of soft pink hands over a beer gut doing its best to push through the buttons on his green uniform shirt.

"Emmett, I've been advised to suspend you from duty, pending an investigation into the shooting this morning. I'll need your gun and badge."

"You already got my goddam gun."

"That's right, sheriff, I took it this morning," Keith said.

"Alright," he said, "In that case, I'll just need your badge."

"What makes you think you got the right?" I said heatedly. "I'm not a county employee. I'm employed by the town of Burr."

"The DA says, as the chief law enforcement officer in the county, I got the right. I ain't asking you to like it."

"What's this all about, anyway, Burt?" I said. "You know that was a good shoot."

"Maybe it was, and maybe it wasn't," he said, rocking his head from side to side. "To tell you the truth, I'm more disturbed about you harassing one of our leading citizens."

Of course. This was all about my talk with Clyde. I knew it, although I was a little surprised he admitted it so fast. "I thought you had more balls than to let Clyde push you around," I said. I didn't think any such thing, but I wanted to shame him.

"Nobody's pushing me around, least of all Clyde Raymer. But it's best for everybody if we do this by the book, and the book says we got to investigate. You're suspended during the investigation. Them's the rules, Emmett."

I might've thought he'd be embarrassed, except nothing embarrasses Burt so long as it takes him a step closer to the governor's mansion. Following Clyde Raymer's orders could help him in that regard.

"So, I'm suspended, then, not arrested."

"That's right," he chuckled. "I guess I jumped the gun a little, didn't I?"

I didn't find it as funny as he did. "Look here, Burt," I said, "Merle Collins was holding up Clyde's plant expansion. Tommy Drury and Dennis Tyler beat him up, and threatened to hurt his family if he didn't give Clyde what he wants. That means rolling over on the zoning changes and selling the land his house sits on. Merle doesn't want to do that, and I don't blame him. For a while now, he and Ona Ray have been getting threatening phone calls. Dennis Tyler was the Chief of Security at WestOK. We checked where Drury's been staying and found an uncashed check for five hundred dollars, made out to him from Elmer Kepley, Raymer's plant manager. I also found an unsigned bill of sale transferring Merle's property to Clyde—notarized by Kepley—and a document in Merle's name, changing the zoning so Clyde can expand his plant—also unsigned, but notarized by Kepley. It don't take a genius to figure out what's going on here."

Burt shrugged and shoved a stick of Juicy Fruit in his mouth.

"On top of that, I got two witnesses who saw Tyler and Drury sitting in Tyler's jeep outside the Butcherville Store when Earl Collins got off the school bus yesterday afternoon, which is the last time anyone's seen him. Tyler and Drury kidnapped him to hold over Merle's head. Clyde's the one who has the most to gain, and given his connection to Tyler, he's got to be a suspect. My God, Burt, the boy's been missing almost 24 hours. I should be out looking for him instead of in here arguing with you."

He picked up a blue plastic fly-swatter and slapped at a fly that had landed on his desk. He missed. He chewed hard on the gum with his mouth half open and slapped his leg nervously. As phony as he is, Burt and I have always gotten along. I could tell he was bothered by being on the wrong side of me. In some ways, he's goodhearted underneath all the political garbage. I think bringing up Earl Collins hit a nerve. I half-expected him to cave-in and say he was on my side, but at the last second, he managed to heroically swallow his sense of basic human decency.

"I'm sorry, it just can't be helped. We're out looking for the boy, don't you worry about that." He held out on open hand and looked up at me—at my chin, not my eyes. "C'mon, Emmett," he said. "I need your badge."

Arguing further would be a waste of time better spent looking for Earl, which was what I intended to do, badge or no badge. I handed it over.

"No hard feelings?" he said.

"That depends on whether we find the boy, and what condition he's in when we find him."

"I can respect that. It's a free country. You can look all you want. You find him, let us know. We'll be looking, too." He stood up and held out his hand. I shook it.

"Who's conducting the investigation?" I asked.

"Me and District Attorney McKinnis."

DA McKinnis being on the case gave me a glimmer of hope. Burt leans whichever way the wind blows. Rex McKinnis can always be trusted to do the right thing.

I asked Burt to keep me updated on my status. He said he'd be meeting with Rex to talk it over first thing Monday, meaning I'd be a civilian over the weekend. I'd gotten the best deal I could, given the circumstances.

"Would it be ok if Keith gives me a ride home?" I asked.

Burt smiled his oiliest smile. "What say, Keith?"

"Glad to," said Keith.

●　　　●　　　●　　　●　　　●

Keith and I got back in his cruiser. "You in any hurry to get back?" I asked.

"You mean back here? I'd rather get some work done, if you don't mind."

I laughed. "Don't mind a bit, buddy. Don't mind a bit."

●　　　●　　　●　　　●　　　●

The drive back to Burr took a quarter of an hour. I tuned Keith's radio to the band we use and called Karen. I asked her to round up my people and have them at the station by the time I got back. My current status wasn't going to stop me from doing what needed doing. I'd given up my Colt, but I still had my off-duty .38 special. As for a badge, well, folks around here don't need a piece of tin to remind them I'm the law. I reckoned to throw Burt a bone and wear civilian clothes for however long I was suspended. I'd also use my pickup instead of the Galaxie or Fury. Not another damned thing would change.

Keith pulled into the unoccupied "Reserved for Chief Hardy" parking space. "Hope I don't get a ticket for this," he said.

"You're ok. I know the guy who runs this place."

"This is just a heckuva day you're having, isn't it?" Karen said as we walked in the door.

"Not as bad as Earl Collins's, I suspect."

The rest of the crew stood or sat around the room either standing, slumping, smoking, or all three. I stood in the middle of the room. "Y'all know I'm not usually in too big of a hurry," I said, "but I feel like we're running out of time to find Earl Collins. The trouble is, I'm not entirely sure where to start. Any ideas?"

"We could go door to door," said Bernard.

"In Burr, and in Butcherville," said Karen.

"We just got that one picture of Earl?" asked Jeff.

"Yeh, and I don't want to go bothering Ona Ray for another one," I said. "One of y'all go over to the library when we're finished here and see if they'll let you make some Xerox copies of the one we got. What's going on with Ona Ray?"

"A highway patrolman and a woman trainee are over to her place, looking after her," said Karen. "Merle is at Baptist Hospital in Oklahoma City, but he should be fine. Unless or until he's at death's door, Ona Ray wants to stay home and wait for Earl to come home."

"A couple of OSBI agents came and went while we were there," Kenny said. "Sounded like they're taking this real serious."

"Well, I guess going door to door beats sitting on our butts doing nothing," I said. "I don't honestly expect it to turn up much. By now, everybody in town must know what's going on. If they knew something they'd have already told us."

"What do we know about where Earl likes to hang out?" asked Karen. "Maybe he's got a fort or a tree house he uses for a hideaway."

I used to build such things out of scrap lumber when I was a kid. I wondered if boys still do that sort of thing. Times have changed, but I doubt they've changed that much. I realized I'd never asked Ona Ray or Merle if Earl had any reason to be hiding from them. I imagined they'd have mentioned it if he did, but I resolved to ask next time I saw them.

"That's a good idea," I said. "Jeff, how 'bout you drive around town and look out for treehouses or forts? It's a longshot, but you never know." He said he would. I asked Karen if she still had that list of Earl's friends.

She rifled through the pages of her well-used yellow pad. "Here you go," she said and ripped it out.

"Kenny, take that list and track down those boys. Ask them if they have any special hideouts. Places they use to get away from grownups. I had Cindy ask them if they knew anyplace Earl might be hiding, but that was yesterday. Maybe their memories have improved." I tossed him the keys. "Take the Galaxie," I said. "Make some Xeroxes of that picture of Earl first." Karen handed him the photo and he took off.

"You got anything in particular you want me to do?" asked Bernard.

Keith broke in. "Emmett," he said, "if it's ok with you, maybe Bernard could take me out to where Tyler and Drury had been living. I wouldn't mind looking around and getting a feel for things."

That made sense, and I said so. "Jeff, you take the Fury. Bernard, you go with Keith. Search Drury's house and that mess of a trailer one more time. You never know. A fresh set of eyes might pick up something we missed."

Bernard tossed Jeff the keys to the Fury.

"That leaves you and me," Karen said when they'd all gone, "and I'm chained to this desk."

I agreed she needed to stay so she could keep tabs on everybody.

"What're you going to do?" she asked.

Good question. "I reckon it might be wise to retrace Earl's steps yesterday. Or retrace the steps I took trying to find him."

"It's only a quarter after three," she said. "The Butcherville Store should be open."

"Yup, I reckon. I want to search the area around the building. I feel like I missed something the first time. I don't know what, but I feel like I need to look again."

"I guess you'll also be going back to Darryl Martin's house," she said.

"Probably at some point I will. What do you know about him and his wife?"

"Nothing, really. Just that he used to be on the Butcherville town council, until he voted to de-annex his property from the town and got kicked off." Her face expressed a sense of wonder. "Folks out there are a breed apart, aren't they?" she said.

"They're something else, alright."

CHAPTER TWENTY TWO

At the Butcherville Store, Cyclops the cat was at his usual spot on the porch. I said hello and didn't get a response, though he didn't lick his privates this time, so I guess that was an advance in our relationship.

I opened the door expecting to find Bonnie, but her mama was there instead, standing in the same spot behind the register as her daughter had the day before, her nose stuck in the same book. *In Cold Blood*. I hadn't had time to stop by the library and claim my copy.

"Bonnie was reading that yesterday," I said.

"We do that a lot—read the same book and talk about it," she said. "We usually take turns, but this time Bonnie got her own copy, so we're reading it at the same time." She marked her place. "The mother of the family that got killed, her name was Bonnie. Bonnie Clutter. According to the author, she had mental problems. Just like my Bonnie."

"C'mon, now. Your Bonnie doesn't have mental problems."

"She thinks she does. She's a misfit, like I was. Like I am." She added softly, "Like Princess Bellchamber."

I remembered the name. It's a hard one to forget. "She's the little girl who lives across the street from y'all, right? Bonnie called her 'my shadow.'"

"Yeh, that's Princess. She idolizes Bonnie. Follows her everywhere. I don't know why I mentioned her. I guess she was on my mind when you came in."

"Well, I haven't met Princess, but as far as you and your daughter are concerned, I'm one-hundred-percent sure there's nothing wrong with either one of you that moving away from Butcherville won't cure. I've been to enough places in this world to know not everywhere is like Butcherville."

"We won't be here long if I have anything to say about it. We just need to save enough money to move. My father bought me this store as a bribe to keep me close to home. It's his name on the title, not mine. I get paid a salary, and not a very big one. I plan to save every penny so we can go someplace else. Far away." She regarded me with a curious expression. "You say you've been to a lot of places. Where?"

"I joined the Marines after I graduated from high school and got sent to Korea. After that I lived in New York City for a while."

"You lived in New York City and you came back here? Why on earth did you do that?" The way she asked, you'd have thought I'd said I inherited a million dollars and used it to build Dizzy a fancy doghouse. Still, the truth is the truth, even if it doesn't always make a lot of sense. "This is where I belong," I said. "I didn't always want it to be true, but it turned out to be. I had to go away to find that out."

"It's not where Bonnie belongs, I'll tell you that," she said. "Maybe I do, but not her."

"She mentioned she was thinking about going to some new police college they got in New York City. That'd be an adventure."

"It would be, wouldn't it?" she said dreamily. "I want her to live her life in a place where people who play Beethoven on the piano or read books by Truman Capote aren't considered crazy."

"All you two need is a bigger pond than Butcherville to swim around in." That got a smile out of her. "Anyway, neither one of y'all are crazy."

"Thank you, Chief Hardy," she said.

"Call me Emmett, I said. "Actually, I came in looking for Bonnie."

"Well, she should be here, but she's not. In fact, I'm a little mad at her right now. Or worried." She tapped the counter nervously. "Mostly worried."

"About what?"

"She was supposed to relieve me an hour ago but hasn't come in yet."

"Where do you reckon she is?"

"I don't know. It's about a ten-minute bike ride or a thirty-minute walk to the store. Either way, she should've been here by now."

"Did you call her to see if she might've taken a nap or lost track of time?"

"The phone at the store is still out. Southwestern Bell says they can't come out to fix it until next week."

My gut started churning. Bonnie wasn't a twelve-year-old boy who might not remember to call his mom if he wasn't going to be home on time. She was a responsible adult, even if she was only sixteen. I tried to put that thought aside for the moment.

"I wanted to double-check some things we discussed earlier," I said. "About the boy who's missing."

"You still haven't found him?"

"No, ma'am. I was hoping Bonnie might've remembered something else that could help."

"Well, I don't know where she is. Wish I did but I don't."

"I'm sure there's nothing to worry about," I said, although after all that had recently happened, I couldn't be sure at all.

"I'll keep an eye out for her while I'm looking for Earl, and tell my people to do the same."

"I can always count on her to do the right thing," she said. "She's been through a lot, with me and her father splitting up, but she's stayed strong through all of it. She's a tough kid."

"I could tell that about her. She seems like a special young lady."

"She is."

"Could she have gone somewhere with Princess?"

"Possibly. I wouldn't be surprised if Princess is with her, wherever she is. Bonnie met her right after we moved into that house, and they took to each other right away. I look out my window every day, and see the poor little thing sitting on her porch swing, waiting for Bonnie to come home. I guess she gets picked on quite a bit at school because of her disability. I forget what it's called, but it makes her move all jerky and makes it hard for her to talk. And of course, kids make fun of her name. Bonnie loves her to pieces, and Princess thinks the sun rises and sets on Bonnie. She follows her everywhere she goes, so yeh, if you find Princess, you might find Bonnie, too."

"We'll find Bonnie."

"Please do."

•　　•　　•　　•　　•

I walked the same path around the store I'd walked the day before. I didn't find anything new. I began to think my instincts had been wrong. I expanded my search into the field behind the building, but still didn't find anything. I was about to give up when I decided to search the ground in the parking lot.

The lot was red dirt, with some scattered chat that had surely been laid down long ago. Most of what remained was ground deep into the clay. I looked closely, determined to take in every pebble, every clod, every tire track. I quickly narrowed the search to where the Willys had been parked the day before.

I found three discarded cigarette butts. Two were Winstons, which I reckon is the second-most-popular brand after Marlboro, so finding them didn't tell me all that much. They could've belonged to Tyler and Drury. Probably did, although it might be hard to pin down for sure.

The other butt was a Tareyton. Tareyton filters are distinctive. Underneath the cork-like paper wrapping is a little piece of charcoal. Tareyton isn't a particularly popular brand. In fact, I only knew of one Tareyton smoker. I'd met him only the day before. Darryl Martin.

I went back into the store. "Mrs. Hubbard," I said, "I can't remember—were Darryl Martin and the fella or fellas in the Willys ever in the store at the same time?"

"They were not. The other men never came in at all."

"Did you see if they spoke to one another?"

"If they did, I didn't see it."

"And where was that fancy pickup of Mr. Martin's parked?"

"On the east side of the lot, almost in the weeds."

That put it a good twenty yards away from the Willys. If Darryl had talked to Tyler and Drury, it would not have happened by accident. He would've had to walk over there. With that big cast on his leg. That's not something he would've done just to be polite.

I thanked her again.

•   •   •   •   •

The radio crackled.

"Emmett, hon, you there?"

Karen, using her unofficial-official mode of address.

"I am, Red. What d'ya got?"

"Brace yourself. Sheriff Murray just strolled in, along with a couple of OSBI agents. Our holding cell has a new guest. Marlon Truitt, Senior. The sheriff arrested him for the kidnapping of Earl Collins."

Not what I expected. I asked if they'd found Earl.

"They did not," she said in a flat, disgusted voice, and told me the tale as best she could. The sheriff had gotten an anonymous tip that Marlon Truitt, Sr. had been run out of Temple City for molesting little boys. I knew there was some mystery about why he'd lost his job and why his wife left him, and why it had been so easy to get him to move to Burr—or Butcherville, as it turned out. It never occurred to me it could be something like that.

I asked what evidence they had connecting him to Earl.

"Burt won't say," she answered. "They're back in your office right now giving him the third degree."

I'd wanted to visit Princess Bellchamber, in the hope she'd seen Bonnie or had some idea where she was. But if Sheriff Murray was questioning a suspect in the Collins case, I needed to be there—especially since he was doing it in my office. Someone else would need to speak to Princess. I explained to Karen about Bonnie going AWOL and how Princess might know where she went. I told her to have Kenny drive out there and talk to Princess. He's great with kids and has the most sympathetic ear of almost anyone in the department except for Karen.

"While you're at it, send Bernard out to check on Darryl Martin," I said and told her about the cigarette butts I'd found. "Maybe it's nothing, but it could mean Darryl knew Tyler better than he lets on. Have Bernard lean on him and see what he can find out. Tell Burt I'll be right there."

"I don't think that's such a good idea. He's liable to just tell you to stay away. You're suspended, remember?"

"Good point. Don't tell him. I'll just show up."

"How're you feeling, by the way?"

"If you mean, 'Has the guilt kicked in from shooting those two boys?', not yet."

"You're not drinking, are you?"

"What makes you ask?"

"History."

"Well, I'm not."

I've lied about it so many times over the years. Once more won't hurt.

CHAPTER TWENTY THREE

It looked like every cop within one-hundred miles had congregated in front of the Burr Police Station by the time I got there. At least a half-dozen county cruisers were parked in front, along with Sheriff Murray's unmarked Buick Regal. There was a unit from the Watie Junction Police and one from Temple City, not to mention a couple of OHP cars—Galaxies, like my own. I had to run a gauntlet of beetle-browed deputy sheriffs drinking coffee on the sidewalk to get inside. Burt and a couple of OSBI agents had finished questioning Mr. Truitt, for the time being, and were now taking a smoke break in the cramped outer office. I said hello to Karen. She harrumphed, looking none too pleased by the invasion.

Burt introduced me to two OSBI detectives who I did not recognize and whose names I immediately forgot. I asked him for a word and we stepped outside. The agents seemed glad enough to stay behind and flirt with Karen. They did so at their own risk. She doesn't suffer fools gladly.

The deputies crowded around as we came out, like they expected news of a confession. Burt waved them off. We walked a few yards down the street and stood in the recessed doorway of an empty storefront.

"Emmett, you can't be here in an official capacity," he said quietly. "It don't look good, with you being suspended and all."

"How about in an unofficial capacity?"

"That don't look much better, to be honest."

I generally dislike making more work for myself, but sometimes you just got to. "C'mon, Burt," I said. "You know this is my case. You're questioning him in my own office, for chrissakes."

"I know, Emmett. I don't want to leave you out of it, but my hands are tied."

Tied by Clyde Raymer, I thought.

"Listen Burt, I don't need credit for Truitt's arrest." Didn't want it, I should've said, since I had serious doubts that anyone other than Tyler and Drury could've taken Earl. If they had help, there was no reason to suspect it had been Truitt. I'd be perfectly happy to let Burt take full blame for what was shaping up to be a royal catastrophe.

"How 'bout you just let me observe?" I said.

"I don't know, Emmett," he said, like I'd asked to borrow twenty bucks.

"At least tell me what you've got on him. You say he hasn't told you anything about where Earl is?"

Burt smirked. "Nah, he's playing dumb. But he doesn't have an alibi for last night. Nobody saw him at the game, which is strange, since his son is the team's star player. He says he was in his office the whole time. I ain't buying it."

Something about what Burt had just said sounded wrong to me, and it wasn't just the fact that Marlon's dad hadn't come to see him play his first game in a Burr uniform. I couldn't put my finger on it.

I asked Burt what put Truitt in the frame. "I got a phone call," he said. "There're some folks in Temple City who're satisfied he's some kind of a pervert. There was a scandal involving a boy he coached a few years ago. I didn't hear about it at the time. Maybe if I had, Earl might still be alive."

"We don't know he's dead."

"No, we don't, but it ain't looking good."

I hated to admit it, but he was right. If it was Truitt or someone like him, that person could've abused the boy then killed him to cover his tracks. On the other hand, if it had been Dennis Tyler and Tommy Drury, there was a chance Earl was still alive. Especially if they had help.

I realized what it was Burt said that sounded wrong.

"Wait a minute. You say Truitt doesn't have an alibi for last night, but the boy wasn't taken last night. He was taken at four o'clock in the afternoon."

Burt's face turned pale. "Uh, to tell you the truth, Emmett, we were only in there with him for a few minutes. We didn't ask about that yet. I thought we'd wait till we get him back to my office."

Yeh, I bet.

"How about this?" I said. "Corral all your deputies and highway patrolmen and secret agents and whoever else you got hanging out on my sidewalk, take 'em across the street to The Piazza and buy 'em something to eat. While you're over there, I'll have an unofficial word with Mr. Truitt. Maybe I can come at it from a different direction. Get something out of him that way. I'll be the good cop to your bad cop."

He smirked again. "You like being the good cop, don't you, Emmett?"

"I can't be the other kind," I said with a rueful smile. "Tried it once. Got laughed at."

He shrugged. "Alright, have at it, but wait until I clear everybody out of there. I don't want 'em knowing what you're up to."

We went back in. Our tiny front office was overwhelmed by the collective bulk of a dozen or more cops and detectives. Karen's eyes roamed malevolently, like she was trying to decide who to kick in the giblets first. Fortunately, Burt lured them all out the door with the promise of free food before any dispatcher-on-cop violence could occur.

On his way out, I asked him if they'd read Truitt his Miranda Rights. Earlier this summer, the Supreme Court ruled criminal suspects have to be informed of their right to legal representation. I've been doing it on my own for years but Burt's the kind who might accidentally-on-purpose forget.

"He ain't been booked, so we don't have to," he said. "I reckon he don't know Miranda from a hole in the ground, anyway."

I would've advised him not to take Marlon Truitt, Sr.'s ignorance for granted, but Burt's going to do what he's going to do. If Truitt turned out to be innocent, his lawyer (assuming he finally got one) would be free to make hay out of anything Burt did wrong. I couldn't worry about that. My only concern was a having a chance to talk to Truitt man-to-man and get a feel for the truth.

After much milling about, the riff-raff finally vacated, leaving me and Karen in the front, with Mr. Truitt occupying the holding cell in my office. I motioned for Karen to come with me.

"Want me to take notes?" she asked.

"Nope. This is about as unofficial as it gets. Just lend me your ears."

Our little holding cell is positioned catty-corner from my desk. Mr. Truitt sat behind the locked gate on a bunk that folds down from the wall. He glowered as Karen and I entered the office. His five o'clock shadow was in the final stages before officially becoming a beard. Even sitting down, he was almost as tall as me, and twice as wide. His lower lip bulged. The circular outline of a snuff can bulged in his shirt pocket. He held a dirty brown Dixie cup with both hands.

I unlocked the cell and motioned for him to take a seat in the folding chair in front of my desk. There was no other chair in the room, so Karen took his place on the bunk. There's barely room in my office for three people to breathe.

I introduced Karen and myself and we all shook hands. "I'm the police chief here," I explained, "although I probably shouldn't tell you that, since I've been suspended. Miss Dean here is my assistant."

Truitt lifted the cup to his mouth and dribbled some spit. "I recognize both of y'all from the Booster Club luncheon last week."

"That boy of yours is a football player," I said.

He smiled faintly and briefly. "Yeh, he is, but that's not what you're here to talk about."

"No, you're right, it's not. Before we go any further, I need to know where you were yesterday afternoon at four o'clock."

"I was chalking the field," he said without pause.

I asked if there were any witnesses to that. "Someone must've seen me," he said. "There were a few people around. I can't tell you who, though. The field got chalked before the game, and I'm the only one who could've done it."

"I reckon that can be checked easily enough," I said. "Next thing: Do you know anyone named Dennis Tyler or Tommy Drury?"

"Never heard of them."

I watched closely for signs he recognized those names. I saw none. There was no reason I could think of why he should.

"Would you mind telling me what you've been talking about with the sheriff and those OSBI boys?"

He grunted irritably. "Them idiots got it in their heads I got something to do with a missing kid I never heard of."

"Why would they think that?"

He looked ready to take off my head in one bite. "I done gone over it with them. I sure as hell don't feel like going over it again."

"I understand, Mr. Truitt, so let me tell you what they're saying about you, and then you tell me where they're wrong."

He used an index finger to scrape the snuff out his mouth, then deposited it into the Dixie cup. "I know what they're saying," he said, then cleaned the inside of his bottom lip with the tip of his tongue. When he finished, he said, "You go ahead, though."

I wanted to be kind, but there's no nice way to say what I was about to say. "The sheriff suspects you of being a child molester," I said. "He says you got run out of Temple City for loving on little boys."

Truitt smacked his two enormous hands down on my desk. Karen and I jumped. The slap echoed in the small space. I regretted not cuffing him.

"Goddammit, I've lived with this trash for going on two years," he began. "I move here and think I'm getting a second chance—that I've gotten away from the lies. Here they are again, following me around like ...." He couldn't think of anything to compare it to and his voice tailed off.

"You're sure they're lies?"

His eyes darkened and a vein pulsed in his forehead. I think there might have been smoke coming out of his ears.

"Chief, I got enough problems as it is without getting charged for hitting a cop so I think you'd better lock me back in that cell and go out the way you came in before something happens both of us will regret."

I appreciated that he was mad and that he was also very large and could probably put a hurting on me if he wanted to, but I had to ignore all that. If he knew something about Earl's situation, I meant to get it out of him.

"Mr. Truitt, if you want to go home any time soon, you'd best cool off and answer my questions. My job is to find Earl Collins, hopefully safe and sound. I'm not saying I think you took him, but Sheriff Murray seems to think you did. I need to know if he's right."

He did not immediately respond, but instead looked at me with what seemed to be witch's brew of emotions. Of course, he was angry, but there was something else, too: confusion, sadness, or maybe disenchantment. I couldn't be sure.

The window next to my desk was open a crack. The wind whistled and tree branches scraped against the screen. I sensed something surprisingly gentle about Marlon Truitt, Sr.—not what you'd expect from a man as big and strong and angry as he was.

He sighed heavily and slumped in his chair. "Mr. Hardy," he said, "I'd like to explain myself, but I don't hardly know how."

CHAPTER TWENTY FOUR

"I knew that boy of mine was an athlete before he could walk," he began. "When he was a baby, he'd sit on the living room floor and I'd toss him a little plastic football, the kind the cheerleaders toss into the crowd at halftime. He caught it and threw it back to me like he was born to do it. The older he got, the better he got. He's a natural. I played some in my time, and I was pretty good, but young Marlon's a genius at football."

He asked for some water, so Karen went out front and got him some. He drank his fill and dried his mouth with a Kleenex from a box on my desk.

"I knew the boy was meant for great things. I wanted to make sure he took the right path. Temple City didn't have tackle football until boys turn thirteen, but I started teaching him how to catch and throw and block and tackle when he was little. By the time he was ready for pads, I didn't trust anybody to coach him but me, so I volunteered to coach his pee-wee league team. We were good, mainly because of Marlon. He scored almost every dang time he touched the ball. Most of the parents didn't mind him being the star. They just wanted to win, and we did, pretty much every game. There was this one daddy, though—Mr. Daugherty, his name was. He thought his son Clarence should've been be the star, even though he wasn't nearly as good as Marlon. Mr. Daugherty gave me a hard time, nagged me about getting the ball in his son's hands more often. I tried, but he'd lose yardage and I'd have to give it back to Marlon so he could dig us out. Marlon couldn't help being Marlon, and Mr. Daugherty's son couldn't help being who he was. Anyway, it caused some bad blood." He reloaded his lower lip from the tin of Skoal in his pocket. "Trying to quit," he said sheepishly. "Not doing a very good job."

He worked the tobacco in place with his tongue and leaned back in his chair, stretching his arms up and his legs as far forward as the cramped space would allow. "Jesus Lord," he complained to the ceiling, "when is this going to end?" I don't think he expected an answer.

"I used to give some of the boys rides home after practice. Some of their mamas couldn't drive, and their dads didn't get off work in time to pick them up. Usually, Marlon would come along when I took 'em home, but not always. The practice field was only a five-minute walk from our house, so there were times Marlon went home instead of riding around with me while I dropped kids off. You got kids, Chief?"

"No," I said, "I've never been a father."

"Well, if you had been, you'd know how kids get to an age where they'd rather be anywhere else but hanging out with their folks. After a while, I'd take those boys home by myself, without Marlon. I didn't mind."

"What's this got to do with why we're here, Mr. Truitt?"

"Alright, I'll get to the point," he said. "Because Clarence Daugherty was one of the boys I gave rides to. Sometimes he was the only one. He liked to talk when it was just him and me. He used to say he liked how I would listen to what he had to say, because his folks wouldn't. Sometimes we'd get to talking and it'd take longer for us to get home. His folks started getting suspicious. One day, out of nowhere, the county sheriff showed up at my door and started asking questions about what Clarence and I had been up to. Clarence's daddy said Clarence had told him I tried to kiss him, if you can believe that."

I wasn't sure if I did or not. I learned from hard experience to reserve judgment until all the evidence is in.

I asked if the county attorney pressed charges, thinking I would've heard if he did.

"Hell no," he said, "because I didn't do anything. But Mr. Daugherty made sure word got out. He went to my boss at the Ford dealership and told him I was a child molester. That got me fired. I was out of work for over a year before the Burr Boosters told me they'd find me a job if we moved here so Marlon could play football. In Temple City he didn't get much playing time, so it seemed like a good opportunity for both of us."

I honestly couldn't tell if he was telling the truth. I hoped he was.

He must've sensed I wasn't convinced. "Listen, I'd like for you to believe me," he said, his voice tense and even, "but there's nothing I can do about it if you don't. I'm telling you this so you'll know why they arrested me, not to get you on my side. They got no evidence. Just suspicions based on a lie."

The way he said that hit home. "Alright, Mr. Truitt," I said, "I'm an innocent-until-proven-guilty man myself, so we'll leave it there for now. It doesn't matter much if I believe you. The sheriff and county attorney are who you need to convince. My only concern finding Earl Collins."

I mulled over whether there was any reason I should suspect this man—apart from an unproven rumor—and couldn't think of any.

That said, there was still the issue of his whereabouts the day before.

"Sheriff Murray tells me you don't have an alibi for last night. I don't recall seeing you at the game. I figure since it's your son's first game here, that's where you'd be."

His face reddened in embarrassment. "No, I wasn't there," he said. "Not on the field, at least. I spent the whole game in my office behind the gym."

"Why?"

"I'm not sure you're going to understand this, but I couldn't bring myself to go. I used to love coaching. Coaching Marlon and watching him turn into the kind of player he's become was the greatest experience of my life. Then some lying son of a bitch decides he's going to ruin me. I can't go to Marlon's games anymore. I just can't." His voice cracked. "Maybe someday, but not now. The president of the Booster Club—"

"Clyde Raymer?"

"That's right, Mr. Raymer. Well, he made it sound like I had a chance to be an assistant coach, but it didn't pan out. Maybe because of those rumors from Temple City, I don't know. Anyway, that's why I wasn't there last night. I was in my office. I'd take a peek and look at the score once in a while, but that was it. Marlon's a good boy. He understands."

His face creased in a broken smile. "I did see that commotion you boys made in the parking lot after the game," he said. "Saw y'all searching that pickup and everything." He described the scene in the kind of detail he couldn't have known unless he'd witnessed it himself.

I thought it unlikely he'd had anything to do with Earl's disappearance, but I showed him the boy's picture, just to get a reaction. There wasn't one. "I don't know," he said. "I might've seen him before, but not yesterday."

If I thought badgering him any further would've helped, I'd have kept going, but it seemed a waste of time. I didn't know to a certainty that he hadn't molested that boy in Temple City, but I do know how rumors and gossip can destroy peoples' lives.

I was completely convinced, however, that he had nothing to do with Earl's disappearance. "Alright, Mr. Truitt," I said, reaching across the desk and offering my hand. "I'll take you at your word." We shook.

"You believe me?"

"I don't have time to disbelieve you. You try to remember who might've seen you chalking the field, get them to vouch for you, and you should be ok."

"You know what?" he said. "Jerry Chrisco's my boss. He was in the parking lot, getting it ready at the same time I was chalking the field. I'm pretty sure he saw me."

"There you go. Jerry's an important man in town. His word means something."

"Think you could put in a good word for me with the sheriff?"

"I will, although I don't know how much good it'll do you. When Sheriff Murray gets an idea in his head, it's hard to get it out." I stood up to leave. "One more thing, Mr. Truitt. You understand you have the right to a lawyer?"

"No one said anything about that."

"Well, I'm saying it. Get one."

"Why, if I got nothing to hide?"

"You'd be surprised at how words can get twisted. If you ask for a lawyer, they're required by law to get you one. Tell them you want one and don't answer any more of their questions until you get one."

"Alright, I will."

CHAPTER TWENTY FIVE

Burt and his posse were coming in just as I was going out. The Piazza's kitchen was closed, so they had to make do with coffee, which jacked them up even more than they were already. I tried to convince Burt that it was extremely unlikely that Truitt had taken Earl.

"The first question you need to ask is what he was doing at four o'clock," I said. "Get his alibi and confirm it. I expect you should be able to do that without much trouble." I was afraid Burt might decide an alleged pervert in the hand was worth two dead kidnappers in the bush. Politically, the best result for him would probably be to wring a confession out of Truitt. For the sake of everyone involved, I hoped he'd put self-interest aside and admit he'd gotten the wrong man.

A pair of deputies handcuffed Truitt and led him out the door. "Keep your head up, Mr. Truitt," I said. He looked like a condemned man, which I guess he was, in a way. Even if he was cleared, as I was positive he would be, he'd still carry that label he'd gotten in Temple City, and a label can be hard to get rid of. I watched through the front window as they shoved him into a cruiser. Their destination was the county jail, where I guessed they keep their implements of torture. If Mr. Truitt was lucky, they'd follow the letter of the law in his interrogation, but Mr. Truitt didn't strike me as the lucky type.

The office cleared, leaving Karen and me. Technically, I wasn't supposed to be there, but she wasn't going to kick me out. I started to ask her what she thought. She cut me off before I could say a word. "Don't even ask, Emmett," she said. "We both know he didn't have anything to do with this. Sitting here talking about it is just a waste of time."

"Alright, then, what next? I'm open to suggestions, especially from someone as smart and pretty as you," I said in a way that was probably inappropriate. I can flirt with Karen under the most extreme conditions.

She rolled her eyes and might've smiled, too, but I would've needed an electron microscope to be make it out. "Alright," she said, "let's figure out where we're at. What about this new friend of yours, this Bonnie, uh—"

"Hubbard. Bonnie Hubbard"

"Bonnie Hubbard is missing. We haven't done anything about that, except tell the sheriff."

"I don't recall telling you to do that," I said.

"I can figure out some things for myself."

"Oh," I said. "Sorry to interrupt."

"As I was saying, you sent Bernard and Keith back out to Tyler's to look around some more."

"Any word from them?" I asked.

"Not yet," she said. "Kenny's out to Princess Bellchamber's, to see if she can shed some light on where Bonnie is."

"I reckon the next step is to check in with everybody."

"Hopefully they've found something," she said.

"Hopefully."

She got Kenny on the radio. Barely. The signal was so bad, we couldn't understand much that he was saying. She asked him if he could get to a phone. He said something like "I'm ago— uh tentpole, Ka—n," We took it as a yes.

The phone rang a few seconds later.

Karen picked up. "Alright, hon, let's see if we can—" she said, then stopped abruptly and listened. "Oh, I'm sorry Ona Ray, I thought you were Kenny, we were expecting—"

For the next minute she was quiet except for an 'Uh-huh,' an 'Oh, my Lord,' and an 'I'm so sorry, hon.' At some point Ona Ray must've taken a breath, allowing Karen a chance to jump in. She said a few kind words and told her I'd be out to fill her in. They said their goodbyes.

Karen started to say something to me when the phone rang again.

"Oh, hello Kenny," she said, then "uh-huh ... uh-huh ... uh-huh ... well, he needs to go out to Ona Ray's and ... uh-huh ... alright then, I'll tell him. You take care." They said their goodbyes.

Karen started to say something to me when the radio crackled again.

The signal was clear this time. It was Bernard. I motioned for Karen to hand me the microphone. I asked him what was going on.

"Keith and I gave Dennis Tyler's place another going over," he said. "We didn't find anything that connects to Earl or Merle. Over." Bernard likes to use the police radio lingo, although sometimes he forgets.

"Well, I'm not too surprised. We searched it pretty good earlier. While you were looking, did you get a feel for Tyler's brand of smokes?"

"There are packs of Winstons all over the place. Most of them empty. Over."

I asked if they found any other brand. He said they'd found a bunch of Tareyton butts on the ground outside the trailer. Not many people smoke Tareytons.

It was starting to look like one of my key witnesses had withheld pertinent facts. At the very least, it looked like Darryl Martin had known Dennis Tyler better than he claimed. "Bernard, I need you to bring in Darryl Martin. I got some questions for him."

"I went out there a little while ago to ask about the cigarette butts you found at the store, but he wasn't there."

"Well, check again. Ask his neighbors if they've seen him. Or maybe his wife's back from her mother's. Just do your best."

"Ten-four, Chief. Over and out."

I was almost out the door when Jeff came over the radio. I'd almost forgotten I'd sent him out looking for forts and treehouses.

"What d'ya got for me, Jeff?" I said.

"I talked to that friend of Earl's, Will Boston. At first, he didn't want to talk to me because he was embarrassed but I made him feel guilty with Earl missing and all so he finally told me."

"Told you what?"

"Him and Earl got themselves a place they go to smoke cigarettes. He didn't want to tell me because he doesn't want his folks to know. I said we won't tell them if we don't have to. I hope that was alright."

It wasn't Earl being found but it was something. "Yeh, that's fine, Jeff. Where is it?"

"An old storm cellar on a lot next to the Collins place. You want me to take a look?"

Damn. "Jeff, I'm on my way to the Collins's right now," I said. "I looked in that cellar already but I'll do it again just to be on the safe side.

"I get overtime for today, Chief?"

"I reckon we all will, son."

I hoped that at the end of the day we'd deserve it.

I stopped by my house to replenish my supply of Old Grand-Dad. I don't always remember having refilled my fancy glass flask, but I was reasonably sober enough this time for it to have made an impression. I didn't drink any, but figured it might come in handy at some point. I also grabbed my fleece-lined denim jacket and carried it out to the truck. This time of year, as hot as it gets in the daytime, it can get pretty chilly after dark.

I headed for Butcherville not sure who to start with: Princess or Ona Ray. I was worried about Bonnie but Karen said Ona Ray was a mess and desperately needed reassurance. I had more confidence in Bonnie's ability to cope than Ona Ray's so I drove to the Collins's.

Later, I'd wish I'd made a different choice, although in the long run, I reckon it wouldn't have made a difference.

●　　　　●　　　　●　　　　●　　　　●

Someone had driven Merle's pickup home and parked it in the driveway. An Oklahoma Highway Patrol cruiser had pulled-in directly behind it, so I parked on the side of the road. It wasn't very cold out, but I put on the jacket so I'd have a place to hide the flask. I stuffed it in one of the oversized pockets.

At the head of the driveway they had one of those fancy futuristic mailboxes that look like something you'd see on *The Jetsons*, with black and gold stick-on letters spelling out COLLINS. I hadn't noticed that before. The box had a chrome finish. Glare from the late-afternoon sun made it seem to glow from within.

A single trooper sat in a lawn chair out on the front lawn, his feet propped up on the accursed riding lawnmower that had given me so much grief the night before. I realized it had been just a little over 24 hours since this whole thing had started. It seemed much longer.

The trooper stood to greet me.

"Howdy," I said, looking at his nameplate. "Trooper Ramsey, is it?"

"Uh-huh," he said. "What can I help you with?"

I didn't know if news of my suspension had been widely circulated, or if it would get in the way of me seeing Ona Ray, but all things considered, I thought it best to tell the truth about who I was. "I'm Emmett Hardy, chief of police in Burr," I said. "I'm the one Ona Ray called about her boy yesterday afternoon. Me and my people been helping y'all look for him and I thought I'd come and try giving her some comfort. She called the station earlier and seemed real upset."

"Yeh, she ain't doing too good." He swatted at a swarm of mosquitos. "We got a female cadet in there keeping her company." He slapped his forearm and lifted his hand. There was a bloody spot where a mosquito used to be. "Son of a bitch got me."

"The patrol's recruiting women these days?" I said.

"Don't get me started on that."

Something about Trooper Ramsey made me suspect he was a walking and talking argument in favor of women troopers whether he realized it or not.

"Mind if I go in?" I asked.

"Be my guest," he said, then cursed and slapped some more.

Ona Ray sat at the kitchen table, her head rocking and rolling like she had a Slinky for a neck. She still wore the same clothes from before, but the t-shirt and green pedal pushers were now stained by cigarette ashes and beer. Two Pall Malls burned in a plaid beanbag ashtray. Ona Ray seemed to be smoking both. A church key and a half-dozen empty Lone Star bottles sat on the table. She wore the addled, red-eyed expression of someone trying to survive on beer and cigarettes and no sleep. I've seen that face in the mirror a few times.

My entrance went unremarked upon by Ona Ray, but the young woman in an OHP cadet uniform sitting with her was demonstrably glad to see me, even without knowing who I was. I reckon she would've been glad to see anyone at that moment. The cadet had dark eyes, a pug nose and chubby cheeks and was as cute as heck. She reminded me of the actress who plays Gidget on the TV show; I never can remember that girl's name. Her mousy brown hair was stuffed into a Smokey the Bear hat. I introduced myself. She told me her name was Irma Lancaster. "I'm with the Highway Patrol," she said, tugging at her name tag. "I'm a cadet, but I guess you can see that."

"I can," I said. "You been keeping Mrs. Collins company?"

She tried to smile but it might as well have been painted on. "I've been trying to tell her everything's going to be alright. Haven't I, Mrs. Collins?"

Ona Ray glared at her like she would a stranger off the street who'd invaded her privacy at the worst possible time—which, I guess, wasn't far from the truth.

"Why don't you take a break and let me talk to Ona Ray a little bit?" I said. "If that's ok."

"That'd be fine. I'll be out front if you need me." The door did not hit her backside on her way out.

I took off my jacket and draped it on the back of a chair. "How're you holding up?" I asked.

"How d'you think?"

I had no good answer for that.

"How's Merle doing?" I said.

She puffed on one of the cigarettes, snubbed it out, then puffed on the other and snubbed it out, too. "He's fine. They stitched up his face. They say he can come home in the morning, if he wants to."

"Why wouldn't he want to?"

She gestured in a manner suggesting I drop that line of inquiry.

"I'd like to tell you we've made progress in finding your boy," I said, "but so far, all we know is where he ain't."

"Then you don't know nothing."

"I reckon that's about right."

She looked so wretched, I felt the need to do something for her, even if it was something small. Maybe I should tidy up her kitchen, I thought. At least I'd be doing something useful.

"Ona Ray, I'd be lying if I said I know what's going to happen, but I want you to know, I'm not going to rest until we find Earl."

She sighed and coughed slightly and stared at nothing in particular. There have been times when I was so sad it was all I could do to keep air moving in and out of my lungs. I reckon that's how she was feeling.

"I know it's a little late in the day to be asking but you never told me what Earl was wearing when he left the house yesterday morning."

"I already told the Highway Patrol."

"Would you mind telling me?"

"Blue and green plaid shirt," she droned. "Jeans. White high-top sneakers. PF Flyers. And he was carrying that football I told you about." She lit another cigarette. "I think he had on one of those red and white ribbons the cheerleaders sell."

On Thursdays before game days, the Burr High School Pep Club sells little ribbon badges meant to urge our team to victory. Usually there's an image of our mascot committing depredations against the opponent's. They call them "spirit ribbons" last time I checked. Probably still do.

"All right," I said, "that might prove helpful."

Her head wobbled in my direction and she regarded me without any particular interest. I thought she was about to say something but she didn't. She just wiped her nose and got back to being miserable. I said I was sorry I couldn't say anything to make her feel any better. She just shrugged. Her eyelids drooped a few extra millimeters.

Her gloom was rubbing off on me. Not that I needed help, but seeing her sit there mourning her son before we even knew what happened to him was robbing me of what little hope I had.

I needed some of the same medicine she'd been taking, only stronger.

From the cupboard over the sink, I scrounged a pair of mismatched water glasses and poured each of us two fingers of bourbon from my flask. We both threw it back in one gulp. Neither of us said anything for a few minutes—just drank and poured until it was nearly gone. I got to thinking about the drawing of "Old Grand-Dad" they put on their labels. I'd always thought he looked like a demented circus clown who'd gotten caught looking up the bearded lady's dress. He sure looked a hell of a lot more like a sex pervert than Mr. Truitt did. I reckon Old Grand-Dad made enough money selling booze that he could live a life of debauchery without fear of persecution from small-town chiefs of police.

That thought entertained me for a minute or two.

I realized I'd been feeling cold and scared the last few minutes. I put on my jacket. That took care of the cold. The premonition of doom remained.

"Tell me about your boy, Ona Ray," I said. "I've been looking for him since yesterday without hardly knowing anything about him except that he looks a lot like his mama."

She swirled a thin film of bourbon left in the bottom of her glass. It seemed like she didn't want to drink it because if she did we'd be out of bourbon and running out of bourbon might be the last straw. Her eyelids fluttered without rhythm, like she had to concentrate to blink.

"He's a good boy," she whispered.

"Does Earl play football?" I asked, thinking of the football he'd carried to school that had ended up in the toolbox on his daddy's truck.

"Just two-below, with his friends. He's too small to play tackle football. What he really likes is music."

"You don't say? Does he sing or does play an instrument?"

"He had a real pretty voice until it started to change, but he doesn't sing much anymore. Now he plays the saxophone."

"I play saxophone myself."

She nodded, or maybe she was about to pass out. "I think I heard that about you," she said. "Earl's a real good saxophone player. He's first chair in the high school band, even though he's only in eighth-grade."

I thought he could've been lugging his horn when he was snatched. I asked if he would've carried it home with him. "He prolly would've left it at school," she said. "The band 'uz supposed to march at the game. Did they?"

"They did."

She seemed glad to hear it.

I noticed a low-pitched hum coming from somewhere in the room. It started to bug me. I got up and looked around. I discovered it came from a small white plastic alarm clock on a counter next to the toaster. The hum wasn't loud but for some reason it bore into my skull. Edgar Allan Poe had his Tell-Tale Heart. Emmett Hardy had his whirring Westclox.

This is ridiculous, I thought groggily. I need to get up and do something.

"Alright, Ona Ray, I'm going to have that young lady come back in and sit with you so I can get back to looking."

"Do what you want," she mumbled.

I wished I could say or do more to make her feel better, but my mind was marinating in alcohol, and anyway, I'm not good at comforting people. That's why I usually take Karen with me on visits like this. I've probably mentioned this previously, but she's a genius at making folks feel better. She'd have been a terrific nurse. Or doctor, for that matter.

I stuffed the empty flask back into a jacket pocket and rose from the table. "Alright then, I'll come around later to check on you."

She didn't respond. Her eyes were half-closed closed and she was breathing heavily. I'd done enough, which is to say: I hadn't done anything except get both of us drunk—or, in her case, drunker. I showed myself out.

It was dark outside, so I switched on the porch light. The male cop had seemingly put aside his reservations about his female colleague and was standing uncomfortably close to her, both of them leaning on the hood of his cruiser. He was smiling lecherously and telling a joke she didn't seem to think was funny. My inhibitions having been lowered by the bourbon, I was even less hesitant to intervene than usual.

"Cadet Lancaster, you can go back in," I said. "I'd keep an eye on her if I were you. Maybe you should try getting her to bed before she falls asleep at the table."

Irma Lancaster popped up like a water droplet dancing on a hot frying pan. "Yes sir, Chief," she said and blew past me.

Trooper Ramsey kept his cocky smile.

"Did I interrupt something?" I asked.

"I believe you might have. That's ok, I'll get another chance later on."

"I don't reckon that young woman joined the patrol looking for a boyfriend."

"That's ok, I'm not looking for a girlfriend, either."

I considered escalating the situation before I remembered how much trouble I was already in. I settled for giving him a warning. "I know your boss, son. You'd best watch your step."

He pretended to be scared. I took a few threatening steps in his direction and he didn't have to pretend. His hand went to his gun. I laughed. "You're a real chickenshit, aren't you?" I could see his hands shake. I'd made my point.

I walked to my truck. "Yeh, well, I know your boss, too, old man," he said to my back. "I wonder what he'll think when I tell him you were drunk on the job."

I guess he meant Burt Murray but I was past caring at that point. "I'm not on the job," I yelled over my shoulder. "Don't they tell you stupid bastards anything?"

I started the engine, then remembered I needed to re-check that root cellar—where Earl and his buddy go to smoke cigarettes and probably look at *Playboy* and maybe sip beer they'd swiped from their dads. The kind of things twelve-year-old boys do when they're playing around at being men.

I switched off the engine, grabbed the flashclub, and walked across the Collins's front yard, past the overgrown foundation of a demolished and long-forgotten house, to where a twisted cellar door sat, crooked, on rusty hinges.

I pulled it open. The shriek of metal-on-metal and the creaking of rotting wood pierced the quiet. I shined my light into the cellar, but I couldn't see much from where I stood, so I descended the stairs, slowly, in consideration of both my knees and my impaired condition. I stopped halfway down. My light came to rest on the figure of a boy lying on his stomach in a corner. A red-checkered Purina burlap feed bag covered his head, so I couldn't see his face. But I recognized the clothes. They'd been described to me only a few minutes earlier.

A plaid shirt. Blue jeans. White PF Flyers. High tops. Pinned to the shirt, one of those red and white ribbons the cheerleaders sell.

"Earl?" I said, but got no answer.

CHAPTER TWENTY SIX

The way Gary Cooper comported himself in *High Noon* squares with my idea of how a hero should behave, although I never understood why he married that whiny little Quaker gal, when he could've had the saloon-keeper, who was just as pretty and probably smarter. He was probably afraid how the townsfolk would react if their marshal married a Mexican woman. Even Will Kane was heroic only up to a point.

I did things as a Marine that might be thought of as heroic, if that's what you call acts committed under the influence of a toxic brew of emotions that inspires you to take risks that could save some lives and cost you your own. I don't think there's any doubt what I did took physical courage. I'll leave it to someone else to judge whether or not it was the act of a hero. All I know is, there's a fine line between bravery and stupidity, and in war, that line gets crossed every goddam minute of every goddam day.

I don't know if I ever wanted to be a hero as much as I always wanted to do the right thing. I'm not sure I'd want people to notice if I were to do something particularly brave. I want to do right by folks, however. I have to live with myself. If someone suffered harm because of something I could've done but didn't, I'd feel awful.

Regardless of my intentions, as a man, I'm not what I aspire to be. I've fallen short of every measure I set for myself. I'm no hero; that I gave up on my dreams so easy, and came back to Burr to be what I am today, is all the proof you need.

Still, with no real hope of success, I strive.

•　　•　　•　　•　　•

I grabbed the handrailing and wedged one foot between two stairs to stop myself from falling to the floor, further damaging my gimpy knees. I dropped the flashclub. The bulb broke on impact, making the cellar darker than a black cat in a bucket of coal. I fished out the Zippo from the pocket of my jeans. The space was small enough that the flame gave me almost enough light. With my free hand, I untied a shoestring from around the bottom of the burlap sack and peeled it off his head. The face I saw was distorted and his head misshapen, but I could tell immediately it was Earl.

I felt for a pulse. There wasn't one. The bag and the boy's shirt had been soiled with muddy tire tracks and grass stains. His jeans were stained purple with blood. His hands were bound behind his back with duct tape. His legs were twisted at unnatural angles.

He'd been run over and killed somewhere else and dumped here. I hoped death had been quick.

I'd mistimed my consumption of bourbon. Its effects were still strong. As I leaned over the boy, the cellar started spinning and I fell backwards on my ass. My head bounced off the wall. I sat for a few seconds trying to get my bearings, then struggled to my feet and climbed up the steps. It seemed cooler than it had been just a few minutes earlier—not cold, but cool enough for that jacket to serve as something more than just a hiding place for my flask.

I stumbled across the field to where Trooper Ramsey sat smoking in his lawn chair and told him what I'd found. To his credit, he was appropriately alarmed. I suggested he call it in and not tell Ona Ray about finding Earl until the sheriff got there. I didn't want to be the one to do it, just I didn't desire to be around when the reinforcements arrived. Not in my condition. Ramsey dropped his attitude and did what I asked. I staggered back to my truck.

I removed the .38 from the holster in the small of my back, slipped it into the side pocket of my jacket, and tossed the holster to the floorboard.

I was in a fog, but I've been in a fog before and still managed to get things done. Earl was dead, but Bonnie was still out there. I aimed to find her.

•　　•　　•　　•　　•

"Karen, you there? It's Emmett." It took her a few seconds to answer.

"Sorry, I was making coffee," she said. "What's going on, hon?"

"Earl's dead."

Silence. Painful, soul-deadening silence. "Oh no," she **said**. Her response lasted only a second, but her despair was apparent. Karen's tough, but finding the subject of a long search dead is enough to break anyone. Especially when the subject is twelve years old. She recovered enough to ask me where, when, and how.

"I want to be gone before the sheriff's boys get here," I said after I'd given her all the details I could. "Did Kenny get any information out of Princess Bellchamber?"

"No, he didn't," she said flatly. "He said he couldn't get a word out of her. There's something wrong with that poor girl."

"Alright, then," I said, "I'm on my way over there. Maybe she'll talk to me."

"You think there's a connection between Bonnie and Earl?"

"Tyler and Drury killed the boy. Both of them were dead by the time Bonnie disappeared. I don't see how the cases could be connected, unless it has something to do with that third man we've been looking for. Elmer Kepley, maybe. I don't know. I can't rule out anything. I could be wrong about Drury and Tyler. Bes' thing to do is talk to Princess and see if she can help."

I'd pay for slurring that last sentence.

"Dang it Emmett, you've been drinking," Karen said. "Why don't you come back here and pick up one of the boys? Let them drive you out there."

"That doesn't make sense. I'm halfway there already. I'm fine to drive. Anyway I want Bernard and Kenny and Jeff out trying to track down Kepley. Get Keith to help, too, if he's still riding with Bernard."

After all that, I could think of one good reason to drive back to town. "I'll come get you," I said. "I could use your help dealing with Princess. See if you can get Cindy to mind the store for a little while. I'll be there in five minutes."

"I still think you should let Bernard—"

I switched-off the radio. Whatever else she had to say, I didn't want to hear it. I had enough to worry about, already. I tried organizing in my head who I'd sent where and to what purpose, but my mind wasn't working as well as it should. I rolled down my window and threw out my fancy glass flask. I heard it shatter. Must've hit a rock.

CHAPTER TWENTY SEVEN

As soon as Karen clambered into the truck she crinkled her nose. "My Lord, Emmett," she said, "you smell like a distillery."

"Ona Ray had more than me," I said, realizing how childish it sounded before the words even left my mouth.

"That's not the point," Karen said. "You promised me you'd quit."

"Yeh, well I meant to. Don't worry, I'm not drunk. You're just smelling a little bit I spilled on my shirt." I turned the key in the ignition in an attempt to preempt further challenges, but she reached over and turned it off before I could shift into gear.

"Switch sides," she said. "I'm driving."

"C'mon, Red—"

"Don't 'c'mon, Red' me. You want my help? I'm driving." I learned a long time ago not to argue with her when she gets her back up like that. She slammed the door so hard, the truck shook. We switched places.

She backed us out. I know I've mentioned how I feel obligated to make conversation with whoever I'm riding with, but this time I'd have been happy if neither one of us said a word. I was afraid the next thing out of her mouth might be something I didn't want to hear.

When she finally did speak, it was only to say, "We're going to have a talk when this is over."

I reckoned I'd gotten off easy.

We drove north to Butcherville. The thunderstorms that had been forecast did not materialize. The stars shone bright and infinite. A crescent moon shed pale light on the wheat fields and pastures on both sides of US 14.

The memory of Earl's broken body, combined with the rotten-egg odor of sulfur belched out by the WestOK plant, helped to focus my thoughts.

I get along pretty good with young people, but I couldn't count on doing any better with Princess than Kenny did, which is why I brought Karen. She's a natural when it comes to kids. It's a shame she never had any herself.

"What can you tell me about the Bellchambers?" I asked.

"Not much," she said. "There's no Mr. Bellchamber. He either died or left the family. No one seems to know for sure. Mrs. Bellchamber's name is Agnes. She's old for having such a young daughter. Apparently, she dropped Princess on her head as a baby and the little girl hasn't been right since. She belongs in a special school, but no one knows how to get her into one, so she goes to Burr Elementary."

"Bonnie and her mother told me Princess catches plenty of hell from some of the other kids," I said.

"That's awful," Karen said. "Poor child."

We pulled into the Bellchambers's hard-packed dirt driveway. The house was dark except for a pale blue glow coming from a front window.

The door opened at the Hubbard house across the road. Someone stepped out onto the porch. I assumed it was Grace although I couldn't be one-hundred-percent sure; all I could see was a dark figure profiled against the bright light from the house's interior. I waved. "It's Emmett Hardy, Grace," I said.

"Hello, Chief Hardy," she said. We stood a fair distance from one another so we had to talk pretty loudly.

We exchanged information. Neither of us had heard from Bonnie. I withheld what I knew about Earl. She didn't need to hear that, with her girl missing and all. I introduced Karen, and said we were there to talk to Princess. "I tried talking to her myself," Grace said. "Couldn't get her to say a word."

"Well, we're going to give it a shot," I said. "Karen's my secret weapon."

Grace tried to grin but seemed closer to crying. "Alright then," she said, "let me know what happens."

The Bellchamber residence reminded me of the bordellos from back when Butcherville was the Sodom of the Southwest. I always thought Leave it to Bever's was the only one to escape the torch. I might've been wrong. The Bellchamber house was a similar kind of flat-sided, two-story structure— obviously built in a hurry, using the cheapest materials money could buy. Whereas it had once been white with black trim, now, large sections of white had worn or chipped away, to reveal the weathered gray wood underneath, in a random pattern that reminded me of an Appaloosa colt.

It was so ramshackle, I thought it might fall down if I looked at it too hard.

The porch across the front of the house sagged in the middle where the steps led to the door. I groped around in the dark for a doorbell, but couldn't find one. At one time, there had been a knocker, but the part that knocked was nowhere to be found. Inside, a television blared: female voices singing "How Much is That Doggy in the Window." If it was Saturday night, it must be The Lawrence Welk Show.

I banged on the door with my fist. No one answered. I banged again. Harder.

A woman's voice yelled ... no, I believe 'yelped' would be a more apt description, "Come in!" I turned the knob. The door was unlocked. We went in.

It was almost darker inside than it had been outside. I couldn't see much, but I could smell, and what I was smelling wasn't exactly Chanel Number Five. I hadn't taken more than two steps when my foot landed in a box of gravel. I put two-and-two together, and identified the stink: a cat box that hadn't recently—or ever—been changed. I checked the bottom of my shoe. Fortunately, nothing adhered.

The light and noise from the television led us to a surprisingly well-kept, if dusty, living room. The furniture was old and worn, but there was plenty of it. A mangy light-green velvet-upholstered couch took up the most space. In front of it sat an enormous oak coffee table with bronze handles on the sides that made it look like a coffin. On one side of the room were two matching armchairs. In between the chairs was a fancy wooden end table, on which sat a lamp designed like a small gilded bird cage. On the floor was a large woven rug. It had once had an elaborate design, but by now had faded to the color of the inside of a dog's mouth.

The walls were lined with shelves containing hundreds of salt and pepper shakers, covered with dust and yellowed by years and years of cigarette smoke. A salt penguin and a pepper penguin. A Mr. and Mrs. Peanut. Laurel and Hardy. A cartoon Humphrey Bogart and Laurel Bacall. Giraffes, monkeys, pigs, gorillas, Mickey Mouses and Minnie Mouses. Also, for some reason, dozens of owls.

Despite the overall strangeness, everything was orderly. From the living room, I could barely even smell the dirty litter box. There was no trash lying around, in contrast to, say, Dennis Tyler's trailer, which was just one big garbage heap. Compared to that, the Bellchamber residence was a regular Buckingham Palace.

In the center of the living room sat a woman in a light blue house dress, her eyes glued to a black-and-white television set. It was hard to measure her age; she could've been fifty or she could've been one-hundred. However old she was, she looked unwell enough that it wouldn't have surprised me if she'd up and died right there and then. She sat so close to the TV, it almost touched her knees. In the harsh light of the screen, her face looked like it had been molded out of white modeling clay, peeled off and run through a blender, then plastered back on without much concern for which part went where. Her eyes were covered by cataracts and opened to their greatest extremity, as if to absorb every available drop of light. She wore a dark-brown, Audrey Hepburn-styled wig, twisted around so the bangs were in back and the back was in front. She'd pull aside the hair so she could see, but every time she did, it fell back into her eyes. Her chair was the same olive-drab color as the rest of the furniture. I'd lay good money it had started life a darker shade and faded to its present hue.

"Ma'am?" I said. "My name is Emmett Hardy. I'm the chief of police over in Burr. This is my assistant, Karen Dean. Are you Mrs. Bellchamber? Princess's mother?"

She nodded without taking her eyes off the TV. "I already told that Indian," she said, meaning Kenny, I presumed. "She's got a disease. Can't talk."

On the TV, Mr. Welk was giving fatherly hugs to four women in flouncy dresses. "Wunnerful, wunnerful," he said.

"I'd like to give it a try anyway, if you don't mind," I said. "Talking to her, I mean."

The women in flouncy dresses began singing "In the Mood" backed by the Welk Orchestra. I remember my mama used to listen to the original Glenn Miller version of that tune. That was at least twenty years ago, which— judging by the layers of dust covering everything in the room—might have been the last time anyone in this house had opened a window.

Mrs. Bellchamber was riveted enough to ignore my request. I started to ask again. "Shush," she said, her eyes still glued to the TV. She rocked back and forth to the music. "I just love these girls," she rasped quietly. Karen and I exchanged looks and waited for the song to end.

It did finally end, segueing to a commercial for Milk of Magnesia. Mrs. Bellchamber clapped, then pushed aside the short lengths of hair hanging in her face and peered at us for the first time. "Princess has a brain disease that don't let her talk like regular people," she said. Her voice sounded like a broken tailpipe dragging on asphalt. "Y'all go ahead if you want to try. Room's at the top of stairs. Second door on the right, across from the toilet."

We left her to her entertainments and climbed the stairs. The steps groaned and the staircase seemed unlikely to support our collective weight, so we took turns, careful to stay close to the wall and away from the wobbly bannister.

A dim yellow light showed under the door across from the bathroom. I knocked. There was no answer, so I let myself in.

The room was lit by a single thin candle sitting on a nightstand and burning in a holder fashioned out of a can that once contained Del Monte-brand creamed corn. Next to it was a book, lying with its front cover down. The room's single window was covered in Reynolds Wrap, blocking off any light from the outside world. A cot-sized bed was shoved into one corner. A young girl with brown hair sat upright on the bed with her back against the wall. For a fraction-of-a-second I thought I'd found Bonnie. I hadn't.

This girl was much younger. Her head twisted on her neck like a weather vane in a stiff wind. Her arms stood out straight from her shoulders. Her fingers stretched and contorted like she was continually trying to reach something out of her grasp. Her facial expression alternated back-and-forth from slack to constricted. The only thing she seemed able to control was her eyes; they fixed on mine and did not waver. Once a year, an Oklahoma City TV station runs a benefit for folks with a disorder called cerebral palsy. I reckoned Princess Bellchamber might be thus afflicted.

"Princess," I said, "I'm Chief Hardy of the Burr police and this is my partner, Karen. We're looking for your friend Bonnie Hubbard and were hoping you might be able to help us."

At that point, I was about to hand over the responsibility for further questioning to Karen, but there was something in Princess's eyes that made me think it was me she'd been waiting for. With enormous effort, she slowly stretched an arm toward her bed stand. Her stiff fingers reached for the book sitting there. I considered lending a hand, but I reckoned that someone in her condition probably got tired of people trying to do things for her. It took her several tries to turn it over so I could see what it was, but she finally did.

In Cold Blood.

She managed to pick it up and hand it to me. I opened it to the title page.

There was a transcription. "To Bonnie, with love," it said. Underneath was a line from a poem, and a signature. Under that was something scrawled in pencil. Something I'd seen before.

One word.

HELP

CHAPTER TWENTY EIGHT

Princess and I looked at each other with perfect understanding.

"Thank you, sweetheart," I said. "Is there anything else you want to tell us?"

She struggled to lean forward, shaking like a leaf. Her head rocked, as before. She opened and closed her mouth. Nothing came out, but with every attempt, she became more determined.

Finally, with one last, strangled spasm, she shouted, "FIND HER!" The sound of her own voice shocked Princess as much as it did Karen and me. She cringed and fell back against the wall, exhausted by the effort. Her limbs still moved spastically, but her eyes gave the impression of stillness. They stayed locked on mine. They were red with tears. Probably mine were, too.

"I will, sweetheart," I said. "I swear to God, I will."

Karen and I ran down the stairs as fast as their decrepit condition would allow, which wasn't the greatest idea, given my partially-inebriated condition. At one juncture I nearly fell, but Karen caught and steadied me. On the TV, Myron Floren played "Lady of Spain" on his accordion. Mrs. Bellchamber swayed in her chair. I didn't bother saying goodbye.

We got to the truck. I couldn't find my keys.

"I got 'em, Emmett," said Karen. I'd forgotten she'd driven us. She dug them out but made no move to hand them over.

"Give 'em here," I said and held out my hand. "I'm driving."

"Not until you tell me where we're going," she said.

"I know where Bonnie is and we'd better get there damn fast or I'm afraid what happened to Earl is going to happen to her."

She didn't understand but trusted me enough not to ask. "Ok," she said, "but I should drive."

"Not now, Red," I said, and roughly grabbed the keys out of her hand. She let it go. "It'll be quicker if I drive," I said with an apologetic smile. "Don't worry, I'm fine."

I'm not sure how reassured she was but she got in on the passenger side without further comment or resistance. I shifted the truck into gear and fishtailed onto the dirt road.

Again, I said, "I'm fine."

"You said that already," Karen said. "Saying it twice don't make it any more true."

She popped a piece of Dentyne in her mouth. She's been chewing it a lot lately. She's trying to quit smoking. "You going to tell me what's going on?" she asked.

I told her as much as I could, given the hurry we were in. I'd about gotten through the story when the radio crackled. It was Bernard.

Karen picked up. "Chief's with me," she said. "What's going on?

He asked where we were. She told him. "You might want to take a look to the southwest," he said.

I pulled to the side of the road and looked over my shoulder. An orange dome glowed on the horizon.

"What's on fire?" Karen asked.

"Darryl Martin's house and the house next to it," he said. "I'm there now, keeping an eye on things. The Butcherville fire department's putting out the neighbor's house, but they're letting the Martin place burn. I reckon Darryl seceded from the town."

I reckon he did.

I told Karen to ask Bernard if they'd located Elmer Kepley. They had not. At this point, it didn't much matter. I knew who our third man was and it wasn't Kepley.

Karen handed me the handset and I asked Bernard if anyone had been injured. No one had at the neighbor's, but they couldn't be sure about the Martins', where the fire had started. The neighbor had seen a flash at the Martin house through his bedroom window, then heard a vehicle drive away at a high rate of speed. He immediately called the fire department but didn't get a look at the car or truck. He was sure it was set on purpose. Flames blew onto his roof but the firefighters put it out before it could do much damage.

The pace of events had sobered me up considerably. I told Bernard to get hold of Kenny, have him wake someone up at City Hall and find out who owns the empty lot next to the Collins place. I shushed him before he could ask why. "They'll say they can't do it because it's the weekend," I said, "but tell Kenny to insist. I think I know who it belongs to, but I want to make sure."

I asked if he was still with Keith. He told me no, Keith had been called away. I told him to call Jeff and have him take over at the fire, then join Karen and me. I told him where we'd be.

"Ten-four on that," he said. "It might take a little while, though. Do you want me to get some sheriff's deputies or the Highway Patrol out there?"

I should've said yes, but I was afraid they'd bring too much firepower to do the job I had in mind. "Don't worry about that," I said. "Just call Jeff and meet us when you can."

"One more thing, Chief. The OSBI forensic people found something while they were removing Earl's body." He told me what. It confirmed my suspicion. I over-and-outed, shifted into gear, and pressed the accelerator to the floor.

"Don't you think you should've taken him up on the offer to get some sheriff's deputies out there?" Karen asked. "You shouldn't be doing this without backup."

"You know those fellas are more trouble than they're worth. Except for Keith, of course."

"Then get Keith."

"No," I said, pounding the steering wheel. "I don't have time." I felt bad for raising my voice, but I couldn't worry about ruffled feathers. "I've got to do this myself, Red. Just trust me."

She growled in frustration. Karen doesn't often growl. I'd just have to let her be mad. I could apologize when this was over.

It wouldn't take more than twenty minutes to get where I was going, if I drove like a maniac. I intended to do just that.

•　　•　　•　　•　　•

Oklahoma has very few natural standing bodies of water—by which I mean, lakes that weren't created by the Army Corps of Engineers by damming one of the rivers flowing through the state. In fact, I only know of one: Rose Crest Lake, a shallow expanse of brackish water that sits in the middle of the Rose Crest Salt Flats on the northern edge of Tilghman County.

Rose Crest is all that's left of an ancient sea that once covered these parts from western Oklahoma to the Texas panhandle. In the 1800s—and probably long before that—herds of buffalo gathered there and licked as much salt as they could handle. The area also attracts fancy migratory birds you won't find anywhere else in the state: whooping cranes, terns, pelicans, and so forth, on their way north or south, depending on the season. Bald eagles and peregrine falcons nest in the surrounding woods. During World War II, the Army Air Corps used the flats to practice bombing and strafing. People digging for selenite crystals beneath the surface still find a spent bullet or casing once in a while. A few years ago, a Boy Scout found a cache of mustard gas that the military had buried and forgotten about. Lucky for the boy, it didn't go off.

For the most part, the flats remain in the possession of Mother Nature, who does a pretty good job taking care of them. There's been talk about making the area into either a state or national park. Most folks around here hope that doesn't happen. Rose Crest is Tilghman County's little secret. We'd like to keep it that way.

They say the lake is about one-fourth as salty as the Atlantic and Pacific Oceans. It's not huge—maybe five square miles. Sitting in the middle, like a bull's eye, is a small island. If it has a name, I don't know what it is. I canoed out there one time when I was in high school. I walked around the outer edge but was too scared of snakes to venture into the interior. I remember being surprised to discover the water in the lake never got more than a couple of feet deep.

I didn't need the canoe. I could've walked.

•　　•　　•　　•　　•

By the time we reached the salt flats, it was too dark to see much of anything. I cut my headlights anyway. If, as I suspected, someone was hiding on the island, I didn't want to advertise our imminent arrival.

The white salt deposits were hard and made for secure driving. I was able to pull up right to the edge of the water while keeping my eyes peeled for any obstacles that might rise up out of the gloom.

I cut the engine and looked out to where I knew the island to be. If I strained my eyes, I could see its dark outline against the starlit sky.

My booze high was long gone. Instead, I felt alert. Extremely alert. So alert, you wouldn't believe it. Like when I'd faced down Tommy Drury and Dennis Tyler.

Karen had calmed herself. I hoped she'd forgiven me for my outburst, my lying about not drinking, and whatever else there was on the growing list of things I'd done wrong.

I told her it would be best if she waited for Bernard.

"I think it would be best if *you* waited for Bernard," she said.

"If I do, I might be too late. Don't worry. I've got the element of surprise on my side."

She fixed me with a stare. "I swear to God, Emmett Hardy, if you say 'don't worry' one more time, I'm going to clock you."

I had to laugh. "Fair enough," I said. She's a tough broad, that one.

I'd broken the flashclub, so I needed something else to light my way—something better than the Zippo. I felt around under the seat for an old Eveready flashlight I thought was there. It wasn't.

Karen said, "You looking for a flashlight?"

"I am."

"Here," she said. She rummaged around in her purse and took out a miniature version of the flashlight I'd been looking for: a silver tube with a red plastic switch and ring around the bulb and reflector. "It takes those itty-bitty batteries," she said. "It's not that bright, but it's better than nothing."

I don't know what I'd do without that girl.

I reached into my jeans jacket, took out my .38, checked it one more time to make sure it was loaded, then put it back in my pocket. I would've preferred my Colt, but I'd use what I had, not what I wished I had. At least there'd be no hammer spur to get hung up in a stray thread like what happened to Tommy Drury.

"Well," Karen said, finally. "Go on, then."

I leaned over to kiss her on the cheek. She turned and gave it to me full on the lips. "You be careful," she said.

"Always," I said.

"Never," she scoffed, and hugged me. I hugged back. I let go first and felt bad about it. Oh well, I thought, I'll get another chance.

A voice whispered in the back of my head: One of these days, Emmett, you're going to run out of chances.

Maybe I didn't need a canoe, but a pair of tall rubber boots would've helped; the water itself was a lot colder than the surrounding air. Fortunately, my footing was good and the water only came halfway up my shins. I did my best to keep all sloshing sounds to a minimum. I had no hard evidence that who I was looking for was even on the island, but if they weren't, I didn't know where else they'd be. I didn't dare turn on Karen's little flashlight until absolutely necessary. I didn't want to announce my arrival until I was ready.

The trek probably only took a couple of minutes although it seemed longer. My feet were numb by the time I got to the shore. I looked back, hoping to see Bernard riding to the rescue. All I saw was my truck's silhouette against the whiteness of the flats.

This would be a solo performance.

Oh well, I thought. It wouldn't be the first time. It wouldn't even be the first time today.

Rising up only a foot or two out of the water, the shore was lined with thick vines and dense brush, with a few smallish trees mixed in. I searched for a break in the vegetation and waved away assorted winged bugs making kamikaze attacks on my mouth. I couldn't see much in the dark and before long had to switch on the flashlight. It provided a narrow cone of light, just enough to navigate. I found a path to the interior fairly soon. I turned to the truck and flashed the flashlight on and off. Karen knew better than to shine the headlights at me but I thought I could see her wave.

I headed down the trail, shielding the beam with my hand to reduce the chances of being seen in case anybody was on the lookout. My aversion to snakes had not abated in the years since I'd last visited the island. I suspected the presence of water moccasins, so I trod with great unease. The path consisted mainly of packed salt and not much mud. Within a couple of minutes, I saw a fleck of light filtered through the trees. I switched off the flashlight and stumbled forward in the dark. Branches scratched and slapped against my face. I reached a clearing and the source of the light: a small wooden cabin.

There was hardly anything to it. It had a hardwood door like you'd find on any house, with a single window on its left side. I walked slowly and quietly around the structure. There were no other windows or doors. One way in, one way out.

At the other end of the clearing was a narrow, unpaved road. A white-and-blue Chevy C-10 four-by-four pickup was parked in back. It's once-shiny Cragar mag wheels and raised-white-letter tires were caked in mud. Salt water had splashed onto the body and dried. Bad for the paint, I thought.

The window was closed but the shades were open halfway so I could see inside. The room was lit—barely—by a pair of Coleman lanterns. A man sat in a rocking chair, half-turned away from me, talking to somebody out of sight. I couldn't tell who he was talking to, although I had a pretty good idea. The man held a double-barreled shotgun in his lap. A pair of crutches lay overlapped on the floor next to him like the crossbones on a pirate's flag.

I put my right hand in my pocket and curled it around my .38. It could be fairly argued that I should've shot him through the window and been done with it. That's not my style, however, presuming I even have a style.

Instead, I knocked and called out: "Hey, Darryl, it's Chief Hardy. Mind if I come in?"

"Whoa," he said, surprised. "Yeh, c'mon in, Chief, join the party."

CHAPTER TWENTY NINE

Darryl Martin sat in an antique rocking chair in the middle of the room. The chair was fancy and might've been worth some real money if not for the overabundance of chips and scratches and cigarette burns scarring almost every square inch. The back of the thing rose a foot over Darryl's head, and was decorated with a small, faded painting of Abraham Lincoln. Abe is my favorite president. I wondered if him being there was a sign of good luck.

Nah, it wasn't. A side-by-side double-barreled shotgun pointed at you is the opposite of good luck.

I waited to be invited in.

Darryl's anxious, bloodshot eyes mocked the smile he'd pasted on his face. "I'd offer you a seat," he said, "but unfortunately, this rocking chair's all I got, and in my condition—" he tapped the cast covering his right leg, "I reckon I need it more than you."

"That's alright, I don't mind standing." I hadn't entered the cabin, but stood outside the open door.

"Good," he said, "because this thing hurts like a son of a bitch. Slammed it in the truck door while I was getting out. I think I re-broke the damn thing."

He was pale and drenched with sweat. His eyelids twitched and the cords in his neck stood out. A Y-shaped vein pulsed in his forehead. The shrub of curly brown hair around his head that yesterday had been so neatly combed now looked like it had been washed in used motor oil and styled with hedge clippers. His unbroken leg hopped up and down like a tethered jackrabbit. He wore blue Oshkosh overalls with one pant leg cut-off to accommodate the cast. Beneath the overalls he wore a white tee shirt with underarm sweat stains the size of dinner plates. On his good foot was a blue vinyl bedroom slipper.

Darryl Martin no longer looked like the respectable family man I'd spoken with the day before. He'd been reduced to a pathetic, small-time, small-town hustler, broken by pain and his own poorly-laid plans, struggling to hold on to what few marbles he had left.

He braced the shotgun against his body and kept it pointed at me.

"Before we do anything else," he said, "I'd like you to open that jacket and let me see if you're wearing a gun."

I opened the jacket by the lapels and gave him a good long look, hoping it would be enough, and that he wouldn't ask me to empty my pockets. Fortunately, he saw I wasn't wearing a gun belt and seemed satisfied. Maybe my reputation for not carrying a gun had preceded me. I closed the jacket and put my hands in the pockets. That .38 felt good—probably better than it should have, given how deep a hole I'd climbed into.

"What I'd like to know," he said, "is how in heck you knew to come here?" Gone was the glad-handing Darryl of the day before. If he'd ever felt a need to impress me, he didn't any longer. "I swear to God, I never told a living soul about this place." He nodded to a spot to the left and in front of where he sat. "I sure as hell never told him."

I couldn't see who he talking about, but I had an idea. "Damn, Chief, I already invited you in once. C'mon, now. You might as well know what you're dealing with."

I stepped inside. "Just leave the door open," he said. I didn't think it was hot, but Darryl plainly did. He was sweating buckets.

I looked around. Sprawled in front of a cast-iron stove, half the size of the one in the Butcherville Store, was the body of a thin, nearly emaciated, elderly man. He wore a pair of green rubber waders that were way too big for him, twill pants that had once been black but were now a shiny dark green, and the top half of a short-sleeved white dress shirt. Below the collar the shirt had been obliterated by a shotgun blast, along with most of the man's midsection. I could see the broken spinal column through the remaining shreds of tissue and splintered rib cage. Body parts spread in ghastly chunks across and on top of the stove and the floor around it. The man's pale, hollow-cheeked face was fixed in a disbelieving expression. I knew how he felt.

"He found me, too," Darryl said in a philosophical tone. "I bet he wished he hadn't. Guess he never heard that curiosity killed the cat."

My face burned and my heart hurt and I had to struggle to keep from leaping across the space between us and try to shove that shotgun down his throat. But discretion prevailed.

"I'm guessing this is Elmer Kepley," I said.

"Yup. You two haven't met? Elmer, Chief Hardy. Chief Hardy, Elmer." He giggled. "Elmer got nosy and followed me out here." With his good foot, he nudged one of his crutches so that it poked the body. "Should've minded your own business, Elmer," he said loudly, like Kepley was just hard of hearing and not dead.

I heard a muffled cough behind me. I turned and saw Bonnie Hubbard seated on the floor in one corner, her shoulders hunched and knees pulled up under her chin with her hands clasped between them. She wore a red-and-white-striped version of the short-sleeved shirt she'd worn the day before, a pair of blue jeans with the legs rolled above the ankles, and those shiny black combat boots with the gum soles and yellow stitching. Her face was shiny with sweat and her hair was a tangled rat's nest. Evidently, she had not willingly acquiesced to Darryl's demands. More than anything, she seemed to be in mourning for something. Probably not the psychopath currently holding her prisoner. But something.

Bereft is a good word. I think I'll use it here. She looked bereft.

"You ok?" I asked.

She nodded slowly.

"I'm not planning on hurting her," Darryl said with forced good cheer, while real pain remained etched on his face. "You, on the other hand ... well, you shouldn't have come, Chief. You just shouldn't have come."

•　　•　　•　　•　　•

Karen doesn't like that I drink because she cares about me. I appreciate that, I do. If, one of these days, a scientist invents a little pill that eliminates the feelings of hopelessness to which I am commonly prone and gives me the same jolt of self-confidence I get from bourbon, I'll be happy to take it. As far as I know, however, no such pill exists.

So, bourbon it is.

I could try to explain to Karen how it works, but I'm afraid she'll try to convince me there's a better way, and I'm not sure I'm ready to hear that. I'm well aware of the problems involved with excessive drinking. In fact, I'm beginning to experience them more regularly.

But the fact remains: without booze, I'm like a scared little boy; with it, I feel like a goddam world-beater, even when there's the barrel of a shotgun pointed at my belly, which, at the moment, there was. I guess I should've been more scared, since Elmer Kepley's fate looked to be a preview of my own. A smart person wouldn't have given me a nickel for my chances, that's for sure. Maybe I'm not all that smart, though, because a voice in my head was telling me this wasn't my time and this cabin wasn't the place. The voice was a little bit bourbon-fueled, sure, but I listened to it, nevertheless. As long as I had my hand wrapped around the .38 in my jacket pocket, I knew I had a puncher's shot.

"Darryl, I thought we were friends."

"Are we friends? I wasn't aware of that, Chief. I wish you'd told me before. Now it's too late."

"It's not too late, Darryl. You got a lot of years left."

"Years?" he scoffed. "Months, if I'm lucky. Maybe not even that. I'll go to the chair if I get caught. Do not pass go. Do not collect two-hundred dollars." He smirked. "You ever play Monopoly, Chief?"

Yes, I told him. A few times. Was I any good? No, I'm too impatient and I can't manage money. Not even play money.

"I never lose," he said, seeming to forget the pain for a moment. "I don't know what it is, but I'm just great at that game. You'd think I'd be good at business, since I'm so good at Monopoly."

"I reckon you've done alright for yourself."

"That's true, I have. I got me a nice house and a good job, and I bought myself a cheap parcel of land that turned out to be worth a quarter-million dollars."

"That'd be the lot next to the Collins place."

"Bingo. How'd you know?"

"Lucky guess."

He snickered. "I doubt that," he said. I thought I detected a note of respect. I'd have preferred to be underestimated.

"The idea was," he said, "I'd sell it to Clyde Raymer, buy a bigger house and run against Burt Murray for state senate. I'd have won, too."

Unlikely, I thought, but a man's entitled to his dreams.

"Burt doesn't realize the Democrats are finished in this part of the state. I'd run as a Republican and beat him going away and there would've been plenty of money left. It was all set. Until that ignorant son of a bitch Merle Collins ruined everything."

He spit on the floor. The glob landed close to Kepley. "Oops, sorry about that, Elmer," he said, then asked how Merle was doing. I told him he'd pull through.

"Well, praise Jesus," he said contemptuously. "You know all those folks who died would still be alive it wasn't for him, right? Dennis Tyler and that kid he hired to help him, the one with the rotten teeth. Both of 'em would be alive."

That was arguable, I reckoned. Surely in Tommy Drury's case it would've been only a matter of time before someone put him down.

Darryl made a tsk-ing sound. "Erin'd be alive, too," he said, answering a question I'd been afraid to ask. "I didn't love her all that much, but she was ok to be married to. I'll probably miss her if I live long enough to miss anybody."

I struggled once again with the impulse to introduce his mouth to the barrel of that shotgun.

"Y'all find her?" he asked absently.

"Find her where?" I barely was able to keep my voice level.

"You been to my house, haven't you?"

"Not since earlier today. My people said there was a fire."

"Well, there you go, then. That's where she is." He made a regretful face. "I was hoping she'd fry-up so bad y'all would think it was me. Might've given me time to get the hell out of Dodge." He sighed. "Didn't work any better than the rest of the plan."

I was beginning to feel like someone was slowly pressing a sharpened stake into my gut. "What was your plan?" I asked

"My plan? What makes you think it was my plan? Maybe I shouldn't tell you anything at all. What if this case goes to court? I could get the electric chair." He laughed. "Loose lips sink ships, ain't that what they say?"

It didn't seem funny for very long and he stopped laughing real quick. "I know," he sighed. "I'm going to the electric chair anyway unless I can escape from here tonight. Which ain't going to be easy, since I'm not even sure I can get up out of this chair."

He looked over at Bonnie and for a second puffed up like he did the day before when bragging about his wife's biscuits. "Bonnie and I are going away where no one can find us, and we're going to get married and live happily ever after, just like Romeo and Juliet. Ain't we, honey?"

She didn't respond, but only looked sadder—even more bereft—than before, if that were possible.

Maybe Bonnie's lack of enthusiasm for his plan was to blame, but something set him off. He lifted the shotgun and aimed it at my face. He was holding his breath and sweating and shaking all over and I thought my heart might burst through my chest and fly across the room. I stared down the twin barrels for a few seconds before Darryl finally lowered it. He laid it down across his lap and smiled. "Scared you, didn't I?" he said.

Hell yes, but I wasn't about to admit it. More important was the fact that, for the first time since I'd gotten there, the gun was pointed away from me. I calculated my chances of survival as slightly improved. I even considered pulling my .38 while he was gloating over his stunt, but decided against it. I'd try talking with him some more and hope a better chance would come up down the road.

"Darryl, before you blow me into the next county, would you mind telling me what in hell this is all about? I know you didn't kill Earl Collins. Dennis Tyler and Tommy Drury did." That was mostly a lie. By now, I strongly suspected it was Darryl. I just needed to hear him say it to be sure.

"Oh, you know that, do you? I'll bet you also think you know who killed Kennedy." He leaned forward and gave me an evil smile. "I'll give you hint," he stage-whispered. "It wasn't Oswald."

He jerked the gun from his lap again and fired into the ceiling, while screaming incoherently at the top of his lungs. Pieces of wood and roof shingles showered down on us. I could've and should've pulled on him right then, but I'd been taken by surprise, and before I could react, he lowered the gun to chest level and pointed it back at me. I'm no expert on double-barreled shotguns, but I had to believe there was another shell in this one, and it could just as well have my name on it.

"God*dam* this hurts," he hollered, more to himself than me or Bonnie. He was looking sicker and more despairing by the minute.

I'd missed another chance. I was afraid I might not get another.

I withheld comment on his sudden impulse to install a skylight and focused on getting him to tell as much of the story as he was willing to tell. "You're saying you killed Earl?" I asked. "I thought it was those two punks."

That scream had made him sound like he'd tried to remove his own tonsils with a fish hook. "I wish that was true," he rasped. "They kidnapped him, but no, it was me who killed him. I swear on Jesus's name, though, it was an accident. I never meant to hurt a hair on his head. Before yesterday I never killed anything bigger than a field mouse. Now I got"—he counted on his fingers—"five dead bodies on my conscience. Six, if Merle don't pull through, and he's the one I wouldn't mind being dead."

He looked at Bonnie, which I didn't want him to do. I wanted him to forget she was even in the room. "Does that bother you?" I asked, trying to draw his attention back to me.

He looked shocked. "What? Of course, it does. What in hell do you take me for? I only done it because I didn't have no choice. It was either me or them." His face softened. "I got to say, though," he said, "killing Elmer was easier than killing Erin. I reckon killing you will be easier still."

The suggestion that I was to be shot inspired me to take immediate stock of the tight spot I was in. Darryl and I were no more than six feet away from one another. He was in agony, immobile and helpless, but armed with a shotgun and ready to use it. My legs hurt and I could still feel the slight after-effects from the alcohol, but I was in a lot better shape than Darryl. I had a .38 in my jacket pocket that I didn't dare pull, for fear I would end up like Elmer Kepley, with my insides sprayed all over the place. There was a young woman in the room who, I'd decided, I would do anything to protect. I concluded that my situation was poor and, in the near-term, unlikely to improve. In the long-term … well, it was extremely unlikely that there'd be a long-term, unless I could keep Darryl talking until help arrived.

Get the lead out, Bernard.

"Alright then—" I said, but he interrupted. "Chief, I know you're not carrying, but do me a favor and keep your hands where I can see them, ok? You're making me nervous."

I had no choice but to take my hands out of my pockets and count myself lucky. "Anyway," I said, "assuming neither of us is a particular hurry to get me shot, how 'bout you tell me how it is you're responsible for all the bloodletting's gone on over the last 24 hours?"

"Well, I already told you, it's really Merle Collins's fault, but I get your point," he said. "The thing is, Chief, I am in a hurry. I only stopped here because I was hurting so bad and needed a rest." He leaned to one side, like he was trying to keep weight off his broken leg. "If I want to make it to Mexico before the law catches up with me, I need to get a move on." He stopped and cocked an ear. "Did you hear that?" he asked. I told him I didn't hear anything. He listened for another second or two

. "Anyway, I got to get going," he said, "which means I'll have to decide what to do with you real quick."

"Darryl, you don't want to kill me."

"I'd be just as happy not to, but really I can't see any other way."

"You mind if I make a suggestion?"

"Make it quick. I'm not going to sit here and let you stall."

"Just hear me out," I said. "How in the world are you going to get out of that chair and into that truck by yourself?"

"I reckon I'll get Bonnie to help."

Bonnie quietly scoffed. "It looks to me like you had a hard-enough time getting her here," I said. "The girl's a mess." I quickly added: "No offense, Bonnie."

"That's fine," she said limply, like she was accepting my offer of something she didn't want or need, just to be polite.

"I guess maybe you could try asking real nice, but I don't believe she'll be much inclined to help."

"I'll just have to shoot her too, then." He raised the gun at me again. "C'mon, Chief. You're wasting my time."

I held up my hands. "Now, wait a minute, Darryl," I said. "Listen to yourself. You don't want to kill her. You love her."

He glanced at her and I thought I could see him start to question himself.

"Think about it, now," I continued. "You're not getting out of here without help, and we're the only chance of help you've got. You shoot us, you'll still be sitting there when my people come around. What's going to happen then? Are you just going to keep shooting everyone who walks through that door? Sooner or later you're going to run out of shells."

I slowly started to put my hands in my pockets. "No, no, no, no, no," he said. "Those hands are fine where they are."

"Sorry, I forgot."

I hoped at some point the pain would get so bad that he'd faint or at least close his eyes because my chances of successfully pulling on him—never great to begin with—were much diminished with my right hand outside that jacket pocket.

"You know what—" he said, then tried to raise himself with his free arm and healthy leg, while simultaneously keeping me in his line of vision and fire. The rocking chair made it hard for him to get leverage but he was stronger than he looked and made good progress. Something must've snapped, though. He drew his lips tight against his gums and bared his teeth like a rabid dog, cried out and fell back into the chair. All that time, the shotgun never wavered. It stayed fixed on me. How he managed that with the pain he was in, I'll never know.

He banged his head against the chair back, over and over. I reckon he'd accepted he wasn't getting out of there on his own.

"Are you saying you'll help me escape?" he said.

"I'm saying we can make a deal. You let Bonnie walk out of here right now, I'll help you out the door and into your truck. At least that'll give you a head start."

We both looked over at Bonnie. She'd shifted position. Her back rested square against the wall and her hands were folded on her lap. Her legs stretched straight out and crossed at the ankles so I could see the gum soles of her shoes. Her eyes were soft.

Darryl looked back at me. "What happens when you get me in the truck?"

"Nothing. You drive away. Couldn't stop you if I wanted to." I nodded at the shotgun. "You're the one who's armed."

Nobody said a word for almost a minute. The only sounds came from outside the cabin—whirring insects, a trilling bird up well-past its bedtime, the dismal grousing of a bullfrog.

Darryl still managed to keep that shotgun in a position to shoot.

"Bonnie," he said, his voice wavering. "I just want you to know, I wasn't lying about all those things I said. I did love you. Or I do. I don't know how this happened, but I'm sorry." He tried to smile. "I do like poetry, you know. That line I wrote in your book was by that Allen Ginsberg guy."

"I know," she said, her voice less hard than it might've been, but not the voice of a girl in love. More like a girl experiencing the latest in a long line of disappointments. "Follow your inner moonlight; don't hide the madness."

She managed not to smile at the irony.

"Is it alright if I get up?" she asked.

He nodded. She stood up and stretched her arms and legs. "I should've known," she said, yawning—from nerves, I expect. "I should've known. I guess you couldn't help it. It's this place. You grew up here."

Darryl looked puzzled. "What do you mean, this place? *This place*? There ain't nothing wrong with this place," he said defensively. "I know I complained about it, sweetheart, but I love Butcherville. It's the freest town in America. Nuh-uh. I love Butcherville to death."

Outside, a bird sang a song so intricate and beautiful it could've been played by Charlie Parker.

Bonnie glared at Darryl. Seconds passed. I knew he could still change his mind.

A different bird started singing a different tune—just as free, just as beautiful.

"Don't call me sweetheart," she said. Her voice was flat; her face was as blank as a sheet of paper.

She muttered "I should've known" one more time, then walked out the door. She didn't look back.

Darryl didn't try to stop her.

CHAPTER THIRTY

He asked how we were going to do this. "However you want," I said. "You're the boss."

"Well—" he began.

"*But*," I interrupted, "before we start, I have some questions that need answers."

He whined and stomped his good foot like a two-year-old. "Dang it, that wasn't part of the deal."

It wasn't, but what was he going to do? Shoot me?

"It's just that there are a few questions that still need to be answered."

"What questions? I already told you everything."

"Not everything. I want to hear how Earl died. You say it was an accident. Excuse me for saying so, but that's one hell of an accident."

He tap-tapped his cast impatiently with a thumbnail. It sounded like a woodpecker going to work on an oak tree. "I don't see how I can tell you that, without telling you the whole thing, and that's going to take some time."

"My people's hands are full with that fire you set. If they find Erin, like you expect they will, that'll take up more time." I thought of the dog. "What'd you do with that little dog of Erin's?"

"I shot him. Left him in the house. I didn't want him to suffer in the fire."

"Ok, good," I said, not meaning it, although my standards for what is and what isn't humane had taken a beating over the last twenty-four hours. "Finding the dog might slow them down, too. They don't know where I am or even where to look, so it should be a while before they get here, if they ever do. You've got about as much time as you need."

"Well," he said, tapping his cast some more, "I don't know—"

"How 'bout you just give me the Reader's Digest version."

"What does that mean? Short?"

"That's right. Short."

He rocked back and forth and considered my appeal. "Alright then," he said. "I reckon I can do that, as long as I keep it short."

Only it wasn't short. In fact, once he got started, he wouldn't shut up.

·　　·　　·　　·　　·

I'm not sure how long he talked. I'm sure it seemed longer than it really was. You have to consider that while I listened to his story I was also fearing for my life, looking for an opening to shoot him, and straining to detect the approach of a car that I hoped would mean the cavalry had arrived.

In other words: Time didn't exactly fly.

I can't quote his whole monologue word for word, but here's the gist. It's a hell of a long gist.

·　　·　　·　　·　　·

He started by telling me things I already knew. The new councilmen got elected based on their promise to allow de-annexation, then promptly and unknowingly de-annexed themselves out of office, etc. ("I'm sure if we had to do it all over again," he said with great sincerity, "we'd do it different, but what's done is done." Yup. What's done is done. Jesus H. Christ.)

One thing led to another. Merle was named mayor and put the brakes on the plans of Clyde and his lackeys. That should've been the end of it, but of course it wasn't. From this point in the story, the extent of Clyde's active involvement became unclear. What was clear, is that Darryl Martin was in it up to his eyeballs.

Unlike the other councilmen—who, in true Butcherville style, figured nothing in life is worth doing if it requires more effort than it takes to walk to the end of the driveway and check the mail once a day—Darryl was willing to go all-in for the plant expansion. He couldn't make it happen all by himself, however, so he sought help. Dennis Tyler, Chief of Security at WestOK, stepped up, maybe because Clyde ordered him to (Darryl wouldn't say). Tyler suggested his old high-school buddy, Tommy Drury, might be useful, as well. Darryl and Tyler approached Floyd Kepley about paying Drury off the books.

Kepley agreed, although Darryl was cagey when I asked whether Kepley knew what they were up to.

According to Darryl, someone (Clyde? Darryl wouldn't say) briefly considered going to the state legislature to request a ruling on something they call 'eminent domain,' which allows the government to take over private land for the common good. Darryl thought Clyde getting what he wanted was good for everybody, even if some people were too stupid to figure it out. Clyde had enough friends in the legislature to make it happen, but the consensus was it would take too long. Wheels were already in motion. That's why Darryl decided to embark on his scheme even in the lousy physical shape he was in. A delay would cost everyone a lot of money—especially Clyde, I surmised, but people like Darryl, too. They needed to cut through the red tape, which meant forcing Merle's hand, by any means necessary.

Darryl wouldn't say who came up with the plan, but seemed content to let me think it was him. The idea was simple. Kidnap Earl Collins. Hold him until Merle agreed to sell his property and approve the zoning waiver. Papers were drawn up to accomplish both goals, notarized by Kepley, albeit without signatures. I guess the plan was: get Merle to sign and let Clyde fill in the blanks. Darryl was impressed how, after all the problems Merle had supposedly caused, Clyde still offered him top dollar. ("I thought that was pretty white of Clyde," were his exact words.)

Being an observer of human nature on a par with such noted philosophers as Aristotle and Socrates and Huey P. Long, Darryl ultimately thought Merle would realize he couldn't win and take the money and run. ("Anyone with any sense would, don't you think?") Men like Darryl Martin don't have the foggiest idea what makes men like Merle Collins tick.

I suppose the reverse is also true.

Tyler took care of the operation's nuts and bolts. He couldn't wait to get his old high school pal Tommy Drury in on the deal. (Darryl said, "I wouldn't have trusted the crazy son of a bitch to take out the trash," but he could've just been trying to make himself look better.) Elmer wrote Drury checks on his own account, so they couldn't be traced back to the plant. Darryl claimed not to know where Elmer got the money to pay Drury. I think he was lying.

The three men traced the movements of Earl and his dad all week. Earl got off the bus at the Butcherville Store every day. That's where they'd snatch him. Merle stopped by Leave it to Bever's on his way home. That's where they'd snatch *him*. The plan was for Drury to take the boy, tie him up, blindfold him, and bring him to Darryl's house, where they'd hide him in the brand-new storm cellar. While Drury was doing that, Tyler would corner Merle at Leave it to Bever's, tell him they'd taken his son and that if he ever wanted to see him again he'd sign the papers. Once that was done, they'd let the boy go. ("He'd be blindfolded," Darryl said about Earl. "Drury's the only one of us he might possibly lay eyes on, which didn't matter, because Drury planned to drive to Mexico as soon as he got paid.")

As the week progressed, Tyler began to rethink the trust he'd placed in his friend. He and Darryl got together without Drury and changed the plan. In the new version, Tyler and Drury would take the boy. They'd bring him to Darryl, then head over to Leave it to Bever's and double-team Merle. They decided the best thing to do was buy him a shitload of drinks, get him plastered, then take him somewhere and lay down the law.

The day it was to happen, Darryl got skittish. He didn't like sitting around while Tyler and Drury were doing all the work, even though there wasn't much more he could do with that giant plaster cast on his leg. He started to paint his fence to pass the time, but in the run-up to when the school bus was supposed to arrive, his nerves got the best of him and he drove to the store. ("I needed to pick up some things for Erin, anyway. She was going to make biscuits when she got home from her mother's. I'm sure going to miss those biscuits.")

He parked on the opposite side of the lot from the Willys, wanting to stay away from Tyler and Drury if possible so that anybody watching wouldn't know the three were together. Unfortunately, Drury was yelling and carrying on, and Darryl felt obliged to hobble over there—cast, crutches, and all—and do what he could to shut him up. ("I could only do so much, because that boy was crazy, but he quieted down a little bit.") He stood there for a while and they smoked and talked. Drury calmed down. Darryl went into the store, had his brief encounter with Grace Hubbard, then went back to his truck and waited. He saw Bonnie and Earl get off the bus but drove away before the actual abduction. Tyler later told him they'd had to chase the boy down, and that Earl had locked himself in the restroom, which made it necessary for them to break down the door.

Darryl drove straight home as fast as he could, to get ready for the boy's arrival. The way he told it, the kidnapping itself went as well as could be expected, although he couldn't have known the boy left a clue written in that science textbook of his. Tyler and Drury stuffed a sock in the boy's mouth, put a bag over his head, and tied his hands and ankles with duct tape. They took him to Darryl's and hid him in the storm cellar. From there, Tyler and Drury drove to Rachel Drury's place and switched the Willys for the Mustang. Earl's football was still in the Willys—he'd been carrying it when they grabbed him, but they hadn't noticed. They took it with them in the Mustang, aiming to dump it first chance they got. They hit the road to Leave it to Bever's.

Merle was already there. They knew him because they'd been watching him, but he didn't know them from a hole in the wall. Being the trusting sort—at least when it comes to accepting free drinks—he wasn't the least suspicious when they started buying him beers. They kept setting him up and he kept knocking them down. Before long, Merle was convinced he'd met his new best friends.

It got to be game time. Merle got all worried that he was supposed to take his boy but was in no shape to drive. Tyler and Drury told him they'd drive them all to the game. They said they'd pick up Earl on the way, which Merle must've believed, either because he wanted to or because he was so drunk. Tyler thought Merle's truck would be too conspicuous parked in front of Leave it to Bever's, so he offered to drive it to the stadium, where nobody would notice it until after the game—by which time the caper would've reached a successful conclusion. Drury took the Mustang. Before they left, Tyler had a sudden flash of inspiration. He planted the football in the truck's toolbox, in a half-assed attempt to frame Merle in case things didn't go according to plan.

We're not talking about criminal masterminds here.

Tyler parked Merle's truck in the stadium parking lot near Gene Treadway's Corvair, where we found it later. Merle about lost his you-know-what when Drury showed up without Earl, but they managed to hush him up and take him away. I reckon Merle wasn't in the greatest shape to resist. They drove through town, not worrying about being seen, since just about everyone was at the game.

They dragged Merle inside the old wooden grain elevator across from where Nate Gunter used to live. They told him that if he didn't play ball, he and his family were dead meat, then knocked the shit out of him just for fun. When the time came for them to make Merle sign the papers, they realized they couldn't because they'd left them at Drury's place, where we found them later. For some reason, instead of going back to get the papers, they let Merle loose on the highway outside town, where Karen and I found him. On top of everything—as if they hadn't already screwed up the plan beyond redemption—the pair of dumbasses forgot to tell Merle they'd kidnapped his boy, which you'd think would be the first thing they'd do if they wanted to blackmail him.

So far, while painful to imagine, you can almost laugh, it's all so ridiculous.

Unfortunately, there's nothing the slightest bit funny about how it went down the rest of the way.

•　　•　　•　　•　　•

Not five minutes after Tyler and Drury left Darryl's house, Erin returned home unexpectedly. Apparently, she and her mother had a fight that ended with Erin driving back to Butcherville. Normally, Darryl wouldn't have minded. He said he hates his mother-in-law for poisoning Erin's mind against him. Today wasn't a bit normal, however. There was a young boy in his cellar, bound and gagged with a bag over his head, and Darryl didn't want his wife to know.

As if that weren't bad enough, I showed up with Bonnie, who Darryl had been courting on the QT for weeks. He didn't get very far, but she was impressed at how he was interested in artistic pursuits, unlike anybody else she'd met since she moved here. She started spending time with him. Darryl showed her his bird pictures and read to her from a book of poetry by someone named Rod McKuen. They didn't much appeal to her, but she was touched by the gesture. She gave him a book entitled *Howl*, which Darryl pretended to like because he liked Bonnie so much.

Anyway, she was about the last person he'd want to know about his criminal enterprise. Yet there she was, riding in a police car, alongside someone who was asking him questions about the boy locked in his basement. Tyler and Drury were supposed to drop off the papers they'd supposedly gotten Merle to sign, then take Earl someplace he'd be found. Darryl didn't know exactly what time they'd show up, but he sure as heck didn't want me and Bonnie there when they did. He figured the way he'd gotten rid of us was pretty slick. Now he realized he hadn't been as slick as he thought.

Darryl couldn't deliver the boy to Tyler and Drury with Erin around, either, unless he wanted her to find out what was going on, which he did not. Fortunately, Erin said she wanted to go the game, which Darryl saw as a stroke of luck. He drove her to the game. When they got there, he pretended he'd forgotten something and needed to go back home. He dropped her off and said he'd be right back.

By the time he got home, Darryl expected Tyler and Drury at any moment. He decided to bring Earl up from the cellar so he'd be ready to go as soon as they got there. He said he also wanted to bring Earl topside because he felt bad about leaving him down there in the dark, all alone, but I think he was just trying to make himself look better.

That's when things started going completely to hell. Getting Earl down to the basement with Tyler's and Drury's help was one thing. Doing it all by himself—with a partially-healed broken leg and a cast the size and weight of a concrete sewer pipe—was another. Somehow, he made it down into the cellar, but once there realized there was no way in hell he could carry the boy up those stairs. He used a boxcutter to cut the tape holding Earl to the chair but left his hands taped together behind his back. He disguised his voice, told Earl everything was going to be fine, and nudged him up the stairs. Darryl knew Earl would get to the top first but didn't think he'd run off, with that bag over his head and it being dark and everything.

He was wrong.

Darryl held on to Earl's taped-up hands but wasn't holding on tight enough. While he was locking the cellar door behind them, Earl tore himself away and took off running. The boy couldn't see where he was going with that bag over his head, but he ran anyway. He crashed into the newly-painted, still-wet gate, which knocked him down—and stained his jeans—but didn't stop him. He got up and ran some more. Darryl's fence only wrapped around the front of the house; the backyard was open pasture. Once Earl got pointed in the right direction, nothing stood in his way—certainly not Darryl, who, with that cast on his leg, couldn't have run down a three-legged box turtle.

Faced with ruinous consequences if Earl was allowed to escape, Darryl realized the only way he was going to catch the boy was to get his truck and chase him down. Somehow—keyed up on adrenaline would be my guess—he managed to climb into the truck's cab by himself. Earl had gotten a sizable head start, but with that bag over his head he couldn't see where he was going. He zig-zagged this way and that, which made it easier for Darryl to catch up.

Darryl drove across the field to within twenty or thirty yards of Earl when the boy vanished just as quick as if he'd been raptured to heaven. Darryl braked and let the truck idle while he considered what to do next. ("One second, he was there, the next second, he wasn't.")

Darryl set off in the direction he'd last seen the boy, driving too fast as it turned out. The truck came over a rise just as Earl popped up a few feet from the truck's front bumper. Darryl couldn't stop in time.

("He was just *there*," Darryl said. "With that burlap sack over his head, like a damn scarecrow." His voice cracked. "I tried to miss him, but I couldn't," he said. "I tried. I really did...." His voice trailed off.)

He wanted to help the boy, so he pulled the bag off his head. One look and he knew there was nothing he could do. The boy died instantly.

Earl's days of playing the saxophone and flirting with Bonnie Hubbard and making his mama proud were over.

Darryl sat in the grass alongside Earl's body and tried to decide what to do. Two hundred yards in the distance, he saw a car pull into his driveway. He didn't know who it was, all he saw were a pair of headlights. He relaxed a little when he recognized Erin getting out on the passenger side. Erin waved goodbye to whoever was in the car and they drove off. Erin noticed the pickup parked in the field behind her house. It must've puzzled her until she realized it was Darryl. She began walking, then running, toward the truck. Darryl shouted and waved at her to stay where she was, but she kept coming. ("She was never great at taking orders.") Darryl knew that, as bad as things had gone, they were about to get a whole lot worse.

She hollered some things: "What's going on?" and "Why're you out here with the truck after dark?" Darryl tried to head her off before she got where she could see Earl but there was only so much he could do, moving-around-wise. Erin maneuvered past him without any trouble.

She saw Earl—bloodied, with tire-tracks on his clothes, and his head lopsided from being run over—and screamed to wake the dead. ("I thanked the Lord whoever was in that car had gone," Darryl said, which I took to mean he was glad to have one less witness to deal with.)

He managed to hush her up and get her into the truck, put the bag back over Earl's head and lift him into the bed, then get himself behind the wheel. I had to give him credit; all that couldn't have been easy in his condition. Erin wailed and wept on the short drive back to the house. Darryl tried to think of a plausible explanation.

He couldn't think of one, so he decided to give the truth a try and hope Erin's love for him would keep her from helping grease the skids to the electric chair. Unfortunately, his contention that the kidnapping scheme was the Martin family's ticket to a lifetime of wealth and happiness was a hard sell and Erin wasn't buying. First, she got hysterical, then she got mad— flummoxed that Darryl could've done something so stupid and immoral.

Darryl told me he could take the crying, but drew the line at bitching and name-calling. I can remember the rest of what he said pretty well. I know I'll try to forget but I doubt I ever will.

●　　●　　●　　●　　●

"I tried to argue with her," Darryl said, "but she wouldn't shut up, and I couldn't get in a goddam word edgewise. Finally, I had enough. I just grabbed her by the throat and started to squeeze. Let me tell you: That sure as hell shut her up. I didn't mean to kill her, at least not at first, but, well ... this might sound nuts, but her throat felt soft and tender under my hands, like Play Doh. You know how good Play Doh feels when you squish it through your fingers?"

I barely know what Play Doh is. I've seen the commercials on TV, is all.

I shook my head.

"It's cold and gooey," he said. "The harder you squeeze, the more of it squishes through your fingers, the nicer it feels. I couldn't get her throat to squish through my fingers, even though I tried. Her skin felt warm—not cool, like Play Doh—but it felt good in the same kind of way. I don't think I even noticed she'd died. I was just enjoying that feeling, you know? Then I got to thinking about how Play Doh tastes salty, so I licked her face. She'd been crying, and she'd started bleeding from somewhere. Her mouth, I think. Anyway, I licked her face and she *tasted* like Play Doh, too. Not blood, not tears, but Play Doh. I guess it's funny, the kind of things that cross your mind when you're doing something like that. I mean, I'd just killed my wife, and there I was licking her face and thinking about Play Doh. I guess you think that's weird. Maybe it is."

His voice and manner were almost nostalgic—like he was remembering a past vacation that didn't go exactly according to plan but, now that he looks back on it, still had its fun parts. To this point I'd thought he was mostly normal person who'd simply let things spiral out of control. I was wrong. He'd been an unexploded bat shit bomb the whole time.

"I stuffed her in a closet thinking I'd bury her later," he said, "but I never got around to it. Too much else to do. The boys I work with will tell you, I'm always dawdling. It's always later than I think.

"I can see how you're looking at me, you think I'm out of my mind. I know I don't sound like I'm sorry I killed her. I guess in a way, I'm not. I thought I loved her when I married her, but this last summer, when I met Bonnie, I learned what real love is, and I knew I didn't love Erin at all, and never had. 'Course, marrying Erin did have benefits. Her daddy had money and connections. He's the one who got me the job with Clyde, and he's the reason I got promoted so fast. I did a good job and I deserved it, but hell, we all know you don't always get what you deserve. Sometimes it takes luck. It don't hurt to make your own luck. That's what I was doing when I married Erin. Making my own luck." He smiled without remorse. "I reckon if her daddy discovers I killed his daughter, he won't be wanting to help me anymore, but it don't matter, because by the time he finds out, I'll be down in Mexico sipping tequila sunrises.

"I reckon I'll live on the money I was supposed to give Tyler and Drury. I ran into them on the road right after I killed Erin. I had Earl's body next to me, covered by a blanket on the floor of my truck. That Mustang is so low-slung, they couldn't see inside. They'd just finished with Merle and wanted to get paid. I told them, first they needed to get those papers signed. They didn't like it, but said they'd do it in the morning if I gave them an advance on what I owed 'em. I had a couple of twenties in my billfold, so I gave it to 'em. They most likely spent it on beer and table dances at Leave it to Bever's. You gunned them down before they could collect the rest. I guess I'll hang on to it and use it to finance my new life south of the border.

"You know, I think Erin's dad will miss me. He really likes me. Most people do. I'm a likeable son of a bitch. Everybody says so."

• • • • •

I doubted anyone in Butcherville would henceforth find Darryl any more likeable than a case of venereal disease, but if the cost of buying myself time was to nod politely at his bizarre rantings, I was willing to pay. I had another question or two. I thought I knew the answers, but I'd ask to make sure.

"We found Earl's body in the root cellar on the lot next to the Collins place—"

"My property," he said.

"That's right, your property," I said. "How'd he end up there?"

"I took him there late last night, after you left. I parked myself down the road a little ways with my lights off, waiting for you to finish with Mrs. Collins. I thought if I left him there, whoever found him would think his folks did it, since the cellar is right next door to their house."

No one had suspected Earl's folks for even a second. No clear-minded person would. I wouldn't, and my mind isn't always all that clear.

Darryl must've sensed my skepticism. "I'm not saying it was a good idea," he said, "but it was better than him being found in my house."

That was undeniably true.

"What I'd like to know is how you knew I was involved," he said. "I thought I'd covered my tracks."

"I didn't know for sure until I was on my way here. My deputy radioed me and said they found dried paint on Earl's trousers. The same three colors as were smeared on me last night. Red, white, and blue. I realized Earl must've been at your house before or after I was. We knew Tyler and Drury must've had help. For a while we thought it was Kepley, but when I heard about the paint that was found on Earl, I knew it had to be you."

"That damn paint," he muttered. "I'm still going to pay for those pants of yours, by the way. Soon as I get down to Mexico, I'll send you a money order."

Sure you will, Darryl, I thought. "As for finding you," I said, "yesterday afternoon at your house, when you were out of the room, Erin and I got to talking about those pictures of birds on your walls. She told me where you took them. She said you had a hideaway out here at the Salt Plains, and that you didn't know she knew about it."

His eyes glinted in recognition. "That's what you two were talking about when I walked in."

"Yup. I remembered this island from when I was a boy, and how I'd always heard talk of a cabin here. I put two and two together and got four. It looks pretty good for as old as it is. How'd you get a hold of it?"

"I bought it from a guy who bought it from another guy who bought it from someone else," he said. "One of those deals."

"Ah," I said. "Well, I went to see Bonnie's little friend, Princess Bellchamber. She'd been out walking with Bonnie when you tracked her down. I'm sure you know, since you were there. I reckon you must've scared her by the way you acted, and she didn't want to go with you. Probably you refused to take Princess, and Bonnie didn't want to leave her all alone there in the middle of the road. In any case, before you forced her into the truck, she had the foresight to scribble the word 'HELP' on the front page of *In Cold Blood*— right underneath where you inscribed it. She left it with Princess, who gave it to me. I added it all up. Again. Two plus two equals four."

Darryl groaned in pain and closed his eyes long enough for me to put my hands in my pockets. My right index finger curled around the trigger of my .38 and I waited for the opening I wasn't sure would come. I felt thankful he hadn't wondered why I was wearing that jacket. It wasn't really cold enough.

He opened his eyes as wide as he could, like he was trying to clear his head. "There I go, talking and forgetting about what time it is," he said. "Let's get the show on the road, Chief. That fire should've been out by now. No telling when your people will show up."

I felt like I was in a dream, but not necessarily my own. I was playing a part. Someone else was talking through me. I was just mouthing the words.

There was no reason Darryl shouldn't have shot me already, but he hadn't. For a second, I felt like we'd both lost control of our fates—that someone or something else was going to decide how this played out.

If that were the case, whoever or whatever it was would've had the same question I did:

"Darryl, that money you were supposed to pay Tyler and Drury. Where'd that come from?"

He gave me a wary look.

"Where do you think?"

"You know what I think. I just want to hear you say it."

He shifted in his chair, trying to get less uncomfortable. "If I tell you," he said, his voice like a pitiful child's, "will you please promise not to tell anyone where I'm going?"

It would've been easy to lie and say 'yes,' and I was just about to, when Darryl cocked his head and got real still, like Dizzy does when she hears a bird fluttering around outside. Both of us heard it. A car engine.

It sounded like the Fury. The engine quit and seconds later I heard splashes in the distance. Someone running across the lake.

"Dammit to hell, there I go again," Darryl yelled in despair and hopelessness and all those other things you feel when you realize you've screwed up so bad, things can't be fixed. "Running my mouth when I should've been taking care of business."

He looked like a man backed to the edge of a cliff, knowing his only option was to jump, but if he was going over the edge, he was taking someone with him. I was the obvious choice.

Some instinct made him struggle to get up. As he did, the barrels of the gun dropped. Slightly. But enough.

Or so I thought.

Now's the time. I pulled the .38.

My life didn't pass before my eyes, but people did: my dad, whose mind was failing and who needed me now as much as I needed him when I was a kid; Karen, who loved me without reservation for so long but whose love I resisted, out of self-destructive habit more than anything. I also thought of those I'd failed: namely, Erin Martin and Earl Collins. I thought about the night ten years ago when Tommy Drury beat his mama into a coma, and the moment a few hours ago, when his try at putting me in a wood box was foiled by a stray thread in the lining of his jacket.

Darryl recognized his blunder within a fraction of a second. In one motion, he dropped back into the chair and raised the gun to shoot. The odds turned back in his favor. But I'm fast. Faster than just about anyone.

Our eyes locked.

There was a blast and the sound of glass breaking. Then quiet.

I guess I'm not as fast as I used to be.

This time I got beat.

CHAPTER THIRTY ONE

At first, I thought I'd gone deaf. Then I felt blood trickling down the back of my neck and was afraid I'd lost more than my hearing.

The shot came from two feet behind and to the left of me. I closed my eyes out of reflex. When I opened them, I was still there, but the left side of Darryl Martin's face was gone.

Pieces of him mixed with bits of Elmer Kepley on the floor and walls of the cabin. My right hand shook. I looked down at my right hand. The .38 had barely cleared my pocket. I'd never gotten it in position to shoot. I gingerly put it back in my jacket.

I turned around and looked out the window, expecting to see Bernard. But it wasn't him.

It was Karen.

Her lips moved, but the blast had done a number on my hearing and I couldn't understand what she was saying. I put a hand to my ear and shook my head. She vanished from behind the broken window and reappeared in the door, carrying the Winchester .30-30 I keep in my pickup. I dimly wondered why she'd shot through the window when I'd left the door wide open. She leaned the rifle against the wall and came to me. We both dropped to our knees. She held my head in her hands. "Are you alright?" she said.

I said I was fine. To me, my voice sounded like it was underwater, but it didn't to her. She said, "You don't have to shout," laughing and crying at the same time.

Lights went on and off at the edge of my field of vision. There was caterwauling in my head, like I was listening to a dozen different Jerry Lee Lewis songs at the same time.

Karen's embrace would've reduced a block of granite to dust, but I was too numb to feel it.

"Remind me to thank your daddy for teaching you to shoot," I said.

"I taught myself," she replied with a little less sass than usual. She was careful to keep her back to the gory scene. "I'm not going to look over there, if you don't mind," she said. It was truly about as ugly a sight as you'll ever want to avoid looking at.

She helped me to my feet. My knees felt like they'd been scalded with a blowtorch. She suggested we go outside. I followed her out of the bloody, dimly-lit cabin, into the full-on darkness and fresh air of the late summer night.

Bernard burst into the clearing, his service revolver in one hand, and his flashlight in the other. He shined it on Karen and me. By the faint light of the cabin, I watched the fear on his face dissolve into an expression of relief. He bent over, grabbed his knees, and struggled to catch his breath. "Whew!" he said. "I heard a shot—" he panted, "I thought I was—" he panted some more "—I thought I was too late."

He was. Thank God Karen wasn't.

We assured him we were ok and I sketched out what had just happened. He apologized for taking so long, but he couldn't get hold of Jeff and a few folks watching the fire had gotten unruly and he had to straighten that out. Out of habit, I asked him if he'd put in calls to the sheriff and Highway Patrol. He said he had and suggested we sit in the cruiser and wait. He offered to carry Karen across the lake. She offered to slap him. We waded across, each under our own power.

Karen and I got into the back seat of the Fury. Bonnie Hubbard was already in the front, wrapped in a green army blanket. "Have you two met?" I asked them. "Just a few minutes ago, although it seems longer," said Karen. "We've already been through a lot together."

Bernard got a hold of Kenny on the box and told him to notify Grace Hubbard that Bonnie had been found in good shape, all things considered. With little else to do until the state and county boys arrived, he stood next to the car and asked me questions through the rolled-down window. I summoned what energy I could and answered.

"So Elmer Kepley wasn't the one behind this, after all?" he said.

"All I know for sure is that Elmer paid Tommy Drury under the table to work for Dennis Tyler," I said. "Tyler and Drury worked with Darryl Martin to kidnap Earl Collins and get Merle to sell his property and sign-off on the zoning. I suspect they were doing the bidding of Clyde Raymer, but all three of them are dead, so we might never know." I didn't necessarily like talking about Bonnie's grandfather in front of her, but at that point I reckoned it didn't matter a whole hell of a lot.

Bernard wiped his face with a handkerchief. It wasn't hot, but I guess he'd worked up a sweat running out there. "Makes you wonder, don't it?" he said.

"What I'm wondering is what it's going to take to nail Clyde to the cross."

"You're pretty sure it was him, then."

Karen interjected, "Those others were too stupid to do something like this on their own."

I thought about saying, "The whole goddam plan *was* stupid," but I don't like to correct Red, so I didn't.

Bonnie was slumped down in the front seat so that, from where I sat, I could only see the top of her head, and the part in her hair. "It was him," she said in a small voice. "It's something he'd do."

"I think Darryl was about to tell me, when he got distracted," I said. "Before it got to be too late." I didn't tell Bernard that it was the sound of his car that distracted him. He'd blame himself. I didn't want that.

The temperature had dropped into the high 50s or low 60s. My legs were cold and wet and my mangled knees throbbed. At least my full consciousness was more or less restored. One thing for sure: I had become acutely aware how close I'd come to meeting the same fate as Elmer Kepley.

"I thought I told you to stay put," I said to Karen. "I reckon it's lucky for me you never listen."

"Blame this one here," Karen said, poking the back of the seat where Bonnie was. "She scooted across that lake like a duck on water skis. Told me Darryl was about to shoot you and that I'd better get out there quick. With a gun." Her voice trembled a little on that last word. She was still shaken and was likely to remain so for a while.

"I guess I should thank both of you, then."

"Maybe you'll do the same for us, someday," said Karen.

"He already did," said Bonnie. "For me, I mean."

Karen moved close and put her head on my shoulder. She was still mad at me but for the moment it didn't matter.

We sat in silence and waited.

I almost didn't care who was behind the whole deal, or—if it was Clyde—that he'd almost certainly get away with his crimes. All I could think about were the six people who'd died and how their deaths would be chalked up to my account.

I'd never lose a wink of sleep over what I'd done to Tommy Drury and Dennis Tyler. Darryl Martin had to be put down, as well. I'd rather have been the one to do it instead of Karen—she'll have nightmares about it for a long time—but it had to be done. As for Elmer Kepley, I almost hoped he was part of the scheme. I'd hate to think he died just for writing Tommy Drury a check.

Erin Martin and Earl Collins, however, weighed heavy. I couldn't help but feel if I'd done my job better, they'd still be alive. If I'd seen what was staring me in the face—namely, that Darryl Martin was a card or two short of a full deck—this would've ended differently.

Of course, it could also be said that none of this would've happened if not for some folks's willingness to sell each other out for a quick and easy buck.

Six people killed in less than a day. On my patch.

Of course, Butcherville's my patch more by custom than by law.

Somehow, knowing that didn't help much.

CHAPTER THIRTY TWO

Before long, Oklahoma Highway Patrol and Tilghman County Sheriff's Department vehicles arrived. Bright, battery-powered lights mounted on stilts lit up the little island. I was gratified to see that Burton Murray had dragged himself out of bed in the middle of the night to attend to a bit of law enforcement. I think everyone would agree: multiple violent deaths occurring in his jurisdiction within the span of a single day warranted cutting short his beauty sleep.

Indeed, this area hadn't seen anything like this in recent memory. The closest thing was a little over a year ago, when we found a young negro woman with her throat cut on the railroad tracks just outside Burr. Before that, there hadn't been a murder around here in several years—at least, none that resulted in a conviction.

On the other hand, given how lax Butcherville has always been when it comes to preserving the peace, it's a wonder something like this didn't happen a long time ago.

The Oklahoma State Bureau of Investigation sent Agent Ovell Jones to the scene. I knew Ovell to be well-meaning and a good investigator overall, despite having butted heads with him over the killing of that colored girl. He asked how I was doing and commiserated when I told him I'd been better. I gave him the Cliffs Notes version of events. He asked me to come to his office the next day and give him a full statement. I said I'd be glad to. He said he hadn't known I policed Butcherville. I told him no one polices Butcherville, I just come when they call, but in general they don't want anyone's help and I was a fool to try. He nodded. I'm sure he understood.

Sheriff Murray ambled up to me like we were old friends and asked me how I was. I told him I was fine. He asked what had happened. I gave him the same story I'd given Agent Jones. He motioned for me to follow him to his car. He pulled my badge and gun out of his glove compartment, apologized for having confiscated them in the first place, and offered them back to me. I accepted the gun but told him he could hang on to the badge. He tried to press it on me. I said no thank you and walked away.

Burt and the Highway Patrol and Agent Jones questioned Karen and Bonnie. Jeff and Kenny were there, even though, as it turned out, their presence was not required. They nevertheless wanted to know what had happened. Bernard told them what he knew and steered them clear of me. He understood that, as fond as I am of my people, I was sick of rehashing the last several hours. I needed a break.

And a drink.

●　　　●　　　●　　　●　　　●

Grace Hubbard must've beaten the world land speed record getting to the Salt Flats. Her reunion with Bonnie was emotional to witness. I fought off tears with some effort. Karen didn't see the need and cried freely.

As much as I would've enjoyed having them as neighbors, I hoped the Hubbards's stay in Butcherville would be brief. There wasn't anything for them here.

Burt let Grace take Bonnie home. I watched them leave and wondered if I'd see them again.

Clyde Raymer, Grace's father and Bonnie's grandfather, did not make an appearance.

Karen and I ceased to be the focus of attention. We sat on the hood of the Fury without saying much. I tried to apologize more than once. She cut me off every time. I gave up, leaned back and gazed up at the moon. I remembered Walter Cronkite saying men would be walking on it within a year or two. I wondered if it was too late to sign up for the trip. At that moment, the moon seemed preferable to Burr. Or Butcherville. Or Tilghman County in general.

We were allowed to leave after a while. I looked down at my wrist to check the time and saw I wasn't wearing my watch. I tried to but couldn't remember if I'd put it on that morning. I recalled taking a shower after shooting Tommy Drury and Dennis Tyler. Had that only been this morning? I guess so, although I wouldn't swear to it in court. Oh well. Too late or too early. Not much difference.

I dug into the pocket of my jeans and dug out my keys. For some reason, I was a little surprised they were still there. Karen and I got in the truck and we drove away.

The issue of my drinking and the deception associated with it rose like a forty-foot concrete wall between us. I wanted to apologize, but only for the lying, not the drinking. I was afraid if I apologized for the drinking, I'd be obligated to give it up—for real, this time—and I wasn't ready to do that. Especially not tonight.

Still, I had to say something.

"Look, Red, I'm sorry. I won't lie to you anymore. I promise."

She'd turned her back to me, but her window was rolled up so I could see her face reflected in the glass. She wasn't happy.

"You going to say anything?"

She didn't answer. I asked again.

"What do you want me to say?" she said without turning around.

"That you accept my apology."

"I accept your apology." She still wouldn't face me.

"C'mon, Red—"

She turned to me with her jaw clenched. "Emmett," she said, "I'm glad you're—we're—ok. Alright? Can you do me a favor now and just leave me alone? I really don't think you want to talk about this right now."

She turned away again.

We drove some more. The truck's exhaust made a racket, thanks to my trip to Rachel Drury's. I made a mental note to see Wes Harmon about a new muffler.

"You don't sound very forgiving," I said.

"Stop it!" she cried. Her anger and sadness sucked the air out of the cab. "Maybe I don't *sound* forgiving because *I don't forgive you*."

All of a sudden, the words came in a rush. "My Lord, Emmett, it's not even the lies," she said. "It's that you're killing yourself, and you don't care. It'd be one thing if you didn't mind about how it affects me. I could forgive that, even if it meant we couldn't be together. Or even how it affects your dad, who needs you, but doesn't realize it because he barely understands what's going on around him. But what I *can't* forgive is how you don't care about yourself. I'm not stupid. I've known that you were still drinking for a while now. But I let you think you were fooling me, and I spent as much time with you as I could, because the more time you spent with me, the less you drank. But you *weren't* fooling me. I see it when you show up for work not knowing what day it is, or when you wear the same dirty uniform every day." She threw her hands up so that they banged against the roof. "God almighty, Emmett. When you don't stay with me, *you sleep in a chair*."

I felt so lost, I might've driven into a telephone pole if she hadn't been in the truck with me.

"Oh, and by the way," she said, using her voice like a hammer, pounding every word like it was a ten-penny nail, "*I can smell it on your breath*. I don't have a permanent cold. My nose works just fine."

It was my turn to clam up. Not because I was mad at her. I had no right to be. In fact, if I had the courage to face up to what she said, I'd have agreed with all of it. But I didn't, and I wasn't ready to stop doing what I'd been doing. So I clammed up.

We crossed into Burr. The neon sign at Edna's Eats was turned off, but the bartender's car was still in evidence. I thought if I played my cards right, I could get him to sell me a bottle. He'd done it before. I pulled to the curb and told Karen I'd be out in a minute.

She got out of the truck without a word and marched down the street toward the station, where her own car was parked.

"C'mon, Karen," I pleaded, but she'd made up her mind. She got into her car and drove away. She didn't look back.

Edna's bartender offered to sell me half-a-bottle of Bacardi, which I gladly accepted. I drove out of town on US 14. I pulled over on the side of the road, next to the place by the railroad tracks where, 16 months earlier, Bernard and I had found the body of a young colored girl named Sheryl Foster. She'd had her throat cut by a spoiled rich kid, whose house, not coincidentally, I could see in the distance from where I now sat.

That house was dark now. The boy who'd lived there and his father had gone to jail. The mother had left town, likely never to return. At one time, I'd been in love with her, back when were kids. At least I thought I was. When she made it clear my affections were not reciprocated, I started drinking for real. I never stopped. Never really tried.

I sat in the dark, stared at that house, and drank myself unconscious. By the time I woke up, the sun was rising over my shoulder. The rum's effects had faded somewhat. I didn't know how long I'd been asleep. More than one hour, less than three. At least now I could see straight.

The car started with a chug and a roar. I reckoned I'd have to find a new mechanic, wherever it was I ended up. I didn't have a job. I might not have a girlfriend. I could turn back and fight for one or both. Or I could keep going the way I was until I drove off the edge of the earth.

I was less than a mile from the Texas border when I noticed a stray penny stuck in the windshield defroster. I pulled over to the shoulder and pried it loose. I studied the profile of Abraham Lincoln. My favorite president. I wondered if finding it was a sign of good luck.

I flipped it in the air, caught it, and slapped it down on my forearm.

Heads, I stay.

Tails, I go.

I couldn't bring myself to look.

ACKNOWLEDGEMENTS

Once again, I'd like to thank my first readers: my mother, Judy Kelsey, who made me a writer by first making me a lover of books; my friend Gisele Bryce, whose eagle eye caught things that desperately needed to be caught; and finally, my wife, Lisa Kelsey, whose critique and suggestions made this a better story, and whose love and encouragement make me a better writer and person.

NOTE FROM THE AUTHOR

Word-of-mouth is crucial for any author to succeed. If you enjoyed the book, please leave a review online—anywhere you are able. Even if it's just a sentence or two. It would make all the difference and would be very much appreciated.

Thanks!
Chris

Thank you so much for reading one of **Chris Kelsey's** novels.

Discover the original Emmett Hardy mystery

Where the Hurt Is by Chris Kelsey

Winner, 2018 PenCraft Award—Best Fiction Book for *Where the Hurt Is*

*"This sensational small town crime thriller
is a perfect beach read." –Best Thrillers*

View other Black Rose Writing titles at
www.blackrosewriting.com/books and use promo code
PRINT to receive a **20% discount** when purchasing.